Courtney glanced up, then back at me. "I love watching the night sky. Don't you?" She continued before I could answer. "There's magic in the stars and the heavens, Robert. You do believe in magic?" A playful smile teased her lips. "I'd spend hours at home, just lying on the grass, looking up at it. I'd pick out the constellations, imagining I was being spirited across the Milky Way by a handsome prince." Her eyes watched me, then dropped.

"Yes. I believe in magic, Courtney. And your adventure sounds wonderful. Is there room up there for someone else?" I asked.

"There might be." She stared up at me, curiosity and wonder mixing on her face. "Are you applying for the position?" She came closer, her look a heady blend of innocence and invitation.

She stood too close in her silky nightgown. I found myself watching. With each breath, the sheer bodice outlined her breasts. The soft breeze blew the skirt against her hips and legs.

Don't do this, Robert, I warned myself. *This is a fantasy. She's a beauty, but you have someone waiting for you. Don't tease yourself. You'll wake up and be sorry.*

Praise for Kevin V. Symmons
and
RITE OF PASSAGE

"An intriguing read. The characters are very strong. It has the sense of foreboding on a summer day. Sort of the feeling when a thunderstorm is approaching. You know it's coming but you don't know when it'll crash around you or what damage it will be caused."

~Jo Ann Ferguson, best-selling author
~*~

"A haunting period piece with memorable characters and all the paranormal bells and whistles. Breakneck pace, romance and clever plotting."

~Arlene Kay, author
~*~

"A delightful read. A wonderful mix of Wiccan ritual, fantasy, destiny, and karma woven together to create an imaginative and engrossing tale. I recommend it highly!"

~High Priestess Ellen Anne Donovan Townsend

Rite of Passage

by

Kevin V. Symmons

Rite of Passage

Cover Art by *Kim Mendoza*

The Wild Rose Press, Inc.
PO Box 708
Adams Basin, NY 14410-0708
Visit us at www.thewildrosepress.com

Publishing History
First Faery Rose Edition, 2012
Print ISBN 978-1-61217-387-0
Digital ISBN 978-1-61217-388-7

Published in the United States of America

Dedication

To all those who had faith:
my loving wife Joan, my children,
and my fellow writers.
Thank you.

Prologue

March 21, 1947
Three Months Prior to the Summer Solstice

Twenty years of patience, hiding in shadows, changing his name and face. The high priest sat, surveying the Druid elders. *Soon it will be over, and you will have brought me my revenge.* These Druids viewed themselves as the elite of the pagan world. The high priest wore a scornful smile beneath his hood. In the months since becoming their leader, he'd driven them toward a dangerous precipice. A place he could find the closure he sought. The twelve men and women seated at his front were tools to support his brutal plan. Nothing more.

He stood, knowing his stature intimidated them. "Twelve weeks until the summer solstice," he began. "The night she'll be sacrificed." He pronounced the sentence without emotion.

As the dying sun filtered through the thickets, the high priest scanned the low hills bordering the nemeton, their sacred place of worship. He could allow no witnesses to this ritual. Nothing moved. Only the vagrant breeze stirring branches on the ancient oaks.

The spring equinox symbolized rebirth and fertility, a harbinger of celebration and joy. The meeting on this sparkling evening had a more ominous purpose. They would sanction the flawed pronouncement he had duped them into believing.

The twelve met at their ritual site on the Welsh island of Anglesey—where the Romans had

1

slaughtered their ancestors in the first century. His heart quickened imagining the magnificent carnage. Heads skewered on pikes, shamans impaled by Roman short swords, and innocent women and children dragged to slavery in chains. The Druids had been a peaceful people—philosophers, scientists, and teachers. More primitive interests motivated him. The high priest allowed himself a moment of optimism. No conscience. No emotion. He had one purpose: repayment of a long overdue debt.

He surveyed his companions. Membership in this innermost circle was coveted and anonymous. They knew each other by a secret name. His was Gottfried. Membership and elevation to their leadership was a testament to his guile, ingenuity, and the gullibility of these fools.

They represented others, descendents of those who ruled this land before the Romans and the Christians corrupted it. Their ancestors used the planets, stars, and the monoliths surrounding them to predict the future.

The group sat on worn granite pediments facing their leader. Two concentric circles surrounded them. Each of the outer monoliths was in perfect alignment with its mate on the opposite side. Despite many centuries, the stones still enabled their users to find meaning in the heavens.

The inner circle held smaller stones. These azimuth stones predicted planetary paths to help foretell significant events. The high priest made an impressive show, using the stones to confirm their fears, assuring this small band that his observations predicted a cataclysm of such cosmic import it would force them to take action. Hazelwood torches flickered, illuminating the circle's perimeter. As if drawn by an invisible force, the thirteen stood in unison.

"For centuries," the high priest commenced

"we've awaited this terrible event. It will occur on the night of the summer solstice. The witches intend to celebrate their chosen one's rite of passage. They'll invoke the ancient spirits to make the young beauty the embodiment of a goddess. That will bring catastrophe."

"But she'll be gone," protested a figure. "And human sacrifice is against everything we believe in."

"You question me?" the leader asked, knowing his followers must never guess his purpose. "Everything has been planned to the smallest detail." He closed his eyes while fingering the gold medallion that adorned his neck. He would succeed.

"We will not be deprived," another celebrant agreed. "The natural order will be restored."

He'd waited for this: *her* sacrifice. Twenty years was a long time, but not too long. Three short months and his patience would be rewarded. The debt repaid. He'd used these Druids, warning that her ascendance would bring havoc. By the time they realized the extent of his lie, he'd be far away and anonymous once again.

"She is the fortieth in her line," said another in the circle. "That signifies great power."

"It could be." The high priest nodded. "But it will be of no use. She's mastered their craft. But she'll find her way to our altar nonetheless." He shook his head in mock regret. "Taking the life of one so innocent and so beautiful cannot be viewed lightly, but we must do it," he added, *"for the greater good!"*

"Yes. She is a witch, young, sentimental and devoted to the occult," another agreed. "A sad, sweet creature. Mysticism and meditation rule their lives."

The high priest nodded again. "It will be her undoing." He stared at the elders knowing the chain of events he had set in motion. "Enough!" he commanded. "No more debate."

"How can you know all this?" asked another.

"Are you a telepath?"

"No," he lied. They could never know his true identity and the powers he possessed. "I have more practical methods. A confidant. Someone close to them. When our task is complete," the high priest promised, "nature and mankind will be in balance once again."

"Yes." All repeated the chant in their ancient Celtic tongue. "Nature and mankind will be in balance once again!"

****

Early May, 1947
Six Weeks Prior to the Summer Solstice
Briarwood Estate, Gloucestershire, Western England

The tall man bent, watching the young woman curled up in the silk comforter. Duncan Wellington watched Ellen's daughter impassively. She'd grown into a beauty. Innocent and shy, Courtney carried the look of an angel. But she was a burden he'd borne far too long. That would soon be over. Moving in her sleep, the girl's dark curls fell in disarray across her pillow, cascading over the stuffed horse she clung to.

"Courtney's become a beauty. Has the look of her mother," he observed. His words were bitter. He turned to Megan McPherson, his daughter's Scottish nanny. "It's her mouth," he said as Courtney's lips parted, curling into a dreamlike smile. "Striking and sensual. Just like Ellen's."

"Aye, sir, my Courtney does have the look of Mistress Ellen," the old woman said, brushing aside the tears on her ruddy cheeks.

"It's best if she leaves as soon as possible," he whispered. "She needs to get away. Too many bad memories—of Ellen, the accident." Wellington's words trailed off. He sighed deeply, taking one last look at the sweet, wounded young woman he was banishing. Backing out, he closed her door as he turned toward Mrs. McPherson.

"Sir?" She stood, searching his face. "Please, sir." Mrs. McPherson clutched her employer's arm. "This is where she belongs—with us, with me. She's still a child in so many ways and loves Briarwood so much. Miss Courtney *needs* to be here," the woman pleaded. Her words echoed past the ancestral portraits standing guard in the hallway.

"This is not a debate, McPherson," he said, removing his servant's hand. "I've spoken to Gretchen, her aunt. She's agreed to allow Courtney to live there." He played with his mustache. "Have her things packed by the time I return."

Mrs. McPherson raised her hand.

"One more word and you can draw your salary."

"All right." She walked past him in defiant resignation. "I'll pack Miss Courtney's things and then"—Mrs. McPherson stopped, downcast eyes showing resignation—"I'll draw my salary. I'm through, sir!"

Chapter One

June, 1947, Eight Days Prior to the Summer Solstice
The Evanses' Estate, Southern Maine

Life can be cruel, displaying forbidden pleasures, showing us things we want desperately, things that remain just beyond our reach. That was Courtney, a vision of innocence and perfection I could worship but feared I could never possess.

Entering the dining room on that June evening, I walked through the thick air, my shirt clinging to my skin beneath my dinner jacket. My mind wandered as I surveyed my surroundings, drained after my long drive from Boston, an afternoon in the June sun, and three games of billiards with my host.

"This is Robert McGregor. You may remember him." He slapped me on the back. "Going to Harvard Law this fall. Wonderful lad! Harvard summa, looks of a matinee idol, and tore up the playing fields to boot." Jonathan Evans, my father's best friend, slapped me again, displaying me. The prize bull at the county fair. "Hasn't been to one of our events since before the war, but I think of him like a son," he added, smiling with the flush of too much wine.

I shook my head. "Please, Uncle Jon." I was less than half the age of those surrounding me. I wished again that I'd turned a deaf ear to my mother's pleas to attend. I dreaded playing the role of mascot for this group.

Some of my two dozen dinner companions approached and pumped my hand. None under forty.

This would be an interminable weekend. Waterford crystal filled with red and white from the Evans cellar rested in their hands as they withdrew, smiling and nodding, consuming the canapés that drooped in the damp air.

I took a glass of vintage red from Jon's magnificent cellar. Men patted my back. Middle-aged women shared looks of admiration and provocative smiles. Clumsy flirtations from those old enough to be my mother. The names of my admirers were lost as I moved from one to the next.

We stood, playing out a scene from *Gatsby*. My companions were oblivious, untouched by the countrymen who'd paid dearly to maintain their opulent lifestyle. I thought of my brother, Michael, and what three years as a officer had done to him.

The Evanses' home was spectacular, a grand estate covering acres of birch and oak groves, surrounded by undulating, manicured lawns. The complex dated to the turn of the century, insulated and private, a monument to those who'd benefitted from the recent World Wars. It rested on a secluded cove on the southern shore of Maine's Lake Sebago, a freshwater sea spanning thirty miles.

The main house commanded a low rise, offering splendid views from all its long, east-facing windows. The somber, imposing architecture belied the welcoming interior. The main house had twenty-four rooms. The adjoining guest house offered another half-dozen, all fronted on the swimming pool and courtyard, which separated the main building from its companion. The massive complex embodied the confidence, hope, and arrogance of post-war America.

I stood nearby as Jon and his wife, Gretchen, called us to dinner. He surveyed the smoke-filled room, pudgy face dark and flushed, mumbling between clenched teeth, "Where is that girl, and why is she always late?"

"She'll be here soon, I'm sure. She's been at the stables." Gretchen paused. "Please. Be patient, Jon." Her pleasant face showed concern. "You know what she's been through."

"She should move to the stables. Spends all her time there. I am so sick of hearing about poor—" Jonathan stopped. Three dozen pairs of eyes turned toward the entrance. I stood, interest piqued, hoping this tardy guest might be someone interesting. A vision materialized in the doorway, her striking face and figure framed by the massive arch.

"Good evening," the young woman offered as she entered. I loved her accent. Formal and British, its subtle, delicate quality had elegance. The way she carried herself suggested breeding. She was incredible—part woman, part goddess. Electricity shot through me as her eyes caught mine and held them. My fatigue evaporated.

"My wife's niece, Courtney Wellington." Jonathan waved his arm. My *wife's* niece. Odd choice of words. Like something out of another time, the young woman curtsied, reminiscent of a scene from Jane Austen. Some of the women returned the gesture. I held my breath, watching. The men let their eyes linger. It was difficult not to. Courtney was something to behold.

She wore a fitted white silk blouse, a dazzling multicolored scarf tied around her neck, and a snug, floor-length navy skirt. A silver pendant peeked from beneath her scarf. As she approached I noticed unusual engraving and a small, dark stone at its center.

"Robert, would you escort Courtney to her seat?" Gretchen gestured toward the far end of the table.

"My pleasure," I agreed, moving to join her.

"Hello, Robert," she whispered, eyebrows raised and nodding as she touched my arm. "I am late." She shook her head, resuming her study of the Tabriz oriental covering the dark walnut floor. "It's become a tedious habit of late."

"It's a pleasure to meet you, Courtney."

Her lips curled up for a moment. I hoped she might smile but was left in disappointment. The thick, warm air drifted through the open windows, holding the scent of lilacs and roses, competing with the exotic fragrance surrounding Courtney.

We'd spend the evening with men and women of stature. Too much wine spawning tales of the tragedy the last few decades had witnessed. We would hear how they had saved humanity while the world was held captive. I attended the reunion reluctantly, knowing it would give me a chance to see my brother. My father and Jonathan had been best friends. Despite the lack of a blood relationship, we had always been like family. I'd been absent for years. Why this striking young woman was here was a mystery. I promised to find out and make our evening as bearable as possible.

"I'm a friend of the family."

"Yes, Robert, I know." She nodded. "I saw you at the pool this afternoon."

"Really?" I said, wondering how I could have missed her.

She shrugged.

Courtney was spectacular. Tall and slender, her dark brown hair shone, cascading over her shoulders. Her pale skin looked lustrous in the soft light from the chandelier. Large, dark eyes recalled images of a doe. They flanked a perfect, lightly freckled nose.

It began as she took my arm—the excitement, the wonderful, hollow feeling in my stomach. Energy flowed between us with that first touch. Courtney tightened her grip. I followed each graceful stride as she headed to her seat.

"I have no idea how I missed you," I repeated.

"I can explain." Her voice was soft and hypnotic. I could have listened to her all night. "Thank you, Robert," she offered, inclining her head as she sat down. "I saw you from my window," she confessed. "I'm on the second floor." A smile emerged. It was subtle but radiant, the glow of dawn after a dark night. I glimpsed flawless white teeth. This was no young woman. Courtney was an angel masquerading as Gretchen's niece.

"I see." I nodded, taking the seat beside her.

Before I had the chance to continue, the woman on my left took my arm. She was forty, on her way to being drunk, and quite loud. Reluctantly, I turned, making polite conversation. Her breath smelled of wine and spicy canapés. I recalled Jon introducing us earlier. I did my best to answer her questions: Where did I come from? *Boston.* What did I do? *Harvard Law School in the fall.* How old was I? *Twenty-three.* I allowed the middle-aged woman a few minutes before turning to Courtney again.

Just as I did, Jonathan stood unsteadily. "Ladies and gentlemen." He tapped his glass, then raised it, directing it toward me. "I want to offer a toast to Everett McGregor. His son is seated at the far end of the table. As you know, Everett was my closest friend. I think of Robbie and his brother like sons. It's been a while since they've favored us with a visit." He took a swallow of cabernet. "Robert. I want to toast my dear departed friend, your father, and wish you and your family all the best. And rumor has it there may be wedding bells in the future." He winked at me.

"Hear, hear," the cry rang out in unison as everyone stood and drank, followed by a robust round of applause.

Conscience tugged. I thought of Rachel, my girl back in Boston, as I stared at the captivating young

10

woman on my right. While not perfect, I thought myself loyal. I turned to see Courtney take a long swallow of wine, holding up her glass to have it refilled. She looked so young.

"Twenty-one next Friday, and I've been enjoying wine since I was twelve," she said, reading my thoughts. I stared in amazement. I was about to ask her how she knew what I was thinking when she offered, "Congratulations, Robert. You must be very happy. Auntie never mentioned your wonderful news." Her chestnut eyes grew dark and moist as she spoke. They had an opaque quality, changing from brown to green depending on the light. Turning, Courtney grew silent. She stared at the table, fidgeting with the flatware, scarcely touching her salad or the soup that followed.

Ambivalence consumed me. Rachel and I had discussed many things, but graduate school awaited—she to medical school and me to Harvard Law. We had no agreement. She was determined to become Mass General's first female surgeon. Now, as I sat next to Courtney, my fidelity was being tested. "Jonathan shouldn't have suggested I was engaged."

She sat, wide-eyed, watching me, playing with her hair. For an instant her lips curled up slightly. I thought she might smile. Instead, she pushed her chair back.

"Excuse me," she whispered as she stood, squeezing my shoulder as she passed. Turning, she offered a contrite, I'm-sorry look.

"Humph. I've never seen the like." The woman next to me shook her head, scowling. "Spoiled, petulant girl."

I didn't hear any more. Courtney was gone. I sat, overcome by a sad, empty feeling. I'd known her less than an hour, but suddenly, it mattered. Mattered a great deal.

****

Many guests had gone to bed, dulled by wine, rich food, and the humidity. Bedrooms in the main house had the new room air conditioners that gave them respite from the heat. I tried not to think about Courtney, but she'd bewitched me. I had to know more.

"Ellen and I hadn't been close since she married Duncan," Gretchen explained, speaking the name as though it were profane. "I met him briefly when I went to fetch Courtney. He was cold and uncaring. Ellen and I hardly saw each other and seldom wrote. Courtney's turning twenty-one next Friday." She stopped, a faraway look crossing her face. "Ellen died in a riding accident this spring. She and Courtney were incredibly close.

"They lived on an estate," Gretchen continued, patting her neck with a hanky. "In Gloucestershire. It was lovely but isolated." Her eyes grew distant. "I only saw it once." She shook her head. "Ellen was a wonderful horsewoman, a champion. According to the owner of the local stables, Courtney's following in her footsteps."

"And her family?" I asked.

"She's an only child. Her father"—Gretchen stopped, jaw tightening—"travels a lot." She forced a smile. "He and Courtney were never close. She had a nanny, a kind Scottish woman, a grandmother figure. But Ellen was Courtney's world. That child worshipped my sister."

"See you tomorrow." Gretchen waved good night to a guest. "That man sent her here," she continued.

"Why? She seems so shy and innocent. What has she done to deserve exile?" I protested.

"There was mystery surrounding Ellen's death. Duncan may blame her. I don't know." Gretchen frowned. "I watched her with you, Robert," she said, squeezing my arm. "This evening's the first time she's shown more than polite disregard in weeks. It

12

might be an imposition, but could you spend time with her? You're so close in age. I think she'd like that."

I hesitated. "Me? Are you sure?"

"You could try." She shrugged.

"I could," I answered. "If you think it would help." I pictured Rachel, remembering the touch of her hand, her lavish blond curls and hypnotic gray eyes.

"Be careful," she warned. "Courtney's lovely, brilliant, and desperately needs someone to be kind to her. I've tried. But I saw the way she looked at you." Gretchen, smiled and touched my cheek. "I think you could be friends. But remember. She's fragile, vulnerable."

Gretchen turned, not finishing her thought. There was no need.

Chapter Two

It was past one when I walked through the courtyard toward my room in the guest house. My wrinkled dinner jacket hung over my shoulder. Bending over, I dipped my fingertips in the swimming pool, rubbing it on my forehead and neck. A hint of mist rose into the thick air. I was tempted to jump in fully clothed.

After my conversation with Gretchen, I challenged Jonathan to another game of billiards, hoping to discover more about Courtney. Her vulnerable look haunted me. When I mentioned her name, Jonathan stared, clearing his throat. "She's beautiful, Robert. Also headstrong and aloof. Your father was like a brother to me, so be careful. Remember who you are." It was a warning. "There's more to her than you want to know," he added. That was the end of it. I pressed the point without success.

"Do you know how lucky you are, my boy? We live in the greatest country in the world. We're strong, resilient—the most awesome industrial giant in history." He rounded the billiard table and slapped my back. "Your father knew that. Think of your opportunities. After Harvard Law, with your brains and social connections"—he nodded—"there'll be no stopping you."

"What about the Russians, Communism, the bomb?" I thought of my brother and the millions who never came home. "Didn't we just 'fight the war to end all wars'? Now we may have to do it all over again."

"Russians, Communists. Fools. They snagged a few German scientists and think they're our equal. Patton was right. We should have marched to Moscow. Put an end to them." He shook his head. "Business, world trade, and the law. Stick with those and you'll end up like your father did."

I tried to absorb his wisdom. Jon and my father had taken a run-down factory and created the mighty corporate giant that had paid for this estate. It also put my father in an early grave. I thought about Rachel, her ambition, and my own. I pictured eighteen-hour days capped with too much alcohol and too little warmth. Was that what I wanted? Thinking about that sterile, loveless image, another came to mind: Courtney. Her face; the soft, hypnotic voice; the electricity when we touched. A mixture of guilt and excitement swept over me.

"May I use your phone?" I asked, remembering my promise to call Rachel. Perhaps hearing her voice would help. He showed me to his office and left, closing the door. After tapping the receiver several times the operator's voice came through. "Number please."

I gave it to her. After an endless delay, I heard Rachel's voice, scratchy and distant.

"Robbie?" she whispered.

I'd awakened her.

"Sorry, Rach. I didn't realize how late it was."

"What time is it?"

I looked at my watch. "About twelve -thirty."

"It's okay, but I've got to be in early this week." She volunteered at Massachusetts General Hospital.

I was silent for a minute. "I just wanted to hear your voice." And I did. To yank me back to reality. A reminder of that pleasant, satisfying existence Jonathan talked about.

"That's sweet, but can we do this tomorrow?"

"Sure. Talk to you then." I hesitated, adding,

"Love you, Rachel."

"Me, too," she whispered and hung up.

I stood staring at the desktop. I had the world within my grasp. Why were these strange desires consuming me? I shook my head as I left the office, looking back at the phone. So much for intimate conversation.

****

Courtney dropped her sheer white robe on the fallen log and stood barefoot on the blanket of pine needles. Only a fragrant headband of jasmine leaves and holly remained. The sacred site stood secluded, out of sight of the estate, behind a stand of white pines and hardwoods that overlooked the lake. She inhaled deeply. The perfume of the neighboring forest greeted her, hanging in the thick, moist air.

She'd fallen in love with the estate and her surroundings. And America's grandeur and plenty awed her. Parts of Britain and much of Europe lay in ruins—plagued by shortages of everything from cigarettes to petrol. Once prosperous centers of commerce and art resembled skeletons.

Simon Phillips, Courtney's grandfather and teacher, had taken her to the Continent to see the devastation firsthand. Simon had a reason behind that journey. "After you and your mate are joined on the night of the solstice, this will never happen again," he promised her. "Traditional warfare is tragic enough. But the new threat—the use of atomic power as a weapon—must be feared most. Humans wield it like a child does a sharp stick. We will use our powers to see it's controlled." No one need give Courtney pep talks. She knew the import of her task.

Before walking to the ritual site, Courtney had fasted and taken a ritual bath with the spices used for purification. Beginning her meditation, she consecrated and charged her sacred tools. Next, she defined the boundaries of the ritual circle using her athame, her witch's knife. After cleansing the sacred space, Courtney drew forth symbols of the elements: air, fire, water, and earth. Then she called on the spirit. Her small altar stood in the north of the circle. All her sacred implements were in the proper place.

After lighting the candles, she began, calling on the deity, opening her mind to the goddess's guidance and wisdom. *Focus on your destiny*. The message was clear. But her task was proving more difficult than she'd imagined. Why was Robert so kind, so charming, so beautiful. So much more than the simple vessel she'd envisioned.

Emerging from her trance, Courtney extinguished the candles, took her athame, and walked widdershins, counterclockwise, to take down the witch's circle. Replacing the ritual objects in her paisley satchel, she donned her robe and walked back to her room. The next act was about to begin.

Courtney sat at her window, watching the courtyard and waiting. Cepheus jumped onto the windowsill, purring loudly. "It's all right, Cephy. I'm ready," she assured her four-footed companion. But Courtney wasn't fine. Not at all. Her stomach growled as she twirled her hair on her finger. The enormous black cat, who'd been one of her familiars, tilted his head. He studied her, meowing loudly. He sensed her conflict.

"I told you, *I'm fine*," she said through tight lips. "We knew this wasn't going to be easy." Courtney continued playing with her hair. Her emptiness had nothing to do with hunger. Courtney closed her eyes and breathed deeply as she remembered his touch and the heady sensation it sent through her.

She recalled seeing him at the pool that afternoon. Courtney pictured his bathing suit hugging his lean body. Robert was tall, wiry, a delight to watch. His muscles were tight but subtle, like coiled vipers ready to strike. Courtney wondered how his arms would feel when they surrounded her. The thick dark hair, his strong, cleft chin, and the gray-blue eyes that recalled the sky on a winter's day sent shivers through her. Despite their steely look, those translucent orbs had softened, showing warmth and kindness when he spoke to her. Courtney shuddered. Her face burned from the fire within.

She opened her eyes, staring at the moon. Seven days until the ritual. What would he say when he knew the truth? How could she have known what it would be like to be close to him, how his life force would flow between them? And what about his relationship with this woman? No one had told Courtney about the girl. Should she care? Perhaps not but she could not help herself. She did.

Cassiopeia joined them, rubbing against Courtney's leg, adding her feline voice to the mix. "Yes, I know. He's coming," she told them. While Courtney's soul had migrated through many lifetimes, part of her was simply a young woman. That part was intensely attracted to Robert McGregor.

But years of preparation could not be wasted. She'd play her role to perfection. Courtney lit her jasmine incense, turned north, then east. Closing her eyes, she chanted a blessing in an ancient Welsh tongue.

Footsteps echoed in the courtyard. Courtney opened her eyes, extinguishing the incense. Regardless of what passions Robert awakened in her, Courtney had a destiny. She sighed, watching him approach, knowing it must be fulfilled.

Chapter Three

Threading my way between the chaise lounges surrounding the courtyard, I replayed my conversation with Jonathan. I stopped, looking up at the brilliant display of stars.

A voice echoed from the main house. Her voice— soft and elegant. I could never forget it. I scanned the empty courtyard and surrounding windows. All were dark and closed except—

"Hello, Robert. Up here." She stood, silhouetted in her window, her white nightdress lustrous. She waved, my exquisite Juliet, her smile reflecting the moonlight.

"Have you ever seen anything so beautiful?" she asked, searching the heavens.

"Never," I answered, imagining her face.

"Where are you going?"

"To bed," I told her. "It's late."

"Can you wait a minute?"

I should have said no. But before I could find my voice, she stood in front of me, flanked by two large, majestic cats, wrapping themselves around her supple legs.

"Hello." She found my eyes in the moonlight.

She wore a sheer white nightgown. No robe. I tried not to stare, wondering why a well-brought-up young woman would appear that way.

"I'm glad to see you," I whispered. "You left too soon. I had to put up with the whole group by myself. I needed an ally."

Her face turned upward, moonlight shimmering off her skin and the dark brown ponytail held in place by a white silk ribbon.

"I'm sorry," she said. Her eyes lingered on mine and narrowed. "I'm not sure Uncle Jonathan is pleased I'm here. I wanted to talk to you, but"—she stopped suddenly—"I had something to attend to." She blushed and changed the subject. "It must be nice to be in love. Is your intended very pretty?"

"Yes." I hesitated. "She's lovely. But she's not really my intended," I protested, trying to explain. She refused to let me finish.

"I'm glad." She nodded, suddenly shivering. She closed her eyes momentarily. I stood, watching, a light breeze playing with her ponytail and the trees. It helped the moonlight make elaborate patterns on the courtyard.

I cleared my throat. "What are you doing up so late?"

"I don't sleep much," she confessed. "And I have my companions to take care of." Courtney paused, bending as she stroked the black cat affectionately. "Cepheus is the black fellow." She tickled his chin as he purred loudly, winding himself tightly around her ankles. "And Cassiopeia is this lovely white lady."

Courtney glanced up, then back at me. "I love watching the night sky. Don't you?" She continued before I could answer. "There's magic in the stars and the heavens, Robert. You do believe in magic?" A playful smile teased her lips. "I'd spend hours at home, just lying on the grass, looking up at it. I'd pick out the constellations, imagining I was being spirited across the Milky Way by a handsome prince." Her eyes watched me, then dropped.

"Yes. I believe in magic, Courtney. And your adventure sounds wonderful. Is there room up there for someone else?" I asked.

"There might be." She stared up at me, curiosity and wonder mixing on her face. "Are you applying for the position?" She came closer, her look a heady blend of innocence and invitation.

She stood too close in her silky nightgown. I found myself watching. With each breath, the sheer bodice outlined her breasts. The soft breeze blew the skirt against her hips and legs.

Don't do this, Robert, I warned myself. *This is a fantasy. She's a beauty, but you have someone waiting for you. Don't tease yourself. You'll wake up and be sorry.*

She saw me staring, immediately covering herself with her arms. "I'm so embarrassed. I should have worn my robe." She blushed and shook her head. "Growing up in the country makes one careless."

"Here." I took my wrinkled dinner jacket and offered it to her.

"Thank you." She moved closer, taking it and throwing it across her shoulders.

Standing only inches away, the fragrance she wore surrounded us.

"Your perfume. What is it?"

"It's something special my grandfather gives me. Made from jasmine blossoms. Do you like it?"

The scent was intoxicating. "It's wonderful. I've never smelled anything like it."

"I'm glad." She turned, nodding toward a lounge chair. I fell into step, sitting down next to her.

"Gretchen told me about your mother, Courtney, I lost my father this past winter."

Her soft, warm facade grew dark and tight as she held herself in an embrace, shivering. When she looked up, tears filled her enormous eyes, spilling onto her cheeks.

"I'm so sorry. I shouldn't have..."

"I don't want to think about it!" she protested.

"I understand," I reassured her.

"I can see her lying there," she continued, burying her face in her hands.

I moved to her side, kneeling by her chair. I took her hand, letting my fingers surround hers. "It's all right, Courtney. I promise." I tightened my grasp.

She shared the intimacy briefly, then stood and pulled free. I started after her. She turned, holding up her hand.

"Please don't." Her head dropped. She stood mute.

I froze.

"I'm all right," she whispered. "I'll see you tomorrow." She began to walk away but stopped suddenly. "Do you ride?" she asked, turning toward me.

"Ride?" I shrugged.

"Yes. You know, ride—horses?"

"I love to. Why?"

"There's a wonderful stable nearby. And some dazzling scenery. "

And? I wondered. Was it an observation, an idle comment, an invitation? I had no idea. And no idea what Courtney was. But I wanted desperately to find out. Wanted it more than anything I had in a long time, to explore the attraction drawing us toward one another.

"You're sure you're all right?" I called, still curious about her "stable" comment.

She nodded, smiling warmly, "Thank you, Robert. I am now." She snapped her fingers. "Come along." The grand felines fell into step.

Suddenly, she stopped and turned. Crossing the few yards that separated us, Courtney put her hand around my neck and pulled me toward her. Her fragrance hung between us, her soft breath warm and sweet as she brushed my cheek with her lips. She blushed and retreated, looking back, wearing an expression that showed regret and anticipation.

"Till tomorrow." She turned slowly

Is this really happening? I asked myself.

She got to the main house. I watched, spellbound as the entrance swallowed her. I watched, confused and dazed, wishing desperately it was morning.

Chapter Four

I returned to my room, undressed, and took a long, cold shower. I emerged still flushed. The rooms in the guest house had no air conditioners. I pushed the dial on the window fan to its maximum setting. It rattled into action.

I lay down, reliving the evening. Before Courtney entered that dining room, I was perfectly content. I had everything: a girl with beauty and ambition, a law career launched at the Ivy League's best, elevated social position, and all the other trappings of success. Suddenly, none of that mattered. I *had* been bewitched.

Was this infatuation? When I awoke tomorrow would my fascination with Courtney be gone? Part of me hoped so. Another part desperately wanted it to continue. And Courtney? Was she attracted to me? Had I misread the signs? This was no novel. Could two people meet and be consumed with each other in a single night?

I got into bed and lay, trying to placate my conscience. There was no doubt. Courtney was exquisite and sensitive. But no matter what sensual visions danced through my mind, I needed to follow Jon's advice and keep myself in check—do exactly what Gretchen asked of me: be a friend to Courtney. Nothing more. Satisfied with my heroic self-control, sometime after three my eyelids drooped. I fell into a fitful sleep.

****

America of 1947 was a contradiction. At least it seemed that way to me. While most of Europe and

Asia struggled, slowly rebuilding their economies, infrastructure, and populations, we had escaped destruction, at least at the physical level. But you need only spend time with my brother, Michael, and his fellow veterans to understand that while our structures remained intact, those who had given years of their lives had not. They didn't congregate and swap robust stories of victory and battle. They had troubled, sleepless nights, keeping a solitary counsel of the horrors they had witnessed. While Michael tried to masquerade it, I'd seen it. Shame dogged me over the injury that had kept me from serving.

The reunion ignored those who had given so much to preserve our way of life. The site rotated. This year the Evanses had the task of hosting aging family members and friends. I came reluctantly when my mother sprained her ankle, knowing that the location would allow me to see Michael.

Since his homecoming, my brother had been sullen and introspective, disappearing for long periods, traveling to unknown destinations. When he returned for our father's funeral, he informed us he had accepted a teaching position at Dartmouth. This summer he was renovating a ski lodge and insisted I visit. I wanted to see him and witness how he dealt with civilian life after three grueling years in Europe.

The weather had been unusually hot. The weathermen described it as "brutal." I tumbled from my damp sheets sometime after nine. My sleep had been haunted and restless, filled with strange dreams and visions. I awoke feeling guilty about my fixation on Courtney, especially when I pictured Rachel.

I showered and dressed in light cotton trousers, a polo shirt, and a pair of walking shoes. The dining room was half-empty by the time I appeared. Some had chosen a brisk swim or boating on the lake. Others elected to challenge Point Sebago, the region's finest golf course. I greeted those still eating, making conversation before heading to the table occupied by my hosts. Whatever the misgivings, I was on a mission. Despite Jonathan's comments in the billiard room, I was determined to find out more about Courtney, if only to satisfy my curiosity.

My plan for the day was to take my roadster over the spectacular countryside to Naples, a quaint community known for its freshwater salmon and magnificent vistas of the lakes and mountains that ringed it. That evening I planned to visit my brother.

By the time I entered the dining room it was almost ten.

"Good morning," I offered, smiling. "May I?" I asked, gesturing to one of the empty seats.

"Of course." Gretchen motioned to the one next to her.

"They say it may be a little cooler today," I said as I sat and asked the server for coffee.

"A little," Jon agreed absently, studying the *Wall Street Journal.*

"What are your plans for the day, Robbie?" Gretchen asked.

"Well, I'm no golfer and I get my fill of the water. Thought I'd drive over to Naples, take in the scenery, and buy my mother a present. I understand they have some great woolen shops. And I hear their freshwater salmon is the best in New England."

"Well, I think there are a few places that might argue with that," Jon said as he put down the paper. "But it is damn good."

Gretchen looked at me, brows raised. "Have you thought about what I asked you? About spending time with Courtney?" she asked. "I feel so badly. Except for her daily visit to the stables she's stayed to herself. I've tried to get close and get her to go to the local dances and meet other young people, but I've had no luck breaking through the wall she's built around herself."

This could be an invitation to disaster. But how could I refuse? "If you think she'd open up with me, I'll try." Why not volunteer? *Kind, friendly, platonic.* I reaffirmed my pledge from last night.

Jonathan scowled. Gretchen looked annoyed and batted his arm.

"Give her a chance, Jon. The poor girl has been through so much. Her mother's death, being sent here to live with us."

"Yes, and why do you suppose your charming brother-in-law sent her here? Because she's an angel, the perfect child he couldn't stand to be away from?" He shook his head. "I did some investigating." He looked at me, then back at her. "If you're going to be her babysitter, there are some things you should know."

"You're ridiculous," she said bitterly. "Jon has some friends in the press. They dredged up this drivel about a mystery behind Ellen's death and other odd things that happened around Briarwood, her estate in Gloucestershire."

"*A mystery!*" he threw back at her. "You be the judge," he said, directing his comments to me.

"Ellen died in a fall from her horse. They said she broke her neck. Courtney claimed the animal was spooked by lightning, but her mother was the best horsewoman in western England, and no one saw so much as a rain cloud that afternoon. When the constable went to the site of the accident, there were strange markings near her body. Markings that the locals claimed were associated with witchcraft. On top of that, there were other mysterious deaths in the previous five years, when Courtney and only Courtney was—" He stopped in midsentence.

We turned to see her enter the dining room dressed in riding clothes. She walked with fluid strides, like a thoroughbred.

I found myself frowning at Jonathan. "Gretchen, do you believe any of this…"

"…nonsense?" She finished my thought, giving her husband a tap on the wrist. "No, not at all. Jonathan has visions of Olivier and Fontaine at Mandalay." She scoffed. "Courtney is a sweet, beautiful child. Nothing more. She's lonely, hurt, and in need of a friend."

"Don't say I didn't warn you." Jon narrowed his eyes as he looked in her direction.

"She's looking this way." Gretchen pushed me. "Please. Go talk to her, Robbie."

"I'll remember your warning. If she tries to turn me into a frog, you'll be the first to know." I chuckled, as I took my coffee cup. Courtney and witchcraft? I remembered her question about magic and my strange dreams from last night. I had to admit I found the idea intriguing. The occult had always fascinated me. I gave her a wave. She looked up and showed a shy smile when she saw me. I headed toward her table.

"Good morning. I see you've had your exercise." I put my cup on the table. She looked up, her enormous eyes bright. "Anyone sitting here?" I asked.

"Hello," she said quietly, reaching over and pushing out the chair. "No one but you. I usually sit by myself. I get rather fragrant after a ride, especially on a warm day." She turned up her nose and showed an apologetic smile as she moved her helmet, gloves, and crop to an empty seat.

Her thick, dark hair looked damp, tied in a loose braid. The riding clothes she wore looked utilitarian—something for a workout, not show. I

28

watched her, taking in each feature. She wore little makeup. Her face was dotted with beads of perspiration, but Courtney was still a vision.

"Oh, Robert, I'm so sorry," she burst out.

"Sorry. For what?"

"You're being too kind." She blushed, raising her eyes. "For behaving like an hysterical school girl last night. It's just that…"

"Shhh," I whispered. "No need to apologize." I touched her hand. Her eyes shone.

"I think it may be a little cooler today," I said, withdrawing my hand as I changed the subject.

"You couldn't prove it by me. It was hot riding this morning." She lowered her eyes, pushing a loose strand of hair behind her ear.

"So, what are you doing for the rest of the day?" I asked.

She shook her head, pushing her lips together. "Actually, I'd love to get away, visit some of the countryside," she said quietly. "It's beautiful here and some of the riding trails are exquisite. But I've been here for weeks and haven't left. Not that I'm complaining. Auntie Gretchen's been a jewel."

Spend time with her, be her friend, break down the walls. Gretchen's words echoed. I played with the idea of asking her. It sounded so innocent. Was I opening myself to an emotional train wreck? What would I say if Rachel asked how I spent my day?

"What about you?" she asked, looking up as she drank her tea and spread jam on her toast.

"Well, I was thinking of taking a ride around the lake up to Naples and…"

"May I come? *Please?*" Courtney dropped her toast, putting her hands together in mock prayer. "It would be so nice to go for a drive, and I'd love to spend some time with…" She stopped. "I mean, it would be such fun to see the scenery. If you think it proper. I mean with your situation and all." She lowered her gaze and her face flushed.

"I'd love to have company," I confessed, watching as she raised her eyes to meet mine. "We'll have a wonderful day. And there's nothing improper about it." I nodded, tapping the table.

Her smile shone in the sunlight.

I cleared my throat. "Well, how about meeting in front of the garage in an hour?" I looked at my watch. "About half past eleven?"

She gulped a quick swallow of tea and grabbed her gear. "See you in thirty minutes," she said, beaming as she jumped up and headed for the door, her high boots clattering on the hardwood. As Courtney reached the door, she turned and waved.

"Thirty minutes," I agreed, nodding. *For God's sake, stay in control.* I repeated the mantra. But as I watched her disappear, a sense of anticipation and excitement filled me. My stomach had that wonderful hollow feeling again. I looked at my watch, wishing the minutes away.

Chapter Five

I left the dining room, giving Gretchen a thumbs-up. Jonathan looked on, frowning. I wondered what was behind his mistrust of Courtney. She was young, pretty, and aloof. Did he have an interest in her? Could it be that simple? No. That was ridiculous. I dismissed the thought. I'd known Jon since I was a child and *lecher* wasn't a name that rang true. And despite Gretchen's attempt to poke fun at him, I found her comments odd. Jon was the most level-headed person I knew. My father told us Jon was a rock, the compass that headed their business in the right direction. No. It was difficult to imagine him being stirred by a pretty face or things that went bump in the night—unless they affected his bottom line.

I dashed across the courtyard and into my room. I brushed my teeth, ran a brush through my hair and added a generous splash of Creed, the expensive aftershave Michael had brought from England.

I went to the garage to get the Jaguar so we could leave as soon as Courtney was ready. Throwing the canvas cover off, a stab of guilt hit me. No matter how I tried to rationalize the trip, Courtney was driving this adventure. I could hear my father—my moral compass. The most honest man I had ever known. *If you can't tell a woman what you're doing, you shouldn't be doing it.* He was right. I'd always been honest with Rachel. But it was too late to back out now. *Control, Robbie. Just be friends.*

****

31

Courtney studied her foggy reflection in the bathroom mirror as she dried her hair. She frowned, trying to decide what to wear. She wanted to look attractive. *Was she dressing for the role she was playing or for Robert?* The question angered her, because she knew the answer.

Courtney searched for her feline companions. "Well, help me," she whispered, pushing her lips into a pout and twirling a strand of damp hair on her finger. "This dating thing is new to me." *Dating. Is that what this is?* She knew that was how she wanted to think of it. At home, she'd attended hunt balls and parties. It was expected. But her mother and Simon had insulated her from the social opportunities she might have found. When suitors came to call, the young men were politely turned away, because Courtney had a purpose. A significance beyond anything the world could suspect. She had no time for courting. She had to learn, hone her powers, and study the craft. Becoming the embodiment of a goddess required every minute of every day.

Courtney brushed the mist from the mirror as her stomach tightened in knots. Strange emotions swept over her, stirring her in ways she could never imagine. Was it guilt because of Robert's lady friend? No, though she did feel the strange new sensation of jealousy, her purpose precluded proper behavior. This was something else. Courtney shook her head. *Stop it!* she scolded herself. *Stay in control.* She was fulfilling her destiny. Seeing that the prophecy was fulfilled. But if this was simply a role, why the euphoria? Why the enchantment since meeting him? And why did she suddenly find herself breaking into a grin every time she imagined Robbie's strong, perfect face, or the way he looked in his swim trunks?

Courtney bit her lip and frowned as she turned

and headed for the door. She sneaked one last look at her reflection, pleased with what she saw. People told her she was pretty, striking, even beautiful. Courtney saw the way men looked at her. She never cared what they thought. Until now. She closed her eyes and pictured Robbie, wishing, hoping he'd think she was beautiful. For the first time in her life, it mattered to Courtney what someone else thought. And it thrilled and terrified her.

****

I pulled the car up to the large gate that bordered the courtyard and checked my watch: 10:45. Courtney could never be here this soon. She had to shower, change, make arrangements for her pets and...

"Hello." I felt a tap on the shoulder and turned. She stood there. Had my watch stopped? I must have looked curious. A grin crossed her face.

"How did you manage to...?" I shrugged.

"Didn't I tell you?" Her eyes had a mischievous sparkle. "With magic! I'm a witch," she whispered, looking around playfully as she laughed. I found myself joining her as I glanced toward the dining room, thinking of Jonathan.

"I'd heard that about you," I said as I opened her door.

"Oh my God, a Jaguar convertible!" She ran her hand over the leather. "And a 1500."

My face flushed. "You know your cars."

"I love sports cars, and this is my favorite. And in British Racing Green. I can't wait to get started." She swooned.

"About the witch thing. Could you do me one favor?" I asked.

"Try me." She raised an eyebrow.

"Don't turn me into a frog."

She studied me, the playful look returning. "Don't worry, Robbie, we only do that to princes."

She patted my shoulder. "You're safe unless you get promoted."

Had she called me "Robbie"? It had a warm, intimate feeling. I felt an incredible connection with this girl I'd only known for less than a day.

I pulled out my cigarettes. She sat, watching, her head tilted to one side. "Would you mind?" she asked quietly. "I know I shouldn't, but I sneak one now and then."

I lit the cigarette and gave it to her. She inhaled deeply, closing her eyes. She handed it back to me. "We could share."

"Sounds good." I loved the simple, intimate gesture.

I sneaked a look at her as I slid into the driver's seat. She caught me.

"Do I pass inspection, Mr. McGregor?" she asked, suppressing a smile as I pretended to study her.

She reached over and pushed me.

"You'll do," I assured her.

She wore tailored shorts and a short-sleeved linen blouse. Navy-blue knee socks and walking shoes—like mine—completed her outfit. A multicolored silk scarf adorned her neck. As she returned the cigarette, I noticed the silver pendant and chain she wore last night. Her hair looked lighter. It had a chestnut tone. Like everything about Courtney, it seemed perfect. A large white silk ribbon decorated the end of her dark ponytail.

"You don't look too bad yourself, Robbie." Courtney's light, playful expression disappeared. She hid a sigh. "Your lady's one lucky woman," she whispered, turning as I eased the Jag onto the narrow two-lane road that would take us north around Sebago.

We rode for thirty minutes. I gave Courtney the map, appointing her lookout and navigator. She took to the task, pointing out everything—a special mountain or lake view, a field of wildflowers, the occasional deer, even small herds of horses or cattle that nodded their approval as we sped by. About halfway to Naples she spotted a small roadside stand that offered homemade ice cream and a small petting zoo.

"Can we stop?" she asked, pointing to the small building and series of corrals.

"Why not?" I agreed.

It was lunchtime and several families walked around the animals. I pulled into the dusty parking lot and turned off the ignition.

Courtney tilted her head. "How about an ice cream?" she suggested.

I nodded and motioned. "I have to go out back. You know."

She crinkled her nose. "You go first. If it's too bad, I think I can wait till we get to Naples."

"Fine." I opened her door and she got out, loosening the ribbon and running her fingers through her thick hair. A gust of wind twisted it into a tumbling swirl of chocolate brown. I watched her as she closed her eyes, twisting her neck to ease the stiffness, remembering she'd already spent time on a horse that morning.

When I emerged, I looked at the stand expecting to see her. Instead, she knelt in front of a homemade fence with a large sign that read, *Stand back! Beware of the Animals.*

Several children, their parents and two older folk, a man in overalls and a woman in a worn print dress, stood six feet behind her, motioning and whispering to each other.

As I approached, the man in overalls looked at me. I began to speak but he put his fingers to his lips. He backed toward me, grinning through a poorly maintained smile. "Is that little lady a friend of yours?"

"Yes." I nodded. "Why?"

"Never seen nothin' like it." He took off his straw hat and scratched his head. "She got them animals eatin' outta her hand." He shook his head. "I mean *really* eatin' out of her hand. They ain't usually that friendly."

I turned to watch. Courtney smiled while a collection of animals and poultry nuzzled her hand and rubbed up against her arm. She turned and saw the small crowd watching.

"Never seen nothin' like it," the man repeated.

The small group gave her a round of spontaneous applause. Courtney blushed and motioned for the children to join her. "They'll be fine," she promised the parents.

She stood, supervising as the children followed her lead. The animals licked their hands. The small group broke up as the families went back to their cars after filling the tip jar to overflowing.

Courtney came to me, a shy smile on her face.

"How was it?" She nodded in the direction of the outdoor toilet.

"Anyone who can do that"—I motioned toward the animals—"can handle it."

"Use ours." The man in the overalls overheard her. He pointed to the farmhouse down the road.

"Thanks." Courtney raised her eyebrows at me and walked quickly to the house. "I'll take a chocolate cone with those sprinkle things. Get whatever you want. It's my treat," she called over her shoulder.

"Ice cream's on me, too," the man said, directing me to the stand.

Courtney ran back to join me after her visit to the farmer's home. We ordered extra-large chocolate cones. Sitting on the hillside, the lake was a sparkling blue jewel in the distance as we fought a losing battle, trying to finish our cones before the midday sun took them.

"How'd you do that thing?" I asked. "With the animals?"

"I told you. It's *magic*!" She raised her eyebrows, giggling. "Actually, just too much time spent alone on our estate," she offered. She took a napkin, put it to her lips and leaned over, wiping the ice cream from my mouth as she held my eyes. "That's better."

She stood and held out her hand. "Shall we?" she asked, nodding toward the Jaguar.

"Sure." I followed, resisting the urge to put my arm around her as we headed to the car.

Chapter Six

We drove for forty minutes. Courtney seemed relaxed, even animated by the wildlife, the spectacular vistas, and the lavish green-and-gold of the June landscape. Halfway to Naples, she grew quiet, donning a pair of sunglasses. Tying her hair back, she rested her head against the soft leather. In five minutes she was purring like a kitten.

It was past noon when we reached Naples, a little vacation community separating Long Lake from Sebago. Downshifting, I pulled up in front of a cluster of stores facing the lake. I recalled coming here with my dad. It seemed thriving—more active today.

"Hey, sleepy head," I said softly, pushing the clutch in and putting the Jag in reverse as I shut off the engine. She awoke with a start, turning as she realized she was resting on my shoulder.

"So sorry," she whispered hoarsely. "I never fall asleep like that." She fingered the pendant hiding beneath her scarf, as if checking to make sure it was still there.

"I won't steal it. I promise," I told her. "As long as you don't turn me into a frog."

"Don't worry. I wouldn't let you." She laughed as she awakened. "Did I miss something? Did you become a prince while I was asleep?"

"The Prince of Naples," I said, pointing at the surrounding shops and diner.

"May I be your princess, Robert?" She raised her eyebrows.

Our eyes met. Hers were soft and warm. If eyes

were the mirror of the soul, Courtney *was* a princess.

"For as long as you'd like," I whispered.

She pushed her lips into a mock pout. "I don't think I believe that."

"How about until we get back to Jon and Gretchen's?" I asked.

"Sounds like a bargain," she agreed, breaking into a smile as she stuck out her hand. We shook, letting the grasp last a moment longer than we needed.

Getting out, we strolled along the block of stores. I pointed to Scotland by the Yard, a shop advertising handmade, imported woolens.

"Would you mind? I want to get something for my mother."

Courtney nodded and followed me inside. We studied the scarves and sweaters. She pointed out the strengths and weaknesses of each piece with expertise.

"Your young lady knows her wool," said a gray-haired man with a thick Scottish accent. His heavy gray mustache hung long, covering his upper lip. He was tall and wiry, wearing a fine-looking kilt in place of trousers.

"What a beautiful tartan," Courtney observed when she saw him.

"Thank you, missy." He smiled broadly when he heard her accent. "Where are you two from?"

Courtney blushed. "I come from Gloucestershire." She touched my arm. "My friend is from Boston."

The man directed us toward the rear, bringing out a beautifully knit cardigan.

"It's the best we have." He beamed. "Finest imported wool and hand-woven. For you folks," he whispered, looking around to make sure no one overheard. "Fifteen dollars." The price tag said twenty-five.

I took it and held it up, trying to judge the size. Courtney held it to her chest. She examined it, expertly feeling the wool, turning the threads between her fingers as she nodded her approval. "This is a delightful piece, Robbie. It would be perfect for your mother. Wonderful material and finely made."

"Keep it," I said, giving the man a twenty. He wrapped it in brown paper. I took the parcel as we thanked him. He followed Courtney with his eyes. As she headed out the door, he took my arm.

"That's one bonnie lass you've got there." He slapped my back. "You're a lucky man."

Courtney turned and stood in the doorway, framed by the verdant backdrop of the mountains and the striking blue of Long Lake.

"Thank you," I nodded, shaking his hand and wishing with all my heart that she was mine.

Chapter Seven

The afternoon was as magnificent as the company. A northwest wind had descended, bringing relief from the heat and humidity. The fresh breeze sprinkled tiny whitecaps over Long Lake as feathery clouds hurried across the deep blue of the June sky. Courtney and I were willing spectators as we moved along the walk next to the lake.

"Tell me about your home." I asked. "It's in the west?"

"That's right. Briarwood. It was lovely." She looked at me. "Thanks to the war, we couldn't travel much." A faraway look crossed her face, adding, "Mother and Grandfather were very protective." Courtney stopped. "I kept myself busy exploring on the estate," she continued. "Endless riding trails, lovely streams, and hardwood groves. It got lonely. Little companionship except for Mummy, my nanny, and Simon."

"Simon?"

"Yes, that's my grandfather." She looked up at me. "I thought I'd mentioned him. I hope you get to meet him. He's unlike anyone I've ever known." Her eyes showed something akin to awe. "You'd like him."

"I hope so, too, Courtney. What about your father?"

"Ah, the inscrutable Duncan." Courtney shook her head. Melancholy transformed her features. She cast her gaze down. "When he was at home, and it wasn't often, he treated Mummy and me as if we were strangers. I dreaded it."

I tensed, having no right to ask. "Courtney, did he ever...?"

She raised her hand, anticipating my question, a harsh expression frozen on her face. "No. Never laid a hand on us." She paused. "I sometimes think it would have been better if he had." She shuddered and laughed. It was brittle and cold. "At least that would have been something. Recognition we existed." Her words trailed off. "He sent me here. Gretchen came to fetch me. I never knew her. She's been very kind." Her words were clipped. "I think my father was angry Mummy left me her estate," she said, frowning. "But I have to be twenty-one." She shrugged. "I'm not a young lady of means for another week." She sighed. "So I may have to keep begging your cigarettes." She laughed. I joined her.

Courtney beamed. "I did have another love."

Was that jealousy gnawing at me?

"The Holsteiner my mother gave me on my twelfth birthday." She sighed. "I named him Romeo after my favorite hero." Laughing softly, her eyes found mine as she played with her hair.

I breathed a sigh of relief.

"He had the most incredible coat, Robert. Black and lustrous." She touched my hand softly. "It shone like glass after our workouts. He stood sixteen hands high. There was nothing we couldn't do together. I miss him dreadfully." Her eyes found the sprinkling of clouds overhead.

"Will you be going back to England?" I asked hesitantly, not sure I wanted to know.

She looked up at me, eyes wide and curious. "I miss so many things I left behind, but I think I may stay here awhile." She blushed.

Suddenly, she stopped and sat on a bench facing the water. I sat next to her, our shoulders touching. "What about you? Auntie told me so much. I want to hear everything." She looked at me, eyebrows raised.

"Sorry to disappoint you, but there's not much to tell."

"Nonsense. I must hear every detail," she said, touching my forearm.

"I went to Exeter, a private school north of Boston, then Harvard."

She nodded.

"I just graduated. I'd tried to enlist before the end of the war but they rejected me for a bad knee."

"You're conflicted about it. Part of you feels relieved but another feels sorry you didn't serve."

She'd read my thoughts again. "You're incredibly perceptive."

"No. But from what I've seen of you, I know that's how you'd feel." She touched my shoulder. "Robbie, we're all called upon to be heroes in different ways. I'm sure that when your time comes, you'll do the proper thing."

"I hope you're right," I whispered, studying the lake. "Anyway, I'm going to law school in the fall. I live on Boston Harbor, played center field on the baseball team until my knee gave out, and—"

She'd listened politely to my brief résumé, not letting me finish. "And have a brilliant beauty waiting for you back in Boston. And what does she want to be?" Courtney whispered, finding my eyes. "Besides Mrs. Robert McGregor."

"I told you we have no agreement..."

She interrupted again. "Robert. Please. Stop dodging the question."

"All right. She wants to be the first female surgeon at Massachusetts General Hospital. Rachel's very ambitious."

"Are you worried?" she asked.

"Worried?"

"Yes, Robbie. Being here with me while...?"

"Rachel."

"Yes, while Rachel's in Boston thinking you're

spending the day with my boring relatives. Isn't that what you're going to tell her?" Courtney's smile teased.

"I suppose so," I admitted. "What should I say?"

"That you showed a lonely English girl a bit of the countryside." She laughed. "Don't take me too seriously."

"All right." I needed to change the subject. "I know about your magnificent horse, your two cats, Cepheus and what's her name?"

"Cassiopeia...*C-a-s-s-i-o-p-e-i-a*!" she spelled out.

"Oh." I grinned. "I forgot. You have so many animal friends with unusual names, it's hard to keep track."

She nodded, laughing.

"What about people? You must have someone besides your aunt and your nanny."

She lowered her lashes and turned. When she raised her eyes, finding mine, I felt my heart race. She touched my shoulder again.

"I think I've found someone." Her fingers walked lightly down my sleeve. I swallowed.

"Is this another tease?" I whispered, waiting for her answer.

"No. I don't play those games."

"Then you have," I told her.

"Well," she said, exhaling as she removed her hand. "Enough philosophy, McGregor."

I stood, still tingling from her touch.

"I owe you some cigarettes," she said, looking thoughtfully toward the small collection of stores. "I'll go get some and then we can try that salmon you were raving about. My treat."

"You don't have to keep buying things. I thought you were short of funds."

She laughed. "I can manage. You're a cheap date. After all, I talked you into bringing me along, boring you with stories about my life and pets."

I took her by the shoulders. If she was searching for compliments, I'd gladly oblige. "I wanted you to come."

She twisted her lips, doing her best to hide a smile. "Thank you." Her face grew flushed. "I hoped that was the case, but it's nice to hear you say it," she confessed. "Come on." She quickened her pace, heading toward the general store. "Cigarettes, then salmon."

"Interesting menu," I joked and hurried to catch her.

Chapter Eight

It was almost three when we left the small restaurant. The inside had been spare and utilitarian, offering little charm or atmosphere. Cracked red vinyl covered the seats, worn red Formica the tabletops. But the salmon and the view—of the scenery and my luncheon companion—were superb.

Courtney devoured two servings. We drank beer served in paper cups. I think there were others around us, but our eyes never left each other. We talked about her education—she'd attended a private girls' school she detested. The other girls were dull, giddy, and vacuous. Worse, it took her away from her beloved Briarwood and Romeo.

"Did you graduate?" I asked. She was brilliant and talented. Courtney could be anything she wanted to be.

Her mouth twisted into a pout. "Yes. But I'm taking some time off from formal schooling. Thinking about my options." Her smile was shallow. It looked forced.

I wanted to pursue the subject. It made no sense. Someone with her potential and means could attend any exclusive finishing school, Oxford or Cambridge. Why home study? But she looked around, playing with her hair and the silverware. I wondered if her father was to blame. I let it pass, telling her about my life at Harvard, my friends, activities, and my sailboat, avoiding mention of Rachel.

I told her about my father's death. He was my

hero, always there with sage advice or a willing ear when I needed one. I hoped my brother could fill the vacuum. Courtney's eyes grew damp when I spoke about my father's death.

"I understand." She squeezed my hand. "My mother was like that."

"The salmon was great," I said as we left the restaurant. "Thanks for the treat but, I wish you'd let me pay."

"It's the best I've ever had," she enthused, rubbing her stomach as she closed her eyes. "And I wouldn't hear of it. I wanted to be a proper young lady and give you something for letting me tag along."

"I told you. I wanted you to come." I held her eyes with mine. I sneaked my arm around her waist and squeezed playfully.

"Hey," she squealed. "Be careful. You may see that fish again."

"That's an image I'd rather not think about." I laughed and let her go, looking at my watch.

"Got an appointment?" she questioned.

"Actually, I'm meeting my brother at 7:30."

"Oh." She looked deflated. "Then you...you won't be at dinner tonight?"

I shook my head. "Sorry. No." And I was. "Let's take a quick walk up that trail overlooking the lake. I'll bet the views are spectacular." I gestured toward the narrow path at the end of the sidewalk.

"I'm sorry, Robert." She stopped, hanging her head after a few yards. "We can head back." She turned toward the lake, her face strained and taut. "Being with you makes me feel alive and happy again. But I'm fooling myself," she whispered.

"Being here with you is no flight of fancy, Courtney," I reassured her. "It's real. Very real." I wanted to tell her she was the most beautiful and exciting woman I'd ever met.

"I want to believe you, Robbie, but even if there was no one else in your life…" She turned away, but not before I glimpsed the moisture in her dark eyes.

"Can we talk about it?" I asked.

"It's complicated," she whispered, searching the distant mountains with her eyes. She headed up the trail, leaving me behind. When I followed, a hidden root caught my foot. Hearing a loud snap, I fell to the ground in pain.

Courtney turned and rushed back, kneeling next to me. "Robbie, what happened? Are you all right?"

"I don't know. I think I sprained my ankle. Maybe worse." I rolled onto my back, grasping her hand. "Courtney…"

"Shhh," she whispered, putting her fingers to my lips. "We'll sort it out."

"But I…"

"Please. Be still. We'll sort it out. I promise," she insisted with a reassuring smile as she examined my ankle. It was already swelling. My walking shoe felt tight.

I shook my head. "Can you drive?" The ride back to the estate came to mind.

"Don't worry." She squeezed my hand. "It'll be fine. Robbie, do you believe in me?"

"Believe in you?" I asked, not sure of her meaning. "Of course."

She bit her lip, closed her eyes and touched the pendant beneath her scarf.

"Shhh. Close your eyes and take my hand."

I started to protest, but as soon as she touched me, I was at peace in a way I'd never known. Energy flowed through me, like a mild electric shock. She touched my ankle and the pain disappeared. It was wonderful, like a strong dose of morphine, only better, much, much better.

I tried to speak.

Courtney whispered in a language I'd never

heard. My head grew very light...

****

Courtney massaged his swollen ankle, blue energy radiating from her fingertips. Slowly she lifted her hand and knelt on the trail in front of Robbie, studying every line and feature. She let her other hand run through his thick black hair, down and over his chiseled chin, touching every angle on the face that now consumed her. It had sounded so simple. Come to America, find him, attract him, use him for the ritual. Then what? They'd been waiting a millennium to fulfill the prophecy. Robert was the key. The chosen one.

Find him, attract him, use him. *So simple,* Courtney thought sadly, brushing the tears aside. But it was not simple, not anymore. She stared at Robert, smiling, warmth and happiness overflowing as she thought about every precious moment with him. The emotion was so new and different, unlike anything Courtney had known.

Love. She'd heard it spoken of so often. It had become a cliché. Now she knew what it felt like. Her mother used the word each night as she tucked Courtney in and kissed her goodnight. "Good night, princess. I love you." But this love was something so different, so all-consuming and so beautiful she had no way of comprehending it. It filled her.

Courtney leaned forward and found his hand. Taking it, she bent to his lips, eyes closing as she kissed them softly. "Good night, my prince. I love you," she whispered as she opened her eyes.

She stood, trying to focus, to understand what was happening. Courtney had no idea how her emotions had grown so strong so quickly. It wasn't supposed to happen—not so quickly. Not this way. She should be immune, insulated from human feelings. She repeated the mantra. *He is a vessel, a means for fulfilling the prophecy.*

Love at first sight, Courtney thought as she watched him. She'd heard the expression but never believed it. Something from novels and the cinema. She was wrong. Studying him, she was angry and delighted over this strange unexpected thing that had taken control of her. No matter. She must be strong. Putting her hands on his temples, she rubbed them gently. "You will awaken and feel refreshed, Robert. Remember none of what has happened."

Courtney backed away. Yes, she loved him. Desperately. But Courtney had a destiny. She had no choice. She must complete the ritual and keep her emotions from destroying them both.

****

"Hello," I said as I awoke. "Sorry. I must have fallen asleep." I yawned, feeling refreshed. "I had no idea how tired I was. Let's head back," I said, checking my watch.

"Maybe you should just sit. Relax for a minute," Courtney suggested.

"I'm fine." I stood. A dizzy and disorienting sensation filled my head. I braced myself against a tree. It passed quickly. "I'm sorry, but I have to get back."

"If you're sure everything's all right." She smiled weakly, playing with her hair. She looked drawn and weary. "How's your ankle?" she asked.

"Ankle? Which one?" I looked at them, curious at her question.

"No matter," she said. "I thought you might have twisted one on the trail."

"No, I'm fine," I assured her as we headed toward the village. "Never felt better."

Chapter Nine

We arrived at the boardwalk just after four. Courtney walked back toward the car—silent, wearing a pensive, strained expression as she stared straight ahead. Her enormous eyes showed dark circles beneath them.

"Are you all right?" I asked.

She shot a glance at me. "I'm fine," she whispered.

I held the door for her. She got in, eyelids drooping. I followed her into the Jaguar and depressed the clutch. I turned the key. The four-cylinder engine purred to life and I backed out, heading toward the southern end of Sebago and the estate.

"So you're really going to disappear for dinner?" Courtney asked.

I nodded. "I don't want to." And I didn't. "Michael's my brother and we haven't seen each other for months." I offered my best I'm-sorry look. Besides, I needed to talk to someone about what was happening. Someone objective. Michael was not only my brother, he was my best friend and confidant.

"That's all right, Robert," she said coolly, turning to study the countryside. "I think there's a dance tonight. Auntie's been after me to go for weeks." She shrugged. "Might give it a try."

Was she trying to provoke me? Searching for the answer she wanted to hear? "That's up to you," I countered, feeling guilty about confessing my feelings earlier.

My imagination conjured up an endless line of

young men waiting to dance with her. But I had to be strong. This was a dream, a self-indulgent fantasy. It had no place in my well-ordered life.

"Perhaps I will," she offered, pushing her lips together. "I'll be the proper young lady and dress in my finest frock!" she said, continuing to look away, studying the pleasant countryside in the orange glow of the late afternoon sun.

I tried to see her face, but the winding road demanded my attention. I had to settle for snatching a quick glance when the road straightened. Our delightful afternoon had turned dark. I was torn between conscience and emotion, wanting to reach over, take her hand in mine and tell her that I cared for her, knowing I could not.

The little convertible hummed along the narrow roads toward Jon and Gretchen's. Courtney closed her eyes, dozing, a frown spoiling her face. Conflict consumed me. I'd been wrong, flirting with her and allowing her to flirt with me. But as I looked at her, all I could think of was taking Courtney in my arms and kissing her till she was breathless.

No, Robbie, I warned myself. *Get a grip. You have a full life, a loving girl waiting in Boston, and you know so little about Courtney.* But no one had ever made me feel this way. Courtney was the most beautiful and exciting creature I'd ever known. I found the mystery and vulnerability surrounding her overpowering. Being around her was like a dream you hoped would never end.

"*Robbie*," she whispered in her sleep. She pushed closer, snuggling into my arm. I put my hand down, letting my fingers surround hers. Last night I'd thought about my feelings in the abstract, one of those what if games. Suddenly it had all become very real. What if was no longer a question. I remembered my earlier thoughts about an emotional train wreck, knowing I was heading there at breakneck speed. As an image of Rachel danced before my eyes, I let Courtney's hand slip from mine.

Just before 5:30 we arrived at the estate. I let Courtney out in front of the garage.

"Thanks for a lovely day. I enjoyed getting away and seeing the countryside," she said, shaking my hand.

"It was my pleasure," I said, holding her eyes. Emptiness filled me as I pulled the Jag inside. She waited, looking downcast and defeated when I came out. The cool wind from the northwest continued, sending a shiver through her. I used my arm to warm her.

She turned, looking up at me. "That's all right," she whispered.

I nodded, letting go as we headed back through the massive arch leading to the courtyard. Emptiness greeted us. Our fellow guests had played and drunk their fill, retreating to their rooms for a pre-dinner nap.

As we crossed the pool area, someone called, "Hello there," Gretchen said. "Did you have a nice day?"

"A wonderful day," Courtney answered quietly, eyes lingering on me. "Robbie was the perfect tour guide."

Gretchen gave me an I-told-you-so look.

"Splendid. I look forward to hearing the details." She turned away.

"I'm meeting my brother in Jefferson," I explained. "I'll be back later."

"We'll miss you, won't we, dear?" she asked Courtney. "Oh, Robbie, I almost forgot. There was a call from Rachel. I told her you were out for a drive."

"Thanks," I said, trying to hide my frustration. "I'll call her back."

Gretchen strode inside.

Courtney stood, lips tight, staring at the pool

apron. She touched my hand briefly. "It's all right, Robbie." She sighed, running inside before I could move. I kicked the gravel, turned, and headed for my room to shower.

I threw open the door to my room, furious with myself, my feelings, and fate. On the bed sat a large manila envelope. My name was scrawled on it in rough letters. It was filled with newspaper clippings. Headlines jumped out at me: "Another Mysterious Death at Briarwood." "Young Mistress Witnesses Another Tragedy." "Coroner Mystified by Woman's Death," and others, "Is Witchcraft Alive and Well, Living Under Our Noses?"

I stuffed them back into the envelope and threw it on my bed. Jonathan again, trying to poison my mind? Why? I clenched my fists, anxious to find him, but there was no time. I wanted to find Courtney to make sure she was all right before I left.

I headed for the bathroom, my mind swimming. I shaved, took a quick shower, and went back to the bedroom. I stared at the envelope. Pouring the contents out a second time, I scanned the details. There was nothing damning, just tabloid headlines to attract attention. Mysterious deaths and the occult were always popular. Michael had spent time in England. I wondered if he'd have any insights.

I looked at my watch and seeing the time, threw on a plaid sports shirt, my light cotton trousers, and walking shoes. After splashing Creed on my face, I grabbed my jacket and headed for the door.

I opened the door, hoping to find Courtney. There was no need. She waited, sitting on a lounge chair, still dressed in her clothes from our trip. When she saw me, she got up, closing the distance between us.

"Sorry about running off like that." She held my eyes with hers.

I tried to smile. "I understand. It's been a

confusing day."

She nodded. "More so than I'd planned."

She reached down and touched the envelope. "Taking something to Michael?"

I studied her face. *More so than I'd planned.* Curious comment.

"Robbie?"

"Yes. No. Nothing special. Just some newspaper articles."

She brightened, accepting my explanation. "Perhaps later?" she asked in a whisper, raising her eyebrows.

"Maybe we can catch up after the dance."

Courtney bit her lip and looked up at me, face flushed. "I'm not going." She turned and gave me a wave. "Got to clean up and get dressed for dinner."

I reached out, grabbing her arm. "Walk me to the garage please."

She nodded. "All right."

Seeing no one, I reached for her hand. Our fingers intertwined. Once inside the garage, Courtney closed the door and put her arms around me. She held me briefly then followed me to the large doors that opened onto the gravel drive.

She stood facing me, eyes glistening as she gave me a smile. "Have a good time," she whispered, reaching up to kiss my cheek. "I'll be thinking of you."

"Me, too." I hesitated, wanting to stay with her. I settled into the Jag, started it, and left the garage. I found myself watching her reflection in the fading sunlight, mystified by what had happened since last night and what I was going to do about it.

Chapter Ten

Courtney watched the taillights of his small roadster disappear in the twilight. But despite her fixation on Robbie, her mind was far away. She possessed many gifts. Both her parents had been powerful witches. Courtney was the most sensitive and perceptive telepath her fellow witches had ever seen. And she'd mastered something even more difficult. Courtney could pick and choose whose thoughts she read. She'd become a high priestess at the tender age of fourteen. Her skills were razor sharp and like Ethwyn, the goddess who'd told of the prophecy and her predecessor from antiquity, those skills had proven flawless.

But for the role she would play in directing mankind away from the violence and cruelty that seemed integral to its makeup, she would need every ounce of skill and intuition. How these manifold intuitive abilities related to one another would be of consummate importance in helping her. Now, these abilities raised an alarm.

At first she thought her surprising attraction to Robert had upset the delicate balance her powers required. But by the time Courtney returned to the estate she knew it was more. Telepathic signals, she'd learned after years of practice and study, resembled radio waves. They could be sent to far-flung destinations with ease one day while sending them across an open field proved impossible on others. It was this eccentric quality of transfer that had kept her from concern for much of the day. She simply couldn't be sure what she was sensing. By the time Robert drove off for dinner, Courtney's attraction for him was not the only thing bothering her.

A deep evil invaded her thoughts, something so sinister she could no longer ignore it. She recognized she had been so consumed with her unexpected passion for Robbie she'd let those emotions mask the other, more foreboding images. Courtney needed to talk to Simon. Needed to do it very quickly. Her powers were not whimsical. They were both accurate and frightening. She was certain that somewhere a force was working to defeat what she and her fellow witches had been planning for 1100 years. If these unknown invaders succeeded, the world could be thrown into a state of chaos that would last for decades, perhaps centuries and leave few survivors.

****

On the thirty-five-mile drive to Conway, I thought about what to tell Michael. We planned to catch up. Since his return from the war, Michael had been distant, a recluse. He accepted the teaching position at Dartmouth and moved out of our Beacon Hill townhouse last year. I'd hoped to break through the wall surrounding him. Now, I had something else in mind, something more immediate and more selfish. My brother was brilliant, kind, and compassionate. Qualities I needed tonight. How would he react when I shared the details of the last twenty-four hours? Could I explain my feelings for Courtney I wondered as I studied the envelope on the seat beside me.

My mind kept returning to Rachel. I should have called her. Until I walked into that steamy dining room last evening, I thought I loved her. I knew better now. Love was what I felt whenever I thought of or saw Courtney. The mysteries surrounding her were multiplying by the minute, but rather than be put off, I found it all intoxicating.

Like reading a great whodunit. You were terrified and exhilarated at once. I couldn't wait to get to the next chapter.

I followed Michael's directions and pulled up in front of the rambling farmhouse. It stood fifty feet above the gravel turnaround, nestled in a wooded swale between two gentle slopes leading to a ski tow. The war had left Michael a shadow of what he had once been. But whatever he had become, he was still my older brother. Someone who listened thoughtfully and told the truth.

Before I had even put the Jaguar in gear and applied the hand brake, his burly frame came ambling down the winding stairway. I held out my hand. Michael pushed it aside and grabbed me in a bear hug.

"Come here, you lucky son of a gun." He released me, backing away as he wore a broad grin from ear to ear. "Let's see what it looks like to be a man about town. Mom keeps sending me the newspaper articles about you. And now there's a special girl I understand?"

"Hi, Mike." I nodded. "How's it going?"

He put a massive hand on either side of my head, eyes narrowing as he searched my face.

"I'm doing all right. But...what about you?" He searched my face and frowned. "I expected upbeat, robust." He shook his head. "Hell, you look like you just lost your best friend. Hell, I thought that was me, so I hope it's not the case."

He put his arm around me and ushered me up the long staircase into his spacious living room. The interior belied the rambling farmhouse look. It had the appearance and feel of a hunting lodge without the trophies.

The rough-hewn pine beams gave the room a pleasant scent, intersecting and bridging the high ceiling twelve feet above us. Simple hand-crafted chairs and a long, overstuffed couch were the main furnishings. The walls were covered with photos of his time in the army and his ski adventures. In the rear, an expanse of glass offered a spectacular view of the slopes.

A well-stocked pine-paneled bar said Mike still enjoyed a good drink. He pushed me in that direction and insisted I sit on one of the stools. Despite the rough, utilitarian look, I settled comfortably onto the leather seat.

"The place looks great. I love it, especially that window in the back," I said, taking in the comfortable surroundings. It struck me that the interior of the house was the perfect embodiment of my brother.

He went behind the bar, took out two ice-cold beers, chilled mugs, and poured. "All right, is this gonna be easy, or do I have to get you shitfaced before you tell me what's happening?"

I took a long draft of the beer. It went down too easily—like ice water. "I may need a couple of these." I smiled as I shook my head. He kept studying me. "Keep 'em coming."

"No kidding, Rob, you look like shit."

I took another long swallow of beer.

"Well, at least tell me about the lady in your life. Rachel? That should cheer you up."

I groaned inwardly.

Three beers later, Mike stood on his deck, concentrating on the two massive tenderloins sizzling on the grill. He kept watch on me as he applied his secret marinade.

It had taken the better part of an hour. I told him about the reunion and Courtney. He tried to come to grips with my explanation. "Come on, Robert, we all see sexy kids." He gave me that patronizing guy-to-guy look.

"Whoa!" I stood, grabbing the bar for balance.

"It's not like that. Courtney's twenty, not some teenager I'm leering at. I really like her. More than that"—I swallowed hard and vocalized the thought I'd been fighting—"I...I think I'm falling in love with her."

He waved, dismissing my words as he narrowed his eyes. "Come on. You've only known her for a day." He threw down the barbecue tools and shook his head. "Maybe this is denial. A reaction to getting serious with your girl in Boston." He shrugged.

I rolled my eyes as I weaved behind the bar to open my fourth beer.

"Michael, you're—not—listening. It's not denial," I repeated. "Not some crazy weekend fling. I..." The words stuck in my throat.

He left the barbecue and looked at me. "Jesus. You're serious, aren't you?" He shook his head. "What do you want from me—my blessing?"

"I don't know, Mike. I needed to talk to someone and you drew the short straw."

"Okay. Let's acknowledge love at first sight and assume that you and this English girl are the perfect pair." His comments sounded patronizing. "Have you really thought this through?"

He took the steaks off the grill with a giant fork and went to check the corn boiling on the stove.

"You two are going to be love birds. Are you really going to dump Rachel and piss off all our important friends to play house?" he asked. "Have you taken leave of your senses, Robbie?"

"Well..." I had no rebuttal.

We sat down to eat, Michael's eyes burning a hole in my chest.

"Look," he began. "I know you've always been a charmer, but is it possible she's a gold digger? We have a well-known family name, money. Do you think that—"

"No!" I interrupted. "She's due to inherit a

fortune. She doesn't need my money. And she didn't even know me until two days ago."

"Okay, maybe she's a tease, a girl who decided to screw up your life just for kicks. There are girls who enjoy that kind of thing."

"Hell, Mike, I know that stuff happens, but I can't buy that either. She's more confused and frustrated about what's going on than me."

"All right, option three—the hard one. What you're feeling is real, just what you say it is."

"Okay. Where does that leave us?" I asked. The juicy tenderloins remained untouched. I looked at him. He looked back, shaking his head.

"Shit, Robbie, how do I know?" He exhaled.

I paused, wondering whether to show him the envelope. Why not? He already thought I had punched a one-way ticket for the nearest asylum.

"There's something else."

"What more can there be?"

I left the table and went outside, stumbling down the long staircase. When I got to the Jag, I took the envelope and came back inside.

"This. Someone slipped it under my door today."

"Someone did what?" Michael asked as he spread the contents on the table. He scanned the articles, looking up as he did. Mike was the role model for the term "quick study." After being badly wounded on D-Day, he'd been a superb intelligence analyst. My brother scanned the pieces. I stood and paced. When he was done, he pushed back, balancing himself on two rough-hewn chair legs.

"Whoa." He cleared his throat. His expression had changed. He rubbed his forehead. "Someone's trying to tell you something. Maybe warn you. What do you know about this girl you haven't told me?"

"I've told you everything. Well, almost. I think Jonathan put that stuff in my room. He doesn't like Courtney."

"He doesn't like Courtney," he repeated soberly, shaking his head. "Let's back up to the 'almost' part of the conversation, Robert." He stood and pushed me toward one of the overstuffed chairs in the living room.

"Well, she can communicate with animals and wears this real strange necklace and talks about being a witch and I swear she can read my mind."

He stared at me, shaking his head. "Have you read this stuff?"

I nodded.

"Come on. People die mysteriously and Courtney happens to be the only witness. Signs of witchcraft. And you told me her father sent her away after her mother died in a riding accident? Jesus. Rob, I've served over there. You and I may think this is something out of a dime novel, but I have to tell you, a lot of those folks believe in..." He let his words die as he shook his head again. After a short silence he stood and laughed out loud. "So, my younger brother is involved with a witch."

"Come on. You don't believe in witchcraft, Michael. And if she was involved with those deaths the police would have..."

"Look, Robbie, you're my younger brother and you know I love you. But you have to admit, there's some crazy shit going on here."

Staring at him, I had an epiphany.

"Can you do something for me, Michael?" I begged.

"Hell, for my baby brother, I'll try. What?" A frown spoiled his face.

"You know people over there. In Special Branch and DMI. Don't they call it MI-5 now? Could you talk to them? They may know something, maybe play detective for an old buddy?" I was asking more than I had a right to. But if there was any chance to get to the truth, I had to take it. "If something is out of line, I'll walk away," I promised, knowing I could no more do that than fly the Jaguar across the English Channel. "But if this is what it looks like— smoke and mirrors, grist for the tabloids..."

"Yeah. What if it is, are you gonna ditch your life for this girl?"

"I don't know, Mike. But I have to know. Please." I put my hands together in mock prayer.

Michael checked his watch and put up his hand. "It's three in the morning over there. One of the top guys owes me big time. Saved his life in an air raid. Okay. Can you keep your hands off this British cutie until tomorrow, Romeo?"

I nodded and crossed my heart. "Thanks, Mike. I'll never forget this." I stood up and headed for the door, swaying with the effects of the alcohol on an empty stomach. "Keep the articles until the next time we meet."

"Where the hell are you going, man? You didn't even touch that five-dollar piece of meat in front of you."

"Sorry, brother. I can't." I checked my watch. It was almost ten. "I've gotta get back. I just have to see her again."

"Love. Hope I never catch it! Go ahead. Get the hell out of here." He waved me toward the door. "Expect to hear from me. And drive safely, goddamn it." He slapped me on the shoulder. "You've had a lot to drink and if anything happened to you, I'd never forgive myself and neither would Mom."

Chapter Eleven

I stumbled down the long staircase and jumped into my roadster without benefit of the door. Michael stood on the deck shaking his head as he waved goodnight. The alcohol in my empty stomach took control. Random thoughts and questions swam through my head. About Courtney, my feelings, witchcraft, Jonathan's dislike for her, Rachel, and what to say when I worked up the courage to call her.

The dark, narrow roads shot past in a blur. I had no memory of their passing. In no time I found myself at the estate. I vowed to find Jon and give him a punch in the nose, but there was something I wanted more: to find Courtney and stare into her enormous brown eyes. Maybe I was bewitched. I'd never been a drippy romantic. Every relationship was fun, satisfying, and good for me. This all-consuming passion was something totally new and I wasn't sure how I felt about it.

I was at the turnoff for the estate when I saw the red and blue lights in the rearview mirror. I pulled over a hundred yards from the long gravel driveway, leaning my head against the steering wheel. The officer pulled up behind me and got out of his powerful Ford cruiser. He started toward me. I opened the door and put my foot on the pavement.

"Please, sir," he commanded. "Stay in the vehicle."

As he spoke a vision in a long black skirt and fitted white blouse materialized in the mirror.

"Officer," I overheard her as she approached the

policeman. "This poor man must have been at the hospital. We have a very sick friend and Robert is distraught."

Who could resist that voice, that face, that figure? I turned to watch the show. The trooper surveyed Courtney like a road map.

"Hello." He nodded, giving her a generous smile. As he did, she touched the pendant that adorned her neck, then wrapped her long fingers around his arm.

"Well, miss. If you...say...so..." Was it the alcohol? His speech sounded strange and slurred. I tried to focus. He stood, eyes glassy as he stared at her. She turned in my direction, staring at me. A strange glow illuminated her brown eyes. I felt weak and limp. Imagination and alcohol run amok!

"Just to make sure, Officer...Kent." Courtney turned her attention toward the policeman again. She touched his chest softly. "I'll drive my friend's car the last quarter mile. And as you can tell"—she approached him closely and blew softly in his face—"I'm in perfect condition to drive."

"Ah yes, yes, miss. You certainly are." He took a clumsy step backward, shaking his head. "That's fine." He walked erratically back to his vehicle. "Fine, fine condition," he repeated, still shaking his head as he nodded and got in.

"You've been very kind," she thanked him and waved as she walked to my car.

"All right, McGregor," she said between clenched teeth, pushing me. I tried to clear my head as I slid over the gearshift onto the passenger seat. Courtney put the Jaguar into gear and drove it up the driveway and into the garage.

"I waited for you." She frowned. "Do you know how long I've been sitting on the dock?"

I stared at her. "Really...sorry," I mumbled. "Thanks for help. Whad you do to the cop? He look...hypnotized." I chuckled.

"Don't be ridiculous. I tried to save you from being arrested." She shook her head. "He was right. You should never have been driving. That Michael. Some big brother letting you drive like this."

I turned and watched that lovely profile, those exquisite ears. "D'you know you have the most beautiful nose?" I mumbled, running my finger over it, grinning. My grin spread. I groped clumsily across the bucket seats and slipped my arms around her.

"Oh, Courtney, Courtney," I whispered. My nose rested on her shoulder. She smelled so delicious.

"Come on." She gently pushed me away. "We're getting you some black coffee."

Courtney helped me out of the car. I felt the weight of the keys as she dropped them in my pocket. We left the garage. She walked gracefully. I stumbled next to her.

"Look at that." She stopped and inhaled deeply, pointing as she turned toward the moon. It was almost full, reflecting off her lustrous skin. "Now that's a sight."

I stared at her face. "Sure is," I agreed.

She sighed, resting her hand lightly on my shoulder. "Special things happen on the night of the solstice, the night of the full moon, Robbie. Magical things—things beyond belief." For a moment her eyes seemed to glow again as she stared at the bright orb. I was ready to swear off alcohol. My imagination was definitely running wild. She guided me to the dining room and poured a cup of steaming black coffee.

"Ow," I complained as the hot liquid dribbled down my shirtfront.

"Good God." She picked up a napkin and wiped the hot liquid. "Did you call her? Your...your girlfriend?" Her question had a stern tone.

I shook my head.

"Just as well. You would have sounded

ridiculous. She would have been put off. Come on." She pushed me toward the endless back lawn and sat down, patting the damp ground next to her. "Look at those stars, Robbie. Aren't they exquisite?"

"Yeah...in...in...creble..."

The rest was a blur. I had a foggy recollection of her helping me up, guiding me to my room, and putting me to bed. I had a dream in which Courtney lay next to me. I could smell her perfume, her sweet breath on my face, and somewhere in the dream, she kissed me and told me she loved me. Now that was a dream!

****

Courtney lay next to him, reveling in the pleasure of being close, hearing his soft snoring, and inhaling his fragrance. He whispered her name in his sleep. She felt a grin broaden and work across her face. He loved her. She knew it. Robbie was trying desperately to be faithful to the girl in Boston, but Courtney knew she'd won him. She and Robbie were perfect for each other. There would be no need for spells or telepathy. And both sides of her being— the nascent goddess-in-waiting and the lovesick young woman—were overjoyed. She kissed him softly on the lips and whispered, "I love you."

Slipping out of Robbie's room, Courtney tiptoed across the courtyard heading for the main house. She smiled as she thought about the highway patrolman. But if the policeman had arrested Robbie, it could have been a disaster. Courtney hated using her ability to control others. Visions of a cheap carnival trickster came to mind.

Had Robbie seen the glow in her eyes? If he had, he'd never remember. He'd been so sweet, so adorable, so loving. She assured herself again that he felt the same attraction she did. He had to!

Once inside she walked to Jonathan's office and opened the door, peering down the vacant hallway

67

and casting a cautious glance as she stepped inside. Courtney needed the telephone. Badly. Picking up the receiver, she heard the operator's voice crackling through the line. Just as she was about to speak, the door opened. Jonathan stood facing her.

"What do you want?" he asked with a frown. "Anything wrong?"

She smiled and shook her head.

"Calling Simon," she mouthed.

He nodded, returning her smile. "Good." He crossed the space and sat down in one of the chairs facing the desk. "Mind?" he asked.

"I'm sorry, Uncle Jon," she said. "I need to talk to him alone. In private. If you'd be so kind."

Jonathan frowned. "Is there a problem? I see you tucked your friend in after saving him from the police."

She stared at him as she played with her hair.

He stared for a moment, then stood, his round face showing irritation. Jon was used to getting his way. There was a bit of the spoiled child in him.

"Yes, things are going all right," she said, not quite sure she felt that confident. "I need to talk to Simon in private," she repeated in a whisper, giving him an engaging smile. "Please?"

He nodded. She knew he was cross. "You and Simon are running this show, Courtney. But keep us in the loop. A play is only as good as the supporting cast."

Courtney tapped the phone and spoke into the handset. After a long delay, she asked for the overseas operator and when the woman came on the line gave the woman Simon's number.

"Hello. Courtney?" he answered on the first ring. His rich baritone always inspired confidence in Courtney. But something was different. An edge to his voice. Something guarded.

"Hello, Simon. Sorry to call at this hour." She

checked her watch. It was almost three in the morning in the small Welsh hamlet Simon ruled over.

"How are things progressing?" he asked.

"According to plan." She stopped and inhaled deeply. "But...it's proving more difficult than I thought," she confessed. "Something's happened. Something I had no way of anticipating."

"Really?" He paused. She heard the sound of muffled voices on Simon's end. "Something too difficult for you?"

She sighed, her eyes gazing at the austere portraits surrounding her.

"Are you all right?" he re-phrased his question.

"I will be. After Friday evening."

"What's troubling you, my dear?" he asked.

She was certain he already knew. Courtney brought her eyes back to the desk, playing with her hair as she studied the blotter. "Nothing I can't handle."

"*Courtney?*" He spoke in a strained whisper. "We can have no secrets from one another."

"I've grown very fond of him." She stopped, adding, "More so than I anticipated."

"I see. But of course you'll not let that affect our plans."

"Of course not. I undertand," she assured her mentor. "But it means taking him away from everything in his life. All he holds dear. I have no idea what that may do to him or how he'll feel about me when it's over." She sighed. "But I'll do what I have to. You know that."

He was silent. "I know you will. We knew sacrifices would be involved. You can still use a spell on him. He'll never remember what happened."

"*No!*" she insisted. "No spells." She stopped, knowing Simon understood. Courtney wanted Robert to be her partner without spells and magic.

Wanted him to be with *her*, not under some bloody spell.

He was silent for a moment, then continued, "Now, I'll be there on Sunday. Courtney, there can be no slipups. You do know that." He let it go.

Courtney needed no reminder of how important this was. She thought of mankind's strife and cruelty in the twentieth century. Without the ritual, the prophecy foretold the evil would continue and grow worse.

But Courtney was worried. She knew her mentor. Too well. Had never failed to read his moods, with or without her powers. And now, she sensed he was hiding something. It reinforced her misgivings from earlier in the day. She had the feeling he was holding something back.

"Simon. Is everything all right on your end? Nothing you want to tell me?"

"Everything's fine," he said a little too quickly. His words had a hollow ring. "Good night." He hung up abruptly.

Courtney stood, frustrated, angry, and more than a little frightened.

Chapter Twelve

"Oh," I groaned. The knock grew louder.

"Mr. McGregor, are you in there?" I recognized the housekeeper's voice.

I cleared my throat. "Yeah, I'm here," I answered, checking my watch. My head felt the size of a watermelon, my mouth like the inside of a riding boot.

Nine-forty-five. I never slept this late.

"I have a telephone message for you. From a Mr. Michael McGregor."

Michael! I jumped out of bed, scrambling for my robe. He must have found something. I opened the door, putting my hand over my mouth. I didn't want the woman to faint.

She smiled and handed me a slip of paper: *Got something important. Call me back as soon as possible. Mike.*

"Thanks." I smiled and backed into the room. I sat on the bed, trying to remember the evening. The conversation with Michael was clear enough. The drive home foggy. But I remembered the policeman and Courtney's Academy Award performance. I had a memory of something odd about the way he acted, but it was hazy. She drove my car, got me coffee, a vague recollection of the moon, something strange about her eyes, and memories of the backyard. It was difficult to separate fact from fantasy.

I rose, trudged to the bathroom and took three aspirin. I hopped into the shower, shaved, and spent ten minutes brushing my teeth and gargling with Listerine before heading to the house.

Heading across the courtyard, I hoped Jon's office was free. I shielded my eyes against the sun and my hangover. The heat and humidity had returned, but talking with Michael was my mission.

I waved and nodded to the guests sitting around the pool. Entering the main hallway, I heard someone playing a classical piece. Chopin. The pianist was exceptional. The music stopped. I stole a quick look inside.

There were no lights on, but the large ballroom was illuminated by light from the east-facing windows. Someone sat at the spectacular grand piano. I was about to leave when the pianist launched into Debussy's *La Mer*. I stepped into the room. The artist stopped and turned. Courtney stared at me, her face in shadow.

I applauded. She stood and approached, head tilted. "Please stop it," she ordered. "You're embarrassing me."

"You're wonderful."

She stopped in midstride and studied my face as she narrowed her eyes. The hint of a smile worked across her face.

"I've had lots of practice and some very special teachers."

"Really. How long have you been playing?"

"Seems like forever." She wore a distant look.

I held up my hand. "Don't get too close."

"Don't be silly," she whispered, closing the distance between us.

She stood in front of me, looking perfect again. She wore a plaid skirt, dark-green knee socks, and a long-sleeved blouse. Today her medallion hid behind a dark scarf that matched her socks. She saw me staring and touched it.

"Courtney, I'm sorry about last night. And I wasn't joking. You really don't want to get close this morning. I did my best with Listerine, but I haven't had breakfast yet."

"Actually you were very sweet last night. I like you that way. You let your guard down." Her eyes sparkled as she searched my face.

"Oh. I hope I didn't do or say…"

Her fingers touched my lips. I closed my eyes, inhaling her jasmine scent.

"You were perfect. The proper gentleman throughout." She squeezed my hand.

I offered her a cigarette. "It may kill the smell of the alcohol."

Laughing, she took one as I lit it. "Don't punish yourself." She passed it back to me. "Remember, you're chumming around with a girl who spends her time sweating on the back of a horse or mucking out stalls." She grinned and held her nose. I smiled, wondering what would happen when this magical fantasy ended.

She looked at her watch. "Got to go. Have an appointment. Auntie is taking me to the salon to get ready for the dinner this evening." She raised an eyebrow playfully.

"Me, too." I hoped nothing my brother had discovered would change my feelings for her.

"How 'bout later by the pool?" she suggested.

"Meet you after lunch."

"It's a date. And don't go promising anyone a place on your dance card for this evening." She giggled and waved as she walked away.

I left, heading down the oriental runner to Jonathan's office. The door stood closed. Violence was no longer on my agenda, but I'd determined to give him a piece of my mind.

"Hello," I said, knocking on the massive six-panel door.

"Robbie? Come in." He stood as I entered, holding out his hand. He seemed pleasant. "Good to see you. The reunion with your brother went well, I

73

hope?"

"Very," I offered.

"Is everything all right?" he asked, frowning.

"It's about those newspaper clippings you put in my room."

"What?" He held up his hand, coming around the desk. "Newspaper clippings?"

"Please, Jon." I waved dismissively. "The ones about death and witchcraft on Courtney's estate."

He sat on his desk. "Robbie, you think I'd stoop that low?" If this was a lie, he was doing a good job. "I'd talk to you, man-to-man." He shook his head, gray eyes showing concern.

I wanted to argue. Trouble was, I believed him.

"If it wasn't you, who could have done that? And why would anyone want to? You suggested that Courtney was surrounded by mystery. That she might be involved with…"

He held up his hand again. "I'm glad you dropped by. I had a surprising phone call this morning. I may have been wrong about her."

"Really?"

"Yes. We're going to have visitors on Sunday. That may shed some light on my suspicions, even dispel them." He wore a satisfied look.

"Who's coming?"

"Well." He grinned, enjoying his secret, playing the wizard who'd solve the puzzle. "That must stay a secret until they arrive."

"You're not going to tell Courtney?" I asked. "What about Gretchen?"

He shook his head. "No, but I promise they'll both be flabbergasted!"

He'd decided to keep it a secret. A frown crossed my face. "All right. But I'd still like to know who put those articles in my room."

"Wish I could help." He fiddled with his mustache.

"Well, since I'm here, could I use the phone? I have a couple of calls to make."

He looked at his watch. "I'm polishing my remarks for a talk next week." He gestured toward the chair. "Be my guest. I'll get some coffee."

He patted me on the back. "Gonna call your sweetheart, eh?"

I nodded.

I shook his hand. If Jon was innocent, and it appeared that way, who would have collected all that material so quickly and had the nerve to break into my room? The clippings came from Britain. Some were several years old. Who had a motive to sabotage my relationship with Courtney? I exhaled loudly as I sat down behind the desk. I smiled. So far, life with Courtney had been anything but dull.

Chapter Thirteen

A good man would have called Rachel right away. I dialed Michael as soon as Jonathan closed the door. My brother picked up on the first ring.

"Where the hell have you been?" Michael sounded irritated.

"I'm sorry, Mike. Getting the phone around here isn't easy. What'd you find out?"

"Well," he began. "It doesn't look like Courtney was a suspect in any of those deaths."

I sighed. "Thanks, Michael."

"But there's more," he added. "A lot more."

"Okay, Mike. What's going on? Are you going to tell me she really is a witch?" I forced a laugh.

When he didn't answer, I cleared my throat.

"My friends are MI-5, Rob. They deal in facts."

"And?"

"They had to call their connections in the West Country—constables, country folks, the locals. They put more stock in rumor and folklore."

"Come on. Is this twenty questions?"

"They've come up with some things. My friend's doing me a big favor and still making calls. Can we meet sometime?"

I thought of Courtney and how much I wanted to see her. Who knew how long this star-crossed relationship would last. If it turned out to be our last chance to spend an evening together, I couldn't miss it.

"Okay, just not tonight. Please." I looked at my watch. "I know it's asking a lot, but is there any chance we could meet sometime today? Maybe this afternoon?"

A long silence. "All right. How about 3:00? I'll make it easy for you. There's a place halfway between us called Boone's Bar and Grill, on Route 302. It should only take you twenty minutes to get there. I'll tell you what I have, and you'll be back by dinner."

I stared at the phone and hung up.

I checked my watch, played with Jon's brass letter opener, studied the plaques and mementos on the walls, then finally picked the receiver up to wait for the operator. When prompted, I mumbled Rachel's number into the phone.

After a short silence and a series of clicks, it rang. Once...twice...three times. I thought I might be spared the task of bending the truth. As I was about to replace the handset, she picked up.

"Hello," she said, sounding as if she'd been running.

I pictured Rachel: tall and stunning, blond hair hanging loosely in natural ringlets to her neck, piercing blue-gray eyes, always perfectly lined, her generous figure, concealed by an impeccably tailored outfit. She was the most striking woman I had ever met until Thursday evening.

"Hi, Rach."

"Robbie." Her voice sounded soft, sensual.

"Sorry about your call. I went to Michael's last night and got a little tipsy."

She laughed. "I know how you guys love your beer. It's fine, Rob."

"Well, here I am, a little the worse for wear."

She laughed again. "I just don't want you to forget me." Her voice was sultry. I could feel the heat through the phone.

I said nothing for a long minute. Too long.

"Robbie," she whispered.

I cleared my throat. "Don't be silly. I could never

forget you. I've just been busy."

"Gretchen told me. Ferrying around some little English girl who's lost her mother."

"That's right." I felt the blood rise in my cheeks.

Silence again.

"Robbie, how old is this *little* English girl?" I sensed tension in her voice.

"Twenty."

I could hear her breathing. Her mind was working overtime.

"Twenty!" A long pause. "Robbie, should I be worried?"

"Don't be silly," I lied.

"You're driving around the countryside with a twenty-year-old girl. I don't think I'm being silly." Her tone turned icy. "Please tell me she's overweight, wears thick glasses, and is ugly as sin."

I looked around the room as my conscience brought the walls closer. "Not exactly."

"Look, I hate to leave this discussion up in the air, but I have to go." I heard her breathing into the phone. "Let's pick this up later."

"That's fine. I'll call you tonight or tomorrow."

"All right," she said in clipped tones.

"All right," I whispered back.

"Robbie, is everything all right...with us?"

"Everything is fine."

"Really?" She sounded concerned, pausing for a moment. "Love you," she added, kissing the receiver.

"Me, too," I assured her and hung up. I'd never felt so guilty.

Later, the kitchen staff put together just what my empty stomach craved: bacon, scrambled eggs, and a tall stack of buttermilk pancakes smothered in butter and maple syrup.

After inhaling them I headed back to my room to get my swim trunks. I looked at my watch: 11:30. I arrived at the pool, scanning the area.

No Courtney.

But her absence was acceptable, perhaps even preferable, I mused as I thought about the strained dialogue with Rachel.

An overweight, balding man with coke-bottle glasses sat on a lounge chair. I smiled, watching him concentrate as he thumbed through the July issue of *Life* magazine. I recognized it. The edition showed the summer's new bathing suit collection, including a provocative two-piece style named after an island chain in the Pacific: a bikini. His wife, petite and dark-haired, was engrossed in Laura Hobson's *Gentlemen's Agreement*, the new runaway best-seller. They smiled.

"I've heard they're making that into a movie." I nodded at her novel.

"I've heard that, too," she agreed with enthusiasm. "Gregory Peck's going to star in it. I love him." She swooned and resumed her reading.

I debated heading to the beach, opting for the courtyard and pool. I told Courtney I'd be there after lunch. I took a large towel from a stack near the pool house and flipped it over my shoulder.

Spreading the plush towel over a chaise lounge I lay down in the sun. As I relaxed on the overstuffed cushion, I tried putting my feelings for Courtney in perspective. After the phone call to Rachel, guilt consumed me.

But no matter where I let my mind wander, it was futile. Courtney was always there.

I inventoried the reasons I cared for her. The list was endless: she was lovely, bright, humorous, desperately vulnerable... I stopped at four, knowing I could find a dozen more.

I also knew that no matter how many pluses I found, two negatives outweighed every piece of logic, compassion, and desire: Courtney was cloaked in mystery and Rachel waited for me in Boston.

My mind needed a rest. The problem would have to keep.

I pulled out a magazine, opened to an article on the Red Sox and in minutes, my heavy eyelids drooped as I drifted into a deep sleep.

Chapter Fourteen

I recalled being shaken, hearing the voice that haunted my dreams. Her voice. "Robbie. Robbie," she called softly. I smiled, fighting desperately to stay in the dream. I sighed as her hands touched my shoulders.

"Wake up, sleepy head." Her voice sounded real. "You're getting red. You need to go inside."

I opened my eyes. I must have turned onto my stomach. This was no dream. Courtney stood above me, wearing a frown. "Hello there." She nodded, sitting down next to me. Something was different about her. "This will never do, Robert. You're pink as a freshly caught lobster."

I turned over and sat up clumsily, rubbing my hand across my eyes. "What time is it?" I looked for my watch.

"Almost one-thirty." She reached over, handing me the watch. She touched my chest. Her hand was soft, cool, and welcome. "You simply must get out of the sun." She repeated, shaking her head.

Courtney's hand touched my right shoulder. "Fascinating," she said as she studied my birthmark. Her eyes narrowed. "Just like the new moon," she paused. "I've only seen one other."

"My mother told me my father had one just like it."

"But you never saw it?"

"No." Interesting. I never thought about it till she asked.

"Fascinating," she repeated, as she continued to study the birthmark.

81

"You're right. I should probably go in," I offered, remembering I had to meet Michael at three. "I can feel the sun. I didn't expect to fall asleep for that long."

"Punishment for your behavior last night." She nodded, smiling as she retrieved something from her shoulder bag. "Here, this may help. Has something in it called aloe. Get you feeling chipper by dinnertime," she said, laying a tube of cream next to me. "I'm expecting a proper companion at my side."

"Your hair." I suddenly realized. "That's what's different. It's your hair."

She threw her head back and laughed.

"Bravo." She held out her hands, palms up. "It's about time. I thought you'd never notice." She tilted her head to one side, playing with her lower lip. "Do you like it?" she asked, raising her eyebrows

Her hair had been trimmed. It was much shorter, several inches above the shoulder, framing her face to perfection. It hung, flowing and bouncing with every move. She now had bangs that stopped just above her large eyes.

"I love it," I told her

"I'm so glad. I was afraid you might not...dear." Her face flushed.

The term of endearment took me by complete surprise but sounded so effortless, so perfect.

"Go. Get out of the sun," she ordered, repeating her warning.

Courtney took off her light cotton robe. She wore a black bathing suit with off-white woven into the silky material. It was simple and conservative, fitted in the bodice with a tiny skirt at the waist.

She caught me staring. "Do you like it?" she asked.

"It looks wonderful," I confessed.

"I'm glad you think so." She ran to the water, diving in with grace. Seconds later, she bobbed up in the center of the large pool, urging me in.

She pushed her wet hair aside as she waved.

I stood, knowing I'd become aroused—extremely aroused. I pulled my large towel around me, hoping to hide the evidence.

"Hello, Robert," she called in frustration. "Where are you going?"

"You said I need to get out of the sun." I explained. "I'm going back to my room—got a quick errand to run." I turned away. "I'll see you at dinner." I turned and strode across the courtyard toward the guest house. I smiled weakly and waved. Looking back, I saw her, hanging on the lip of the pool, head tilted.

"Stay—for just a moment longer," she implored.

"Sorry, I really have to go." Closing the door, I threw myself on the bed, waiting for my condition to disappear. I turned on the radio, hoping for something to take my mind off Courtney. Just as I was beginning to relax, I heard a tap on my door. I got up and walked to the window. I pulled back the sheer curtains.

It was Courtney, tube of cream in hand. "Robert," she whispered, looking around. "Open up."

"I can't. I'm not dressed."

"Well, at least open the door so I can give you this. I promise it'll do wonders for your sunburn," she insisted.

I grabbed my robe, pulling it on and headed for the door. I opened it a crack, sticking my head out. She left the cream in front of my door, then crossed the courtyard. Watching her sleek, supple movements was a sight I could never grow tired of. She turned, grinning.

"See you at dinner," she called, wearing the special look I loved. "Don't you dare be late." She giggled.

I threw the tube on the bed and lay down next to

it, picturing Courtney and her new hairdo. As if she wasn't adorable enough. I sighed and closed my eyes.

A soft knocking sounded on the door.

"Robert." It was her again. "Let me in."

I sat up, half asleep. "What is it?" I asked.

"Did you use the sunburn cream?" she whispered.

"No, but I will." I stood and headed to the door. I opened it a crack. She pushed past me.

"You'll never do it properly." She sounded like a nursemaid. "Take off your robe and lie on the bed." She waved me to the bed. "I promise not to compromise your manly virtue." She grinned. "Go ahead."

I looked around and shook my head. "But Courtney," I protested.

"Oh, don't be such a ninny. Lie down," she persisted.

"All right." I gave in.

She poured some of the aromatic cream on her thin, supple hands and rubbed them together. Then, with the delicacy of a masseuse, she rubbed the cool, soothing liquid on my back. A sweet, intoxicating smell drifted to my nostrils.

"My God." I sighed as she applied it.

She stopped and withdrew her hands. "Are you all right?" she asked.

"Just fine," I managed in a whisper.

She leaned over, a few inches from my face, her damp, fragrant hair hanging, touching my cheek. She came closer, her scent filling the space around us. Her lips were so close.

"You're sure?" she asked, a delicious smile materializing as her warm breath caressed my face.

I nodded. Was she naïve or teasing me? I wasn't sure. She resumed the sensuous rub. I was silent, letting her long, fluid fingers wreak havoc. After a few minutes, she took more cream and began to massage my legs.

I pulled her hands away. "Don't, Courtney. Please."

"Why?" she questioned.

"I...I think it might be a good idea if you left."

She stopped and leaned close, whispering in my ear as she touched it with her lips. "But I don't want to leave, not now, not ever...not ever...not ever..." Her words echoed.

I awoke from the dream with a start. I saw by my watch it was 2:20. As I ran to the shower to rinse off, I smelled Courtney's jasmine scent. But that was ridiculous. It had been a dream. Vivid, but still a dream. I threw on a polo shirt, some cotton slacks, and my shoes, grabbed my car keys, and headed out the door to meet Michael.

As I passed through the courtyard, a few guests relaxed around the pool. I threw the cover off the Jag and in thirty seconds I was down the gravel driveway heading to Boone's Bar and Grill. I was terrified thinking about what my brother had found out about the girl I loved.

Chapter Fifteen

At 2:50 I pulled into Boone's Bar and Grill. Michael waited outside, lost in thought, and smoking a cigarette as he paced in front of the entrance.

"Hi, Mike." We shook hands.

"Let's go inside." He nodded, glancing at me as he crushed the cigarette out.

I followed him into the hazy interior. A few customers sat on wooden stools, feet resting on a worn brass foot rail as they stared into the foggy mirror behind the bar. Conversations centered on the Red Sox, politics, and the world situation. Several nodded at Michael as we entered.

"Let's sit back here." He directed me to a table at the rear.

"I haven't got much time and there's a lot to tell. My friends did a good job getting information on such short notice."

"I appreciate it."

"Wait till you hear what I have to tell you," he cautioned. "Some of it's strange, but remember it is from the locals. Country folk love their folklore." He found my eyes.

A massive man in a greasy apron waved in our direction.

"Just a Coke for me," I told Michael.

"Sounds good. Two Cokes," my brother called.

The bartender nodded with a frown. I assumed his usual clientele ordered something with more hair on its chest.

"All right, here goes."

I lit a cigarette while my stomach did flips.

Michael's gray eyes searched the room before finding mine again. "Courtney's mother, Ellen, was beautiful, a champion equestrienne, and heir to a large fortune." He leaned forward. "When she visited England for a riding competition in the mid-twenties, she met a man named Duncan Wellington. He had a fine family name. That was all he had. But he was smooth and handsome. Swept her off her feet."

"All right."

"None of Ellen's family thought much of him, figured Wellington for a gold digger, but she was independent and headstrong. Anyway, she stayed, let him court her and in a few months they were married."

I nodded.

"Ellen's folks were killed in an accident a few months later," Michael continued. "Wellington had it all: a beautiful bride and her fortune. Thanks to the inheritance, they bought Briarwood, a massive estate in Gloucestershire."

"So far, so good," I said, playing with my napkin.

"Things didn't work out the way Ellen hoped. Wellington was distant, surly. He traveled a lot, building an export business using her money. No one understood. Ellen was gorgeous and classy. Because she was such a great horsewoman and since Wellington was away so much, the riding circuit became her life."

"Gretchen told me. Courtney's followed in her footsteps."

He held up his hand and looked at his watch. "Anyway, somewhere she met a man named Courtney Phillips. Great horseman, interesting family background." He paused, eyebrows raised. "Dark, handsome, and mysterious."

"You did say *Courtney* Phillips?" I asked.

"Yeah." He stopped for a minute and lit another

cigarette. "Apparently the big fights between Ellen and her husband were about children. Ellen wanted a family, but Duncan..." Michael stopped and looked away. "Had other ideas. Some even suggest he had, you know, performance problems." Michael shook his head. "Maybe that's why he was away so much. So when Ellen had a beautiful baby girl in June of 1926, the countryside buzzed."

"So then Courtney is named for..." I stopped in midsentence, understanding Wellington's bitterness.

"Her real father." He stopped and shook his head, then held up his hand. "I need a scotch over here," he called to the bartender.

My throat tightened.

"There's more, and this is where it gets strange."

"Go on," I whispered.

"On the day *your* Courtney was born, Phillips died in a car crash. Hit a tree. He and the car burned to a cinder. Some thought it was for the better. Phillips paid plenty of attention to Ellen but he was...let's just say he wasn't a nice guy. In some ways he was worse than Wellington."

"All that must have devastated her mother. First Wellington and then this character."

He nodded, grabbing my forearm. "Here's where the strange part really begins. Phillips and his family came from a long line of witches."

"Witches?" I asked. "Come on, Michael."

"Look, I'm telling you what they say." He shrugged. "Don't shoot the messenger. The real power was Phillip's father, a man named Simon. He's still alive, and if you believe this stuff, the most powerful male witch in Europe. But he had no use for his son. Simon's a class act. Elegant, regal, a real gentleman, even descended from royalty. He was ashamed of his son, disowned him before Courtney was born. "

"Courtney mentioned him." I sat, shaking my

head. "Do you believe any of this? Do your friends?"

He shrugged. "Let me finish. You remember the newspaper articles?"

I nodded, not sure I wanted to hear more.

"Well, during Courtney's lifetime, there have been other mysterious deaths. Friends, staff on the estate, a teacher she was close to. She's always close by, but there's no evidence she's involved—just a terrified witness. Her best friend drowned while they were swimming, her favorite groom was burned to death in a stable fire, and her mother was killed by a freak lightning strike. There were rumors of strange signs near the bodies. Signs that indicate witchcraft."

I heard the words but found it difficult to believe. "Have the local police investigated?"

He nodded. "They've looked at everyone close to her: the father, nanny, staff, even Ellen until she was killed. None of them were nearby or had a motive."

Michael was silent for a minute, then continued. "Except to keep Courtney isolated. Don't you see? Everyone who gets close to her gets killed."

A shiver ran through me as I realized the implication. "I don't know what to say. Are you suggesting that because she and I are...?"

"I'm not suggesting anything." Michael looked at his watch. "I've got to go. But there's something here none of us understand, and you're right in the middle of it. "

"I appreciate what you've found. I just don't know what to do about it."

"Understood, brother. Neither would I. Look, they're still searching so I may have some more."

"Thanks. I want to know everything."

"Rob, what are you going to do?" Michael asked as he stood to leave.

I shrugged. "I have no idea."

He took my arm. "Just suppose you found out Courtney really was...something else?"

I took out a five-dollar bill and paid the check.

"I don't know. There are times I'm sorry I ever met Courtney, but then I see her and it's like nothing I've ever felt before."

"You're sure you're okay?" Michael asked as we left. A lot of what he'd told me was beyond strange.

I shook Michael's hand. "I'll be all right." I stood, looking in the direction of Jon and Gretchen's. "I just need some time to get my mind around this."

Michael nodded. "I wanted to make your problem easier, to help you decide what to do." He shook his head. "I've only made it worse."

"No, you did what I asked. Now it's up to me. Call if you find out anything else." I forced a smile.

I headed to my car, Michael to his Jeep. We got into our vehicles and waved good-bye. I'd be back at the reunion before five. That gave me a couple hours to think.

I thought about Rachel and the picture-book life I had left behind three days ago. Guilt and misgivings continued to fill my mind. Mystery, suspicious deaths, witchcraft? But whatever strange events or mysteries surrounded Courtney, I wanted to be with her, to help her. I was consumed by the intrigue. Odd things were happening—things I had yet to understand, but nothing would change my need to be part of her life.

Chapter Sixteen

Courtney closed the witch's circle, ending her meditation. She covered herself with her white robe, assembling her sacred implements as she headed back toward the house. She'd returned to the ritual site to seek guidance. She achieved a deep trance, attempting to find the answers she sought.

Confusion overwhelmed her. She wanted Robbie so much. Not as a vessel to achieve her purpose for the ceremony, but as a woman wants a man. The stirrings he evoked were like nothing she'd ever known. It was all so new, so foreign, so exciting. Nothing had prepared her for the passion that surged through her.

At first she feared she might need her powers to win him. After meeting him she refused. He must be hers, to want her without spells or magic. Now she knew. He wanted her, loved her as much as she did him.

She knew Robbie held a fascination with magic and the occult. But Courtney refused to read his mind. She reveled in the tempting mystery, in not knowing his thoughts.

Could he deal with the truth? He had no way of knowing who and what he really was—one of them, the chosen one selected to be with her. The family had done their job—throwing mysteries and questions in his path. Would he rebel and run away or become her mate?

She reached the house and put her implements away. Tonight and tomorrow were critical. Courtney wanted Robbie. And before Simon arrived tomorrow night, he would be hers.

She studied her image in the mirror. Her feline familiars looked up at her. "Don't worry," she assured them with a smile. She'd entice him, continuing to make herself mysterious and irresistible. Courtney *had* invaded his dreams. But that was the extent of her manipulation. Whatever happened between them would result from the incredible attraction they shared. It went against all they'd planned, but Robbie would want her without spells, potions, or magic. Nothing had ever meant so much to her. Courtney closed her eyes. "By this time tomorrow, Robert, you will be mine," she whispered.

But as she studied her reflection, her thoughts turned to something more ominous—the dark feelings invading her meditations since last night. Her talk with Simon had done nothing to dispel her misgivings. Quite the contrary. Was someone or some force at work to sabotage their preparation? If so, why? Their sole purpose was to help humanity, to insure peace and prosperity, allow mankind freedom from the threat of war, disease, and terror. Courtney's instincts were never wrong. But something else was. Very wrong. Simon would arrive on Sunday. They needed to find out what and who was at work to undermine their plans.

****

I stood in the shower for a long time, letting the hot water work its magic as I thought about what I'd learned from Michael. The strange deaths, the mysteries, the loneliness surrounding Courtney, even the veiled threats. None of it mattered. Just the opposite. It made me feel closer to her. I found the mystery, the hint of the occult, exciting.

My life had been a romp compared with Courtney's. At that moment I wanted to take her in my arms, hold her, and tell her she'd never be hurt or lonely again. But what about the questions

Michael raised? What about my well-ordered life, Rachel, my influential friends? Suddenly none of it mattered. Not if it meant a life without her. This was no passing flirtation. Being close to Courtney was like standing next to a high tension line. It was electric and energizing. No matter what it meant, there was no turning back, no retreat.

I shaved and dressed in my finest linen suit, a cream colored Brooks Brothers shirt, knit maroon tie, and expensive oxford loafers. Although dinner didn't start until eight, at seven-twenty I headed to the dining room, hoping she'd be early. Like a vision she stood, looking out the large window fronting on the lake, stunning and elegant in a sleeveless white gown. Its front was subtle but revealing. The lower half of the silky evening dress fell into soft folds over her hips. She wore her hair arranged in an intricate braided style with a white silk bow at its base. Her new bangs were separated perfectly to show off her dark, luminous eyes. She heard me enter and turned, rushing over. Holding my eyes with hers, she pulled me down and kissed my cheek.

"Hello, Robert." Her eyes sparkled as she smiled. She wore the fragrance that hypnotized me. A pearl choker rested on her slender neck, matching the iridescent studs in her ears. Below the choker hung the now-familiar pendant on its fine silver chain.

She saw me staring at it.

"You keep looking at this." She touched it lightly. "It's very dear to me, a family heirloom passed down for generations. It's the symbol for the maiden Andromeda. It offers protection from evil." Her eyes dropped as she fingered the small, finely tooled piece. "Do you know Greek mythology?"

I shook my head. "Not really."

"It is rather an arcane subject." She laughed softly. "Andromeda was a beautiful princess sentenced to death because of her mother's vanity.

She was chained to a rock to be sacrificed to Cetus, the sea monster. But Perseus saved her." She looked up, eyes questioning. "We spoke of heroism yesterday. Would you be my Perseus, Robert?" she asked. Her eyes held no amusement.

My face flushed. "Yes," I replied. "And speaking of mythology, where are your friends this evening?"

"Tucked away, comfy in their beds. Thank you for asking." She seemed to relax, showing a demure smile. She stood back to survey me. "You look quite the proper gentleman this evening." She tilted her head.

"You look remarkable, too, Courtney," I began. *Good God*, I thought. *Remarkable*. What a weak choice of words. I wanted to say so much more, to tell her she was the most beautiful creature I'd ever seen.

I studied every feature, letting my fingers touch her arm briefly. She watched my hand, then closed her eyes, exhaling softly. I wanted to crush her in my arms.

"That is such a stunning gown," I whispered instead. "And I love the way you did your hair."

"It's called a French braid," she explained. "And I'm delighted you approve of my frock."

"Very much so."

Her face flushed.

She drew very close, warm breath enveloping me as she whispered, "I've been saving it for a special occasion."

The room was getting warm—very warm. Why was it I never felt this way around Rachel? Why did I love just standing close to Courtney, watching her subtle movements, hanging on her every word and reveling in her enchanting scent?

Before I could think of an answer, our fellow dinner guests began to arrive. Several smiled as they saw us, as if pleased we were together, like the bride and groom at a wedding. Courtney and I separated, talking to our respective companions and stealing discreet looks at one another.

The men hovered around Courtney, flirting shamelessly, watching her move in that delicious gown. I made conversation with the women whose husbands were being entranced. Tonight Courtney was animated and energized, a different young woman from the one I met on Thursday. My ego let me take credit for the transformation.

After an endless separation, Jonathan and Gretchen asked us to be seated. Courtney and I found our places at the end of the table, she seated on my right again. I put my arm around her, squeezing her shoulder as she took her seat. Once seated, I placed my right hand in my lap. She brushed it briefly, blushing as she flashed a smile warm enough to melt the flatware.

Our dinner resonated with laughter and animated conversation, thanks to the abundance and variation of wine provided by our hosts. Courtney and I took full advantage of their cellar, sampling every bottle.

Gretchen watched. Perhaps she disapproved of the fondness we displayed for one another. When I lit a cigarette between the soup and entrée, Courtney reached over and took it from me, lips curling up pleasantly as she inhaled. I loved each small intimacy. But then I reveled in everything Courtney did or said, perhaps more now, knowing what she'd been through.

As the dinner progressed, she seemed to move closer. Shivers ran down my spine when her warm thigh touched mine. I thought of Rachel and my vows to maintain a platonic, distant relationship. As Courtney's leg brushed mine, her soft, jasmine scent filled the smoky space around us, and her adoring smile hung on my every word, my resolve evaporated. I was her captive.

After two hours of tempting foreplay, we adjourned to the great room. It was long and dark with a high vaulted ceiling and walls paneled in mahogany. Somber family portraits covered the finely polished wood. A small orchestra awaited. Many of the older guests looked fatigued, bloated again by the sumptuous meal and too much wine. They said their good-nights and nodded politely, heading off to bed.

"I'm glad you two are joining us," Gretchen said. "Somebody has to take advantage of these fine musicians."

"I wouldn't dream of leaving. Would you, Robbie?" Courtney stared up at me.

Not if I was pulled away by a herd of elephants. I shook my head, thrilled by the prospect of dancing with her, holding her close, feeling her lithe body against mine.

Gretchen raised her eyebrows. "Wonderful," she said, watching us.

The dance floor was sparsely populated. Courtney took my hand, drawing me to a secluded corner. "Let's go over here. I didn't get much practice at home." She winked.

"Let's see about that," I whispered, putting my arm around her waist. I suspected Courtney could master whatever she put her mind to. We worked through a foxtrot—she was good. Then a waltz—she was better. By the third piece, she'd mastered the drill.

"Robbie," she whispered into my chest.

"Yes, Courtney."

"You said you liked to ride?"

"I did," I answered, hoping this was an invitation.

"Could we go for a ride and picnic tomorrow?" She paused. "There's a special place I want to show you before..." Her words trailed off.

I knew what she was thinking. Despite my vows never to leave her, it was the same thought I had, *Before you have to leave and return to your world.*

"Of course."

"Good." She snuggled closer. "Meet you at 7:30 in the courtyard."

We stood in our private space, maintaining the pretense of restraint. When Courtney pressed close, I tried to keep a discreet distance. But by the time the small ensemble played Frank Loesser's "I Wish I Didn't Love You So," my resistance had crumbled. When Courtney clutched my back, I let her. I felt her warm, firm body as she pulled me closer. She clung, breathing heavily as I held her, eyes closed. We stood, barely moving, caught up in the music, the surroundings and the electricity passing between us.

Someone tapped Courtney's shoulder. I opened my eyes. "Cutting in." It was Gretchen. Courtney backed away. "Time to break this lovely couple up." Gretchen took her nieces arm as the dance ended. "This young lady should go to bed."

"Of course," I agreed, looking at my watch and trying to conceal my disappointment. Gretchen looked back, guiding her niece toward the door. Courtney turned, wearing a look of regret.

I left the main house, lighting a cigarette as the damp night air surrounded me. I studied the brilliant stars, searching the constellations and thinking about the conversation on the night we met. Could I really be her Perseus? I wanted to, but I was in uncharted territory. She was beautiful, young, forbidden. She was also everything I had ever dreamt of. I hoped desperately she felt the same way.

"I watched you two tonight, Robert," Jon began. "She is quite the young lady."

"Quite," I whispered.

"She's very taken with you."

"I'm not so sure."

"I am." He flashed me a knowing smile.

I needed something to help me return to reality. "Can I use your phone again?"

Would another well-placed call help to quell this runaway inferno? I doubted it.

"You know where my office is." He pointed toward the house and patted me on the back, weaving off for a nightcap. I went inside, smiling absently at the stragglers returning to their rooms. I threaded my way along the paneled hallway to the polished oak door of Jon's office. I went to his massive desk and picked up the handset, clicking it several times before hearing an operator.

"Number please?" the voice asked wearily.

I whispered the number of Rachel's Back Bay apartment.

"Robbie?" Rachel answered in a scratchy voice. She sounded exhausted. "Is that you again? Twice in one day? It's good to hear your voice. How's the reunion?"

"I'm still here."

"You okay, Rob?"

"Fine," I lied. "Just had to hear your voice before I went to bed."

"You sure you're all right? You sound kind of odd."

"I'm fine," I reassured her.

We spent the next few minutes discussing how we'd spent our Saturdays. She spared me the pain of lying by failing to ask about my new companion. I left out the details of my day: Courtney by the pool, witch stories about Courtney, dancing with Courtney.

"Tell me how much you love me," Rachel commanded. She and I had a pleasant, satisfying relationship. Great rapport, lots of fun, good conversation. But love? I always thought so. I knew better now.

"Madly." I gave in, whispering into the receiver, knowing that my words sounded hollow.

"Gotta go, love."

"Okay, Rach. I'll call you when I can."

"Try. I really miss you, Robbie." Sadly, I knew she did.

"Me, too," I told her.

"Damn," I cursed, hanging up the phone then leaving.

The evening was cooler. A fresh breeze blew across the courtyard, but the weathermen were promising more heat and humidity tomorrow. Our special day together. I sneaked a look up at her window, eager for another late night-rendezvous. It was dark. I opened my door and switched on the light.

The newspaper clippings still troubled me, especially after Michael's revelations that afternoon. Was it possible that someone else knew Courtney's history? Were they warning me? Did this anonymous person think I might be in danger? Was I?

Lying on the bed, my mind drifted back to the evening. The chemistry that played out between us, Courtney's sense of humor, her intoxicating scent, and the way her body and mine melded to perfection.

Chapter Seventeen

I lay on my bed, my mind conflicted with Michael's revelations, the electricity that held me prisoner when Courtney was close, the guilt that consumed me when I pictured Rachel.

I sat up and got out of bed. Pulling on a pair of pants and a T-shirt, I went outside. The moon climbed over the somber, gray façade of the main house as I walked across the courtyard and onto the massive dock that jutted into Sebago. As I passed, I looked up at Courtney's open window. It was dark.

Lighting a cigarette, I sat down in one of the Adirondack chairs at the end. It held a trace of dew, but other things filled my mind. As I watched the dark water moving lazily with the breeze, I thought about tomorrow and spending the day with Courtney. Would it be our last? It was Sunday. My plan was to return to the city on Monday. Or it had been. What should I do? Would pursuing this self-indulgent obsession only cause both of us heartache? What about Rachel, our families, and everyone around us? I thought of Michael, the Evanses, my mother. I couldn't see any of them endorsing my love for Courtney. But how could I leave her?

Checking the luminous dial on my watch I saw it was almost one. I extinguished my cigarette and headed back to the guest house. Walking along the dock, I glanced toward the north. A glow appeared above the forest—as if a bonfire was burning. I stopped. Yes, there was no doubt. I came off the dock and walked toward it, my stomach doing flips. Suddenly it vanished. I stood searching the horizon.

Nothing. I shook my head, turned, and went back to my room, lay on my bed and closed my eyes.

Courtney's image appeared before me, a beautiful vision floating in front of a blazing fire. I could smell the sweet fragrance of hazel logs. Dressed in a flowing white gown tied at the waist with a pink ribbon, she stood at the center of a large circle, surrounded by men and women also dressed in white. They chanted in a strange language. It had a medieval sound.

She moved around the circle fluidly, dancing and spinning in a graceful, erotic way. I felt myself becoming aroused as I watched the enchanting spectacle. The circle was in a wooded place. I watched, hidden behind a thick oak. Shadows from the massive fire lit her lithe, elegant body as she swayed in rhythm to the chanting of those around her. Suddenly, she stopped and looked in my direction. Her dark, hypnotic eyes glowed from within—brown one minute, green the next. Courtney beckoned to me. I found myself unable to resist. She took a gleaming knife and parted the circle. Approaching, she held out her arms. I felt myself moving toward her. Her lips parted as she smiled the soft smile that I loved, the expressive one showing innocence and invitation.

We joined as she took my hands in hers. As we touched euphoria overcome me. I was consumed by a sense of peace and well-being unlike anything I had ever known. Courtney nodded, telling me that I was safe, that everything was all right. Turning, she continued holding my right hand as she led me through the circle toward its center. I looked at the others as I passed. We were surrounded by the people from the reunion: Jon, Gretchen, the couple from the pool. I recognized all of them. Like Courtney, they smiled warmly and nodded as if to assure me I was with friends. As I scanned the circle I saw Michael and even my mother dressed in the same white robes.

As we reached the circle's center, Courtney continued to grasp my hand. She knelt in front of an imposing figure, a giant of a man in a purple robe. She motioned for me to do the same. I did. The man spoke in an arcane tongue for several minutes. Courtney rose. I felt pleasantly light-headed and found myself following her. The circle parted and we passed through to a small clearing. In the fire's glow I could see a bed of leaves and pine needles had been prepared as a place for us to lie. She loosened the pink cord that held her silky robe and shrugged, letting the sheer garment fall to the ground. I saw her magnificent body as the light from the fire flickered. I remember thinking that I had never seen anything so perfect or so beautiful. Courtney smiled and nodded at me. I knew at once that she wanted me to join her. When I looked down I realized I was not wearing my clothes but a sheer white garment similar to hers. I loosened the cord holding my robe in place.

I bolted upright. Wide awake.

Collapsing onto my rumpled bedclothes, perspiration ran down my face. My breathing was heavy and rapid. A tiny part of me was frightened, but most of me wanted desperately to return to Courtney and the dream. While I knew I'd been asleep, Courtney's jasmine scent lingered and surrounded me.

I lay drained, letting my breathing return to normal, trying to remember every detail. I knew I'd been dreaming, but the images were so real, so vivid I found myself wondering. I remembered the phantom glow in the forest. Was talk of witchcraft and mystery invading my subconscious? I turned and saw the small clock on my night table. Two-fifteen.

Swallowing deeply, I slipped out of bed, making my way to the bathroom. After splashing cold water on my face, I pulled out a vial of sleeping pills. I had to sleep if I wanted to be alert for my day with Courtney. Popping one in my mouth, I saw the name of the prescribing physician: Dr. Thomas Worthington. Rachel's father.

Chapter Eighteen

I was up at 6:30, driven by desire. Thoughts of the strange, provocative dream haunted me. I showered, shaved and ran out to the courtyard, knowing I was thirty minutes early. Courtney stood facing me.

"Good morning," she whispered. "I knew you'd be early." She paced, twirling her hair. It was tied into short loose braids, each with a large pink ribbon at its end. A matching scarf adorned her neck. She looked lovely, but there was something different about her this morning. My upbeat Courtney of Friday and Saturday was gone. This was the shy, enigmatic girl I'd met on Thursday evening. Did she question her decision to invite me on this adventure, concerned about what was happening between us? Or was there something else, still another mystery I was unaware of?

"I didn't imagine you'd have the proper attire, so I brought you these." She crossed the small distance separating us and held out a pair of riding breeches, boots, and gloves. I stared at them. "They'll fit," she promised. I examined them. The sizes were perfect.

She glanced at her watch.

"Are you all right? I asked. "You did say 7:30?"

She smiled faintly, nodding. "Yes. You're very early."

"So are you. I couldn't wait," I confessed.

"Neither could I. I want this day to be perfect."

"It will be." She looked so sweet, so young, so vulnerable. I wanted to reach out, take her in my arms, and tell her that she was all I'd thought about since our first meeting. I resisted, assuring her, "I'm just so happy you asked me. I'll go and change." I went inside, emerging in ten minutes.

Courtney continued fidgeting with her braids. She looked at me and then at the ground. "I told you. My life's been solitary. I've never done this—gone for a whole day, alone with a man before. I suppose I'm nervous."

"There's nothing to worry about. Promise," I said. "And the riding clothes are amazing." I gestured toward the outfit she'd produced. "How did you manage it? It's perfect."

"Magic." She shrugged. For an instant the playful gleam returned. "And I was never worried about your being a proper gentleman." She touched my arm as if to reassure me. "I know you too well, Robbie."

I smiled, trying to ignore her mood swing. I stared at her, trying to fathom the cause of her melancholy, remembering what I'd learned about her life—the tragedy, the mysteries, her loneliness.

Courtney was flawlessly attired as always, resplendent in snug, beige jodhpurs, a sheer white blouse, open at the neck, and a pair of highly polished field boots. On the chaise beside her lay a black riding helmet with gloves tucked inside. A black leather crop rested on top of two bulging leather saddlebags.

She studied me, fingering the silver medallion around her neck. A tiny smile crossed her lips. "They have everything else you'll need at the stables. Auntie has an account there."

"All right, but remember what I told you. I haven't done much riding lately."

"You'll do just fine." Her face reddened.

I blushed at the compliment. "All right, but you've been warned."

She tilted her head. "I'll whip you into shape." A

spark of the other Courtney, my Courtney, emerged as she fingered the crop, snapping it as she raised her eyebrows. She touched my arm lightly again, putting a piece of gum in her mouth.

"Breakfast?" I teased.

She shook her head, blushing and putting her hand to her mouth. "No, that's in the saddlebags. I can taste the garlic from dinner last night. I don't want anything to spoil our day together."

"Nothing could spoil our day together," I assured her. Every day with her had been special, perfect. If Courtney bathed in garlic, it wouldn't have mattered.

"Robert," she asked hesitantly. "Will you remember me when…" She couldn't finish.

I stood frozen, trying to avoid the thought of leaving, the possibility of never seeing her again. Despite the circumstances, I refused to consider the idea of leaving Courtney.

"Don't ask me that," I whispered. "You know I could never forget you." My words sounded hollow, patronizing. I wanted to say much more.

She sighed deeply. "We'll remember today," she whispered back, looking away. When she turned toward me, her eyes showed a trace of tears. Her words haunted me. I reached over and squeezed her hand. Our fingers intertwined briefly. A dark look spoiled her exquisite face. "Let's go. It's getting late."

She picked up her helmet, gloves, and crop as she hefted the saddlebags.

"May I carry those?"

"No, I'm fine," she shook her head. "And I'm sorry, Robbie. I'm not trying to be a prima donna."

"I never thought that. I know your life has been difficult." I put my hand on her shoulder. "And don't worry. We *will* make today something special," I repeated, trying to sound cheerful as we headed down the gravel driveway toward the gate. "It's going to be hot. I could drive," I offered, refusing to think about leaving her.

Courtney shook her head. "Thanks. If it's all right with you, I'd rather walk. I find it clears my head."

I nodded. Sweat threaded its way between my shoulder blades.

"I guess I'm what you Yanks call a loner."

"I know you've been through a lot," I said. "But I don't think of you like that. You're charming, thoughtful. You have a wonderful sense of humor."

"That's very sweet. But I've spent so much time alone, there are things I'm not good at. I feel clumsy sometimes. So bear with me." Her words stopped. Her dark eyes looked cloudy. They seemed to be filling up again. She took a deep breath and stepped out with a purpose. This *was* a different Courtney. Where had my sweet, charming companion vanished? Even the way she looked at me was strange. There was something about it—as if she was searching for an answer.

"Is everything all right?" I asked. "You seem preoccupied. If you're not feeling well, or there's something wrong, we don't have to do this."

"No, please." She seemed agitated. "We have to do this today." Her reply had an ominous tone, one of finality. I tried not to think about the meaning.

We arrived at the stables before 7:15. Courtney brightened, her melancholy lost in conversation about the heat, her love of riding, and the evening's fireworks. We entered the office. She was immediately embraced by a slender, middle-aged woman.

"Here's our best customer, come for her workout." The woman spoke with an accent similar to Courtney's.

"Wendy, can I see him?" she asked, then gestured toward me. "My friend Robert needs a tame mount."

The woman nodded as Courtney looked at me, eyes gleaming.

"Be right back. I promise." She touched my arm, running into the stable.

"Very tame, Wendy," I pleaded.

She nodded and held out her hand.

"I understand. I'm Wendy Wilkins. Robert?"

"Yes, Robert McGregor. I'm a guest at the Evanses' for the reunion."

She looked toward the barn and came close. "That's the first time I've seen Courtney smile." Wendy touched my arm. "You're good medicine. She's been our most faithful customer for weeks. Be careful," Wendy continued, nodding. Her light eyes sparkled and her smile was infectious, even captivating. I liked her at once. "She'll put you through your paces. You should see her in the show ring. The finest young rider I've ever seen."

"Maybe she'll take pity on me."

"If you'll pardon my saying it, sir"—her eyes followed Courtney—"I don't think she sees you as an object of pity." Her face flushed.

In a few minutes, Courtney burst in from the stables. "Well, are you ready?"

"Sure." I turned toward the woman. "What have you got for me, Wendy?"

She led us into the stable, the pungent fragrance filling my nostrils. We surveyed the mounts. Courtney had already saddled and bridled her gelding. He was impressive-looking, breathing loudly, snorting, and pawing impatiently at the straw in his stall. I noticed that as soon as Courtney touched his snout he calmed and licked her hand.

Wendy gave Courtney a sly grin. "How about Pumpkin Patch for Robert?"

They exchanged glances.

"The perfect choice," Courtney agreed.

"Pumpkin Patch?" I protested. "Sounds like something for old ladies or little girls."

The two women burst into laughter.

"Don't let his name fool you, sir. He'll test your abilities. Right, Courtney?"

She nodded, heading to the tack room, hefting a blanket, saddle, bridle, and halter. Dropping her load, she went back, returning with a riding helmet. She held it up, judging the size.

"Looks about right. Try it on." Courtney handed it to me. I did. "Come on." She put her hands on her hips. "I'm not doing this by myself." She pointed to the saddle. When I picked it up, she pushed me toward the stall, grinning.

Wendy hid a smile.

Courtney noticed. "Hey, you two. No secrets. Robbie and I have work to do."

Wendy gave me a nod as she headed back to the office.

"Don't forget these." She reappeared with Courtney's packed saddlebags.

"Thanks." Courtney retrieved the bridle and bit. "Let's get back to your mount." She walked me through the process, like a teacher with a slow student.

"I have done this before," I assured her.

I noticed with amazement that every time Courtney touched one of the horses, they grew calm and nuzzled against her.

"That's quite a gift you have."

She smiled, dismissing the compliment. "I told you. It's just a way I have with them."

As we led our mounts from the barn, Wendy waved. "Enjoy your ride."

"Well. You two seemed to hit it off." Courtney stood with a curious look on her face. She tightened her helmet strap and pulled on her gloves.

"What can I say? She warned me to watch out.

Said you might try to take advantage of me." I shrugged.

"Be careful. Wendy's become a good friend." Courtney laughed, holding my eyes with hers, adding, "She may be right." Then turning, she slipped effortlessly up onto her mount.

We proceeded along bridal paths for an hour. At the first fork, Courtney headed west, leading us slowly upward through rich birch and oak groves. We emerged into a spectacular green and golden meadow. Magnificent views of the White Mountains and the fertile valley below appeared, a postcard spread out before us.

Galloping across the lush open space, we reached a stand of ancient fir trees on the far side. We rode side by side when the trail allowed. Courtney was more than a lovely companion. Riding energized her. She described the movement of the tectonic plates, the formation of the distant mountain range, and the last Ice Age like a geology professor. Nothing escaped her eye for detail. Every species of tree, bird, or wildflower was identified at a glance. And all in a pleasant, matter-of-fact way, as if she were telling a child a bedtime story.

"How did you learn so much?" I asked in awe.

"I love to read and discover things, Robert. I told you it was lonely on Briarwood. On rainy days my favorite companions were the *Encyclopedia Britannica* and the *Oxford English Dictionary*. When the weather was pleasant, I spent hours riding and exploring the meadows and highlands from horseback. Mummy and Simon were wonderful teachers." As she spoke, she reined up and looked at me. "You could say I'm wise beyond my years." She gave me a coy smile, nudged her horse, and moved on.

Courtney amazed me. But despite her intellect, delightful sense of humor, and graceful movements, my mind was more on biology than nature studies. She presented a striking, fluid figure as she and her mount moved effortlessly along every trail and across each meadow.

When the trail narrowed, we rode single file, continuing the casual conversation about the scenery or wildlife when we could, working our way up the easy, rolling slopes that crested on a bluff overlooking the mountains and lakes of Western Maine.

To call Courtney a wonderful rider was a mastery of understatement. She and her mount took the lead, moving as one, expertly negotiating every rise and dip in the trail. As we rode, Courtney would bend close to her gelding's ear, whispering as if sharing a secret with him. Each time, the animal would shake his head and canter forward playfully.

"It's very hot. Let's stop and rest," she suggested, pulling up after ninety minutes. "I have some things for breakfast."

"Why not?" Having been away from riding for several years, I was already sore and tired in places I hadn't been in ages.

As we dismounted, Courtney stopped to talk to our mounts. Both shook their heads. She joined me, bringing the saddlebags, leaving both horses to graze unfettered. We headed toward the shade of a large, sheltering oak. It was very warm. Sweat soaked through my light polo shirt and Courtney's clothing showed signs of moisture as she walked in front of me. I found it difficult to avoid watching Courtney's graceful movements in her riding clothes. As with everything she wore, the outfit was expensive and fit as if tailored to her figure.

I gathered some grass to soften a place under the massive limbs.

"Thank you so much," she whispered as we sat down.

"My pleasure. I needed something soft after an hour and a half in the saddle. I told you..."

"I don't mean that," she interrupted. "I mean for coming. For putting up with my moodiness." Her eyes were fixed on mine. "You don't know how much it means to me." She touched my arm, letting her fingers linger. Every intimacy heightened my desire. She was the most stunning and brilliant young woman I had ever known. I wanted desperately to take her in my arms. It took all my self-control to resist. I kept wondering what was happening to me. Was I bewitched? Being a lovesick suitor was not me. How had Courtney hypnotized me so completely in such a short time?

"So, what's for breakfast?" I asked and looked away.

Courtney opened one of the saddlebags. She extracted a thermos of orange juice and a water bottle, then unwrapped muffins and croissants.

"You're quite the cook."

She threw her head back and laughed. "I bribed the chef."

We took off our riding helmets and gloves, leaning next to each other, our backs against the giant oak, shoulders touching. She passed the breakfast stash toward me. We devoured our muffins and breakfast rolls, punctuating our eating with long drafts from the orange juice thermos.

"That hit the spot." I closed my eyes, luxuriating as the scent of her body mingled with the wildflowers in the nearby meadow.

When we finished, I lit a cigarette and passed it to her. Courtney inhaled deeply and handed it back. "I think I'm corrupting you," I said, pointing to the pack as I laid it on the ground.

Her face grew soft, lips turned up in a gentle smile. "You'd never do that to me," she whispered, lowering her dark lashes as I crushed out the cigarette.

"Let's save the water for later," she suggested. "We've still got a way to go before we get there."

"There?" I was curious.

She leaned forward, shaking her loose braids. Turning to look at me, she drew very close, softly brushing the crumbs from my face and lips with her hand, the way she had with the ice cream two days ago. I closed my eyes. The scent from her leather glove lingered on her hand, mingling with the telltale jasmine fragrance from her damp blouse.

"Thanks," I said, clearing my throat. "Where's there?" I repeated, fighting to maintain my self-control.

She hesitated, looking up at me from beneath dark lashes. "A special, private place I want you to see."

"I'm all yours," I confessed.

She turned, studying me. "That would be nice, if it were true." Courtney waited, watching me. When I said nothing, she turned and stood abruptly.

I had no idea how to answer. I wanted to tell her that this morning was special, to promise to be hers for as long as she wanted me, but I stood silently. I knew how she felt about me. If last night had left any doubt, her behavior this morning had dispelled it. I wanted to bend over and let Pumpkin Patch kick me.

She sensed my frustration. "Let's go," she commanded.

"Please, Courtney...wait."

"It's all right," she whispered as we retrieved our horses. She slid up into the saddle. "I'm just being silly again. You don't owe me anything."

But I do. I wanted to tell her I owed her so much. Before meeting her, I thought my life was full, rewarding, had a purpose and meaning. Now I realized how shallow my existence had been. Since

Thursday evening, life had taken on its real purpose: being with Courtney. It was all that mattered.

We rode in silence for another thirty minutes, traveling on ever narrower, steeper paths. The unresolved conversation made her quiet and melancholy again. When she spoke, it was curt and clipped. Courtney had taken my silence as rejection.

It was almost eleven. The June sun was high and warm as we emerged from the pine forest. Beyond, stood a small turquoise lake, fed by a slim waterfall that cascaded down the front of a blue granite cliff. In the foreground was a grand meadow covered by a dizzying tapestry of wildflowers and tall aromatic grasses swimming in the hot breeze. The White Mountains served as the backdrop for this glorious scene.

Courtney cantered toward the lake and pulled up, dismounting twenty yards away. Taking off her helmet and gloves, she ran her fingers over her hair. "This is it." She pointed toward the lake as I came up beside her. "I wanted to share it with you, Robbie." Her enormous eyes were ablaze in the bright morning sun. She exhaled deeply.

I got off my horse and left him, reins hanging, to stand by her side, staring at one of the most incredible vistas I had ever seen. "Thank you, Courtney. It's breathtaking." I touched her shoulder, then took her hand loosely in mine. "Can we go to the lake?"

"Of course." She nodded, tugging me toward the shore. She sat on the grass a few feet from the rocky beach, patting the ground. I joined her.

"I'm sorry," she said, shaking her head. "I know I'm acting like a spoiled brat, but I have a lot on my mind." She shot a look at me.

So something had changed in her life, perhaps in both our lives. I wanted to help, to be her Perseus, that dashing prince, a shoulder if she needed one. "Is it something you can share with me?" I touched her hand. "I want to help if I can."

"No, but thank you." She pursed her lips and shook her head.

"Can I ask you something?"

Courtney looked away. "You can ask." Her shoulders slumped. "I can't promise an answer."

"Does it have anything to do with us?" I waited. Time slowed, then stopped. After a long pause she looked back at me, finding my eyes. Courtney had the most expressive eyes I had ever seen. Today they were unfathomable. What I saw could have been sadness, regret, even fear.

"What do you think?" she whispered, nodding slowly. "Is there anything I've thought of since we met that hasn't involved you?"

I should have been overjoyed but her words had a bitter sound. They held no happiness. I opened my mouth to speak.

Courtney shook her head. "No more questions. Not now. Please."

She sighed, lounging back in the soft grass, staring into the warm sky, avoiding my eyes. I lay down next to her. Our bodies touched. The setting was so tempting, the day so spectacular, and her scent so intoxicating, I wanted desperately to take her in my arms. But after what she said, I resisted.

"Do you like the Bard, Robbie? He's my favorite," she said.

I had no idea what prompted her question, a change of subject, a signal that the other subject was off limits. "Shakespeare? Of course. I love him."

"Really. What do you like best?" She propped onto one elbow, studying me.

"Oh, let's see. *Macbeth, Hamlet, Julius Caesar.* Thunder and heroism, I suppose."

She lay on her back again, her arm pressed against mine. "My God, you are a morbid one." She laughed softly. "I was certain you were more romantic. What about *Romeo and Juliet?*"

"One of my favorites." I was willing to say anything she wanted to hear.

A chickadee flew down and lighted next to her. When she put out her hand, it hopped onto her upturned palm. The bird's mate landed beside her, chirping. Her ability to commune with the animals was disquieting. She raised her arm and they flew away.

I shook my head. "Courtney…"

"Please, Robbie. Enough," she said dismissively. "I told you before. It just comes from spending too much time alone in the forest." She turned toward me. "Perhaps this was a bad idea." Shielding her eyes, Courtney studied the sprinkling of fluffy clouds passing slowly overhead, pushed by the warm breeze. "I wanted to come here with you, so we could be alone."

"It's not that simple," I lied. But it really was. I wanted her so badly it hurt. All I could think of at that moment was pulling Courtney to me, surrounding her with my arms, and kissing her till she begged for air. God help me, Rachel was just a distant memory.

"Come here," I whispered, giving in to temptation. She hesitated for a moment, then grinned, putting her head on my chest. She looked up at me shyly, slowly circling my waist tightly with her arm. Whatever demons she was wrestling with, Courtney was still irresistible. I played with her damp hair, pulling her braids like a schoolboy.

"Ow," she protested, giggling, her eyes closed as she breathed deeply. "Thank you," she said softly, resting her fingers on my shirt.

"For what?" I asked. "You know how I feel."

"I do, but I wanted to be with you so badly," she confessed. "I felt it as soon as we touched that first night—the magic, the electricity between us." Her words were whispered, as if she were telling a secret. "I thought it would be different, that it was my imagination, but it was real and strong and each moment we spend together it grows stronger. I've never felt like this." She continued whispering, lips posed in a tranquil smile. "I'm so happy. No matter what happens tomorrow at least for a few hours, we're here together."

Tomorrow? Since she raised the question, I had to ask. "What if it didn't have to end? What if we could stay together?"

She sat up and stared, her eyes searching mine. "You're serious, aren't you?" Her smile was so gentle yet so inviting excitement surged through my body.

"Of course I'm serious." I took her hand, working my fingers into hers. "Do you think I could leave you after the last three days? When I arrived here, I thought I had a perfect life. Now, none of that matters."

"I'm so sorry, Robbie. I didn't know it would happen like this." She shook her head violently, eyes moist.

"You keep talking like you were performing a script, something you'd planned ahead of time." I raised my voice. "What's going on? Is there something you want to tell me?"

"Yes. But if you care for me, don't ruin this special time together. Please, I'm begging you. Can we enjoy just being with each other for now?"

She put her head back on my chest and hugged me tightly. Her tears dampened my shirt.

"But Courtney," I protested.

"Please," she pleaded. "For me."

I lay with this beautiful young woman holding me as if our very lives depended on it. Perhaps they did. I was sure she loved me. But I had offered her my life, and she balked. I was angry and frustrated, but still her prisoner and so deeply in love, I acquiesced.

I lay exhausted, watching her face move with the slow rhythm of my breathing. I played a game, searching, trying to find an imperfection, some tiny flaw in her face or figure. I found none. After a few minutes she fell asleep. Her thick lashes fluttered lazily as she dozed. Soon, my eyelids grew heavy and I joined her.

I had no idea how long we slept. When I awakened, Courtney was sitting up.

"It's so warm." She exhaled as she stood and walked to the horses, patting them. She came back with the saddlebags. Sitting down, she pulled out the last of the juice and a canteen, moisture dripping off it.

"Pick your pleasure." She glanced at me as she shook the thermos.

"Being here with you," I confessed, my face flushing.

"I know," she assured me.

I reached for the canteen.

She lowered her eyes and played with her loose braids. The warm wind blew across the lake, bringing her familiar jasmine fragrance with it. We sat in awkward silence, taking a drink and avoiding each other's eyes after the deep discussion earlier. Courtney broke the stalemate.

"Well." She cleared her throat. "What happened to the breeze?" she asked, putting down the thermos as she unlaced her boots. She looked in my direction, pulled the boots off, then her socks, putting them next to her helmet and gloves. Standing, she tiptoed over the small smooth stones on the beach, putting her toes in the icy water.

"Oh, it's so cold." She laughed. "I think you're a fraidycat," she said, pointing at me.

"No way," I snapped, joining her laughter as I

pulled off my boots and socks. I walked across the small stone beach and dangled my toes.

"My God," I cried, backing away. "That's the coldest water I've ever felt."

She giggled and closed the small space separating us, putting her arm around my waist as she gave me a playful squeeze.

We bent to retrieve our boots and socks. "Well, what now? Back to the real world?"

"Absolutely not," she protested and took my hand. "We're going to be pioneers, woodsmen, and stay in this beautiful place forever." She let go of my waist and touched my cheek. "Would you like that, dear?" The term of endearment sent shivers through every fiber.

"I'd love nothing more." I took her in my arms as I wanted to so often. Pulling her to me, I let my chin rest on her damp, fragrant hair. I reached down and gently took her face in my hands, letting myself get lost in her luminous eyes. They were soft and inviting. Her full lips parted slightly, her innocent smile waiting, anticipating. What was she thinking? Did Courtney want me to kiss her? I thought so. But once I had, there would be no turning back. It would change our lives forever. I was beyond caring. Closing my eyes, I found her lips. The kiss was soft and gentle, over too quickly, but like nothing I had ever known. In the brief instant our lips met, I was lost in a magical world, hypnotized by the sweetness of her mouth. The taste of Courtney's lips was something I would remember as long as I lived.

"Oh, Robbie." She sighed deeply.

"Are you all right?" I asked. Despite all that was happening between us, had I made a mistake?

"Oh yes," she assured me. "That was wonderful. But I'm not sure I could stop if we..." Her words trailed off. She gave me a shy smile, pushing away, taking my hand as she headed toward the horses.

"Now, you take our friends for a nice long drink while I fix lunch."

"Lunch?" I managed, still lost in a state of pleasant arousal, luxuriating in the memory of our magical kiss.

"If we're going to stay here forever, we have to eat don't we?" She paused. "Or perhaps you've changed your mind already. Are you just going to kiss me and then run off?" she asked, eyebrows raised as she pushed her lips into a pout. "You are a fickle one, McGregor."

I grinned, shaking my head. "You know better."

"Then do the manly thing, get our mounts a drink, round up the helmets and gear and I—will—fix—lunch." She stood, putting out her hand. "Give me your boots or put them on." It was an order.

"Actually the grass feels wonderful." I handed them to her after stuffing my socks inside.

"Thanks so much. You're so good to me." She grinned, holding her nose as she took them with two fingers.

"You seem to be in charge." I shrugged and took Pumpkin Patch and Courtney's magnificent gelding to the lake while she took the saddlebags to a small pine grove. The spot was lovely, nestled into the side of the forest. It was hidden from view, but faced the lake, allowing the warm breeze to blow through. I was careful to make sure our mounts drank enough, promising myself to bring them back after lunch. In a few minutes, I took their reins loosely, picked up the remainder of our gear and headed back to the meadow.

"Should I tie them up?" I called to her.

She shook her head. "They'll be fine. Pumpkin Patch is a dear and so is Romeo. But you could loosen the girth. It's very warm."

I did as she suggested, releasing the cinch on each saddle and left them grazing in the shade then walked toward her.

"You've named this horse Romeo, too?" I asked as I arrived at the grove.

"Of course," she said, lips curled as her face reddened. "Unlike you, I am a romantic."

I was about to tease her when I looked down. There was a blanket, two small bottles of wine, one for each of us, a corkscrew, some cheese, fruit, and a small loaf of coarse bread.

I was incredulous. "Wine, fresh strawberries...you really are quite the cook." I laughed.

She joined me. Standing up, Courtney made a grand gesture of seating me and sat down on my right. I was shaking my head. As I watched she closed her eyes, undid the ribbons and combed out her damp braids with her fingers.

She sighed deeply. "Now that's better. Oh, damn," she cursed. "Can you believe it? I forgot a knife."

"Some witch," I teased. "Not to worry," I volunteered. "I can make one appear by magic," I said, taking my Swiss Army knife from my pocket. I took the corkscrew and handed her the knife, picking up one of the bottles.

"Perfect." She smiled. "I managed to squeeze in a third bottle. It's in the saddlebags," she said, looking content while cutting a slice of cheese, placing it on a cloth napkin with some strawberries and grapes. She did the same with the loaf of bread and pointed toward it.

"Luncheon is served." She gestured. "'A loaf of bread, a jug of wine, and thou.'"

"Omar Khayyam. I am impressed." I handed her the open bottle and repeated the process with the second. I lay on my elbow, taking a piece of bread, then cheese, washing them down with a swallow of the vintage cabernet she brought.

"Do you know how incredible you are?" I asked.

"Yes," she said as she put her lips together.

For the next few minutes, we sat silently, eating and drinking, content to be with each other as we shared our private paradise. I had unanswered questions, but for those few minutes all I wanted was to be near Courtney. Life had a way of working out, I assured myself.

Chapter Nineteen

We finished lunch, sitting warm and tired, watching each other as we wrestled with our thoughts. I wanted to pursue the discussion about the future. Our future. Did we have one or was this all a tease. A bittersweet fantasy? I was willing to abandon my well-ordered life to be with her. But she seemed unwilling or unable to commit. Could I pretend these three days had never happened and go back to Boston, Rachel, and the stuffy social network that had been my life?

I looked up. Courtney was fidgeting with the leftovers, stuffing things into the saddlebags, avoiding my eyes. She pulled out the last bottle of wine and the corkscrew, crossing the small space between us. "What do you think?" she asked, sitting down next to me. Her eyes wore a tired, glassy look.

"I don't know. It's hot and I can already feel the effects of that first bottle."

She shook her head. "You're such a poop." She perked up, poking me in the ribs. "I thought we were going to make this a day to remember."

Courtney stopped, put down the wine and smiled softly as she found my eyes. Her fingertips fell on my shoulders. She began caressing them. Suddenly, she bent down, taking my face in her hands. She pulled me to her. Our mouths met tentatively. I opened my lips. She followed my lead, pressing her mouth against mine. I wanted that sensuous mouth again. Our brief encounter earlier only increased my desire. I played with her lips— above and around them. She followed my lead.

Courtney was inexperienced, but we were lost in a world of ecstasy and anticipation, holding each other as if our lives depended on it. Our hands worked feverishly over our damp clothing. The electricity from the last few days had been a prelude, a tempting overture to what flowed between us, lighting our bodies on fire. The sweet moisture of our lips joined, played, caressed. I let my tongue find hers. She hesitated, backing away, unsure of what to do.

"It's called a French kiss..."

"Shhh," she whispered breathlessly. "Don't stop. I love it." Courtney was a willing student. We inhaled each other, lost in our private ecstasy, in an embrace so tight it was difficult to breathe. I wanted to consume Courtney—take her inside me and never release her. I knew she felt the same. Suddenly, she pushed away, sitting on the ground, gasping as she hugged herself, trembling.

"Oh my God," she whispered, her voice hoarse and full of passion.

I sat, eyes closed, aroused beyond anything I'd ever imagined. My lips could still taste the sweet, salty flavor of hers. "I've never...never felt like that with anyone," I whispered.

"Nor I," she said between quick breaths.

I reached for her again. She held up her hands and backed away.

"No. We can't. Not now." She shook her head. "I'm so sorry. This was wrong, but I couldn't wait. I had to know what it would be like." She touched my lips softly. "To kiss you in the way I'd dreamt of since that first night. To feel you close to me, part of me," she continued, eyes closed, as I kissed her fingertips.

"But Courtney," I protested.

"Please, Robbie. We can't." She held up her hands again.

"But why? I don't care about my life in Boston, Rachel, any of it! You know that. Is there"—I could barely bring myself to say the words—"someone else?"

"Someone else?" she whispered. I could see the pain in her eyes. She shook her head again. "How can you even ask me that?" She took both my hands in hers. Her eyes blazed. "There never was—never could be."

"Then why?"

"I can't explain right now. I'm begging you to trust me." She let go of my hands and reached behind her, producing the third bottle of wine.

I sat frustrated and angry. I did trust her, but...

"Have a sip, please." She opened the wine, watching me. "For me," she repeated, tilting her head.

I took a long swallow. It had a different taste. I handed it back to her. "This is very good. Sweet. Have some."

She took a quick swallow. "I'm all right. It's something very special I brought for you." She took my arm and put it around her shoulder. "May I lie next to you again?"

"Of course." I yawned, drowsiness creeping over me.

Courtney dropped her head onto my chest. I felt her soft, regular breathing, saw her eyes closing, and closed my own for a moment. When she dozed off, I wanted to check the horses to see how they were faring in the heat, perhaps remove their saddles and get them another drink. I was asleep in seconds.

Chapter Twenty

I awoke alone. The angle of the sun told me it was later in the afternoon. I looked at my watch. It was after three. Panic swept over me. But as I surveyed the grove and the meadow everything was in place. The horses roamed freely, playing and grazing. Courtney must have awakened and taken a walk.

"Courtney," I called. No reply. I repeated my call a little louder. My voice sounded lonely, muted by the trees and surrounding vegetation. I rose, pulling on my socks and boots, heading down the path toward the lake. No sign of Courtney anywhere. I decided to walk the perimeter of the grove looking for her.

I called her name again. Still nothing. As I came out from behind a thick stand of pines, a small sheltered area came into view. At its far end was a symmetrical, upright stone. At first glance I mistook it for an altar. What would an altar be doing in the middle of the Maine wilderness?

In the distance, I saw Courtney. She knelt in front of the large rock, holding an object over her head. I watched, about to call. Something made me balk—the mystery, the talk of witchcraft, or the strange dream. Instead, I bent down and crept closer. I stopped twenty yards behind her, finding a spot hidden by decaying logs. When the wind blew in my direction, I could hear her. The language was strange, like the one from my dream.

Suddenly, as if sensing my presence, she turned. Her expression was sad and dark. In the light that filtered through the trees, I could see tears shining on her sunburned cheeks. She took the object in her hands and kissed it. Standing, Courtney walked to the rock formation and placed it in a small container, then put it in the ground directly below a regular discoloration on the rock's surface. She appeared to be burying it.

From behind the logs, I watched through a small gap. Courtney searched the clearing again, smoothed her clothes and headed toward me. It was the most direct route back to our picnic area. Suddenly I wondered. Had she put something in the wine? And if so, why?

I huddled flat against the fallen logs. As she passed, she stopped, raising her head. I sensed Courtney knew I was there, but instead of turning toward me, she continued walking. As soon as she was out of sight, I ran around the grove and found a spot by the shore.

I heard movement across the glade. I turned, sneaking a look toward her. As she approached, Courtney appeared to compose herself, trying to look casual.

"Well, you really dozed off, McGregor. Sorry I deserted you but I had to use the facilities." She was doing her best to keep the conversation light. Nodding toward the horses, Courtney touched my shoulder. "It's time we went home."

****

We rode in silence, retracing our path from the morning. The sumptuous green and gold of the meadows shimmered in the shadows as the sun worked toward the distant mountains. Turning, Courtney paused and watched, searching my eyes, holding them. After a few minutes she slowed. I cantered up to join her.

"Stop!" I commanded, confused, angry, and trying to make sense of all this. I thought about the growing list of mysteries. Her ability to commune with animals, the pendant she guarded like the crown jewels, and the mythology surrounding it. That strange wine and the ceremony in the glade. Michael's stories. And the mysterious Simon. I was in denial, fighting the idea I refused to believe. Was it really possible? This is the twentieth century. We had jets, atomic bombs, air conditioning, and television. Did we really have witches?

"Hello, stranger." Courtney interrupted my thoughts.

Perhaps I was letting my imagination run wild. Was it more simple than sinister? Was she going away and afraid to tell me? I had to know.

"Courtney, what's going on?"

"What do you mean?" She feigned innocence. Her shoulders slumped, betraying her.

"Something's wrong." I took her reins. "Come on. I'm no fool. You put something in that wine. And I saw you in the woods performing that *ritual*."

"It was something I had to do. I told you." She paused. "I'm a witch." She yanked her reins free and galloped ahead.

"That's no answer," I yelled after her, spurring my horse to catch her.

"Isn't that what you expected to hear, Robbie?" She spat the words at me as I pulled abreast of her. "Haven't people been filling your head with sinister stories about me and the mysterious goings on at Briarwood?"

"No...yes. But damn it, I want the truth." I took her arm.

We stopped on the trail. She pulled free, studying my eyes. "You want the truth? Well, here it is. Sorry, but you'll find it very mundane. It won't measure up to the strange, romantic fantasy you've conjured up."

I turned in the saddle, facing her, half angry,

half embarrassed.

"You keep asking about some master plan. Well, dear, I'm sorry to disappoint you." She looked away. When she faced me again her eyes were burning, traces of tears on her cheeks. "Auntie had told me so many wonderful things about you—how handsome you were, how successful. She showed me your picture."

"But Courtney—"

She refused to let me finish.

"I was lonely, angry, vulnerable. I found myself fantasizing about you, playing games in my mind, wondering what you were like, if you'd like me. Silly, schoolgirl dreams. I had no idea about your relationship with Rachel. Suddenly, there you were."

I sat, slumped in my saddle, watching her.

She continued. "So when you arrived and were everything I'd imagined and more, I was already infatuated. And that infatuation has grown into something very deep and very real."

I reached for her hand. She pulled it away.

"And as to the business with the animals you find so unfathomable, it's very common with country folk. I've told you! It comes with practice and patience. There's nothing otherworldly about it."

"All right. I can accept that."

"How kind of you." She shot me a withering glance.

"But today, the wine and that strange ceremony?"

"Yes, I brought that wine especially for you. It was very strong. The weather was very hot and you were exhausted, sore, tired. Is it so strange to think you might doze off?"

"No. I suppose not," I had to admit.

"And the ceremony. My mother was cremated. I was burying her ashes."

"I couldn't have known." I felt humbled, but my

practical side was still raising questions. "Why didn't you tell me? And what was that strange language you were speaking?"

"I didn't tell you, because as much as I care for you, Robbie, it was a very private moment. My mother loved this place. I'm sure you've heard that we were very close. She came here often as a child. That's how I knew about it. She told me. I promised her that if anything ever happened to her I'd do my best to bury her ashes here. My family is descended from Welsh royalty. That was the language I was speaking." Her face grew flushed. "It was an ancient prayer for her immortal soul."

"I'm sorry, Courtney." I felt wrung out, exhausted. Maybe it was all true. Maybe it was the heat and the wine was untouched. Maybe she was burying Ellen's ashes. But I'd always been someone who dealt in logic. And too many things were beginning to raise the hairs on the back of my neck. I opened my mouth to speak. Courtney continued her assault.

"And if you're wondering why I was moody today, it was because I found out that my grandfather was coming tonight with my nanny. I was sad and desperate."

"Sad and desperate?"

"Are you completely blind? That's no mystery. Because I love you. I was terrified he'd want to take me away. I can't stand the thought of leaving you." She sighed and shook her head. "There it is. Does that satisfy your insatiable curiosity, *darling*?"

I sat in silence. Staring at her, every ounce of my being wanted to believe what she'd said. Her performance was perfect. She had a logical explanation for everything that had happened. Trouble is I was born a skeptic. Were her explanations too logical and too perfect?

She looked away and spurred her horse, heading

down the final section of trail. We arrived at the stables, a cold, brittle silence hovering around us. Neither of us spoke over the last two miles. We dismounted and took our horses inside, putting them into their stalls.

"You go back and get cleaned up. I'll take care of the horses," she ordered, refusing to look at me.

"Courtney." I stood, frozen and frustrated.

"Please, Robert, just leave it alone. Leave *me* alone." She continued, staring at the dirt and straw. "Why can't you understand? This is the most difficult thing I've ever gone through." She closed her eyes and pressed her lips together tightly. "I should have kept my feelings a secret, but I couldn't. I'm acting like a spoiled, selfish little girl. I know how much you care for me. But every time I look at you I hate myself for wanting you so badly, for loving you the way I do."

I held out my hand. She took it. "You're not alone, Courtney. I have a stake in what's going on between us. Something incredible has happened to me since I met you. Something out of a fairy tale. "

"Yes, Robbie, of course you have a stake in our future, but I can't look at you and see the way you look at me and not feel guilty. You had a full, rich life before we met. I've stolen that from you. At least that's how I feel. How could we ever be a couple, have any life or future together when I know I've taken you away from everything you loved?"

"What if everything I love is here in front of me?"

She shook her head, releasing my hand and pushing it away.

"Damn it! That's not an answer," I said, raising my voice.

"Robbie, do you love me?" she asked.

"More than I ever thought it possible to love anyone."

Tears streamed down her sunburned cheeks. "Then give me a little time alone, darling. I need to think," she pleaded, forcing a smile. "I'll see you for dinner. Promise."

I sighed and turned, having no idea what to say. Part of me wanted to crush her in my arms and dry her tears. Another wanted to scream at her and demand the truth. As I reached the stable door she ran and caught me.

"I love you so much," she said, as if to reassure herself.

She pulled me to her and kissed my lips, then ran back to the horses. I turned and walked away, hurt, confused, and under her spell. If she'd said the Earth was flat, I would have believed her.

Would this sad, beautiful angel ever open her heart to me completely and let me into her life? I had so many questions. With each step another piece of the dream I'd been living since Thursday evening seemed to crumble and disappear into the trail.

Chapter Twenty-One

I lay on my bed in my dirty riding clothes, glancing at the clock in the fading sunlight. Seven. I took another swallow from the bottle of beer on my night table. My dream had exploded like a land mine. But I was a pragmatist. I believed in reality. I knew better than to think that dreams really came true. I'd made my decision. Pack my bags, kiss Courtney on the cheek, and head back to Boston.

The knock was soft. I knew it was her. Courtney and I had a special intimacy—something almost telepathic. So how could I have been so wrong about so much? I sat up and headed to the door, pulling a cigarette from my pack and reaching for my lighter.

I opened the door. She stood, looking perfect and elegant again. Long beige skirt, fitted white silk blouse, with a monogrammed stock tie. A dazzling set of diamond studs matched the necklace she wore. Her dark hair shone pink in the fading sunlight, held in place by a thick white headband that matched her blouse. It struck me that Courtney's clothing budget could probably support several small European economies.

"Hello," she whispered. "Are you very angry with me?" She bit her lip. Her eyes shone in the twilight. I opened the door. She glanced back toward the courtyard, coming in. "Perhaps I shouldn't." She hesitated.

"I think it's a little late to worry about appearances." I sighed. "Am I angry with you? No. I'm angry with myself. Angry, exhausted, and sick of mysteries. I think it may be time to go home."

"No!" Courtney looked up in disbelief. "You can't." She gasped as if someone had struck her.

I crushed out my cigarette. "I'm kind of dirty. It was hot today, and I was around horses. I recall you being there." It was an attempt at humor. "I thought it might be easier for both of us if I gave you back your life and went to see my brother. I got a head start." I pointed toward the beer.

"No, please, you can't," she repeated. "Robbie, I don't want my life back. Not without you." She looked startled and hurt. "Besides, you can't leave tonight. I'm begging you. I have a special surprise."

Her eyes looked wide—full of wonder and excitement as she closed the distance between us and took my hand. I was sweaty and half drunk. I wanted to pull away but her stare held me. "Oh, Robbie, forgive me. I've done this so badly, but..." She closed her eyes and shook her head. "I couldn't have known what you'd be like."

"Stop it, Courtney!" I raised my voice. "You're doing it again. I have no idea what you're talking about. I want off this roller coaster." I began to turn, but something in her face—love, desperation, vulnerability—captured me.

"You know how much I love you?" She weaved her fingers into mine. "'More than I ever thought it possible.' Weren't those your words?"

"Yes," I whispered as I found myself reaching for her. She fell into my arms.

"Robbie, please stay. Simon and my nanny have arrived. I promise you won't regret it," she pleaded, her head resting on my soiled shirt. "I...I need you." Courtney pushed away and straightened her clothing, looking defeated. She studied me, tears spilling onto her cheeks as she walked toward the door. I took her arm, turning her to face me.

"All right. I'll give this adventure one more night."

"I knew you would." She looked up at me, eyes soft and inviting. "It'll be a wonderful evening, and I promise we'll deal with what's happening between us. Simon's dying to meet you."

Could the fantasy remain alive? More importantly, should it?

"But, you really do need to freshen up, dear." She grinned. "I'll see you at the buffet in an hour." She gave me a coy smile. "While the others are watching the fireworks, we'll steal away. I want to be alone with you. There's a lot to tell you, and we need to make plans."

"Plans?"

"Yes, my love. I think you'll find the evening interesting. Very interesting."

Chapter Twenty-Two

I stood in the shower, trying to make some sense of things. As warm water washed away the residue of our magical day in the high meadows, random thoughts ran through my mind. Not all of them pleasant. She loved me. I knew that. And I loved her. Courtney wasn't playing me—at least about her feelings. But about everything else—the newspaper clippings, the tales of witchcraft and murder, the bizarre events of the afternoon she dismissed or denied—I could only guess. And while it was possible that alcohol let my imagination play tricks, I was certain her eyes had taken on a strange glow more than once.

Yet, in spite of all my misgivings, I had no choice. Staying away from Courtney was like trying to swim the English Channel underwater. It was impossible. I dressed for the lobster buffet and headed off to meet Courtney's guests, wondering if they were the same mysterious visitors Jonathan had anticipated.

When I entered the dining room, it was immediately obvious that the large man standing near Jonathan was Simon. My host stood captivated, fawning over the giant next to him. Uncle Jon doted on his guest like he was a movie star or sports icon. A short, round woman with a cane stood close by, smiling and nodding at the conversation.

My imaginings of Simon suggested a bear of a man. This man was tall, but his lean body held no excess weight. Broad shoulders pushed at the corners of his expensive suit, hinting at the power his six-foot, six-inch frame could unleash. Courtney was nowhere to be seen. As I studied the imposing figure commanding so much attention, a chill ran through me. The giant holding court was the man in the purple robe from my dreams. I swallowed hard and tried to maintain my composure.

I also noticed that despite the promised festivities, the crowd had dwindled. Those who remained were the family members closest to Jon and Gretchen. I noticed with interest that Wendy had joined the ensemble. She nodded and smiled warmly as I caught her eye. She looked quite fetching in a fitted black dress and gray tweed hacking jacket. As I approached, Jon saw me and quickly came over to include me.

"Here he is, Simon. Robert McGregor." He beamed as he directed me toward the new guest. "He's been wonderful to Courtney. They've become quite a pair." He flushed, perhaps realizing the implication.

"I promised you a surprise guest," Jon whispered to me, gloating like a child whose parents have hired a clown for his birthday party.

"So I see. Where did everyone else go?" I asked, gesturing around the room.

"Business, matters at home. Not really sure. Better this way, I think," Jon assured me, surveying the room. "Now, I want you to meet our guests."

"Yes, I've heard so much about you. I feel as if I know you already." Simon approached, studying me, lips curling up. He offered his hand. His shake was strong and warm but non-threatening. I'd never felt a stare hold me so intensely, as if I was being probed. Simon bent his lean body and broad shoulders over my six-foot, one-inch frame. "I'm Simon Wellington, Courtney's guardian. It's a genuine pleasure."

Courtney's guardian?

The accent eluded me. It had none of the formality of his granddaughter's. A touch of Irish, Scottish perhaps.

"Welsh," he volunteered, suppressing a smile. "My family comes from a small hamlet in Wales." He picked up on my curiosity over his speech.

"I see. I wasn't sure."

"I gathered that, Robert. We come from a village in the Southern Cambrian Mountains called Abergwesyn, A-b-e-r-g-w-e-s-y-n. My family's lived there since before the Romans. Our main attraction today is a frightening road known as the Devil's Switchback. The Welsh name for it is difficult enough to spell, let alone pronounce. Too many consonants and too few vowels." He chuckled. "But we're not here for a geography lesson. And since I've heard you're a bright and perceptive young man, you're wondering about my role as your friend's guardian?"

Right again. When he smiled it was obvious where Courtney got her good looks. Simon had a self-assured, pleasant manner about him. His eyes seemed to penetrate while including you in his conversation, leaving the impression of confiding something private and special.

"Well, Courtney has spoken of you often. But yes, sir, I thought she had a father."

"She's a dear child and far too generous." He paused. "And yes, Duncan Wellington is her father, but the poor man disappeared. He and Courtney were never close, but it's a still a tragedy." He put his massive hand on my shoulder and scanned the room, lowering his voice. "You see, Robert, my son Courtney was her real father. I was fortunate enough to convince a magistrate to make her my ward. At least for a while." He chuckled softly, holding up his hands. "When she comes of age, she'll be free to do what she chooses, heaven help us." He rolled his eyes with amusement, releasing me. "Of course, everyone who meets Courtney knows that the real credit for the wonderful things you see in her is due to this fine woman." He nodded toward the gray-haired woman leaning on her cane. "This is Megan McPherson, Courtney's nanny and teacher."

The rotund woman's ruddy face grew red. She pushed back a wisp of thick gray hair as she held out her hand. "Mr. Phillips is far too kind, sir," she demurred. "Miss Courtney is an angel, always has been. Beautiful, brilliant, talented." She paused thoughtfully. "Despite..." She looked at Simon and left her thought unfinished. I caught an imperceptible nod on his part.

"Yes," I agreed. "I've heard some stories. But you're right. She's the most wonderful girl I've ever met." I flushed at having been so open.

"It's all right, Robert." Simon's giant hand fell on my shoulder again. "I know how close you two have become." He smiled. "You're a fine young man. I couldn't be happier."

I wondered what to think. Was Simon encouraging our relationship? I expected reticence, even concern over the affection that had grown between Courtney and I. Especially from a proper British family. Before I had a chance for further introspection, every eye turned toward the massive oak archway.

As was the custom, Courtney's appearance was greeted by silence and stares that anything so beautiful could be real. She smiled warmly and nodded to several of the guests. Courtney approached and stood next to me, taking my arm in hers, leaning against me. Tonight, even Jon smiled at the intimacy. I pushed her gently away. When I looked she wore a grin. Courtney was enjoying my discomfort.

"Robbie, I'm sure that my granddaughter has

mentioned the special event we're celebrating this Friday," Simon began, eyes fixed on Courtney. "Her twenty-first birthday."

I nodded. "She's mentioned it."

"Well, I've spoken to Jon and he's graciously allowed us to plan a small celebration on his estate. I know you may have other commitments, but you and Courtney have grown so close, we'd consider it an honor if you'd join us." He fixed me with a stare. "I can guarantee when the evening is over, you'll be thrilled you stayed."

Courtney had alluded to making plans, promising I wouldn't regret staying. Simon repeated the assurance. It sounded wonderful, but suspicion returned. What could be happening on her birthday to make it a special evening for me? After what I'd heard and seen in the last four days a disturbing image of Christians and lions materialized.

I began processing what staying here would mean. The problem was making excuses. Explanations would have to be made to friends, my mother, and of course, Rachel. There was no way I could do it.

I looked at Courtney. Her delicious smile melted my resolve.

"Absolutely, Simon." I shook his hand. "Wouldn't miss it for the world."

sculptured ears, her delicate nose, and that wonderful mouth I could never get enough of. I took its full measure. As I became aroused she rose to meet me, pressing close as our bodies melded. There never was, never would be another woman to excite me this way. Whatever else was happening, I had no doubt that Courtney meant what she said. We held each other breathlessly. I opened my mouth to speak.

She put her hand to my lips. "Don't even try," she whispered, her fingers clutching my back. "It would be a waste of breath. There are no words to describe what we feel." She released me. "Go. Change quickly, darling. Meet me at the stables. There's a special place where we can watch the fireworks. I'm going to tell you a story. It's a magical story that will change your life, change both our lives forever."

Chapter Twenty-Four

She'd decided to tell me the truth!

I ran back to my room and opened the door. Nothing that happened close to Courtney surprised me any more, so when my riding clothes lay clean and pressed on my bed, I smiled, taking it in stride. I changed in a flash and hopped out the door, pulling my left boot on as I headed through the courtyard and down the gravel path to the stables. I could hear the crowd gathering on the broad lawn by the lake, laughing and singing as they awaited the grand finale.

A single light shone brightly, guiding me to the stable entrance. I opened the office door. As I did, Courtney called to me from the barn. "Come on, Robbie. It's been ages since I've seen fireworks. I don't want to miss the festivities."

Romeo and Pumpkin Patch stood saddled and waiting. There was no sign of Wendy, but that was no surprise. The evening had long ago taken on a dizzying, surreal quality. I didn't give her absence a second thought. Courtney slid into the saddle with her usual grace.

"Ow," I complained as I raised my boot to the stirrup. I was trying to follow her example despite the tired, aching muscles occasioned by hours in the saddle. I let my sore backside down carefully on the unforgiving leather. *Damn, that hurt*, I whined silently, refusing to give Courtney the satisfaction of hearing my discomfort. When we reached the large double door, she pulled open the latch and spurred her mount toward a small hill overlooking the lake.

"Don't be concerned, just follow my lead. I can see the trail perfectly."

How she did I had no idea. The moon was a giant orb rising above the trees in the west while the dazzling Milky Way sprinkled light sparingly on the countryside. Maybe witches could see in the dark. It looked pitch black to my untrained eyes, but I knew better than to doubt Courtney. Her instincts proved flawless once again. In a matter of minutes we traversed the steep, winding path, arriving atop a bare, knobby rise. It offered a spectacular view of the estate below and the cove where the fireworks would be launched.

Courtney dismounted, sliding off gracefully. I did the same, minus the grace. We'd spoken little on the trip up the hill. I was too busy following her. As she had earlier in the day, Courtney pulled the saddlebags off the broad back of her gelding. I noticed a thick blanket rolled up as well.

"What about tying them?" I asked. It was very dark on top of our private retreat. One of the mounts could wander and a misstep might mean a twisted leg or worse.

"There's no need," she assured me, touching them on the snout. Each whinnied and nodded as if to offer me reassurance. I could only marvel. There was something wonderful and fascinating about her kinship with animals.

"You can take off their saddles. We'll put them on this." She spread out the blanket she'd brought. "It'll give us something comfortable to sit on. We may be here a while."

This sounded promising, even provocative, but Courtney's tone was casual. I followed her suggestion and took off the saddles, putting them on top of the blanket I spread on the ground. As if following an imaginary script, just as we sat down, the fireworks began. I rested my sore back against one of the saddles, while Courtney lay, head in my lap, taking my hand. She oohed and aahed, clapping like a child at the county fair seeing fireworks for the first time.

"Isn't this grand?" Courtney enthused.

And it was. Jon and Gretchen had spared no expense in putting on this impressive display of pyrotechnics. Cheers and applause echoed, wafting up from the lawn half a mile to the east.

"Yes," I agreed. My mind was far from the dizzying array of colors playing out above our heads. I was anxious to hear what she was going to tell me, but as she lay laughing in my lap, her sweet fragrance enveloped me. Other urges came to mind. I closed my eyes, my fevered imagination returned to the afternoon and earlier that evening—short passionate moments spent together. I grasped her long slender fingers, enclosing them.

After thirty minutes of aerial magnificence, the show ended with a grand finale. The crowd groaned and applauded one last time. Courtney sat up and reached over, pulling a bottle of wine from the saddlebags. She extracted a corkscrew and opened it, offering me a taste.

I hesitated. "You first," I said, pushing it back toward her.

She smiled. "You have to learn to trust me, McGregor." She took a long swallow and handed it back to me.

As she did, I heard motion behind me.

"Speaking of trust. I knew you might have difficulty believing what I'm going to tell you, Robbie, so I brought an ally. Someone I *know* you trust."

I turned, having no idea who her confidant might be. My jaw dropped when the figure of my brother appeared out of the darkness.

Chapter Twenty-Five

"*Michael!*" I jumped up, looking back and forth between them. "What are you doing here?"

Michael clasped my arm. "Courtney has a lot to explain. Some, you suspect. We left clues for you." He glanced at Courtney, who stood, hands on hips, a reticent smile on her lips. "Actually we did everything but take out an ad in the *Times*. We thought it might help if I was here to tell you she hasn't gone off her nut."

"We. You said 'we'?" I swallowed hard. "Meaning you're one of *them*. You and she are..." I stopped in mid-sentence. My mouth went dry.

"Yes, Robbie. Everyone except Mrs. Mac and the servants are part of our family," Courtney said, looking at Michael. "Maybe we need to sit down and have a drink," she added, looking at me.

Michael nodded.

"Family?" I asked. "I've heard you people referred to as a coven."

"That's true," Michael said as he sat down. "But a coven is usually comprised of thirteen members or fewer. We're much larger. And we find 'family' is less intimidating."

"I see. But Michael. You're my brother. What the hell's going on?" They were casual, uninhibited, exposing their true lineage as if it was routine, even something to be proud of. Each took a swallow from the bottle of wine and offered it to me. "If you're one of them, then..."

"Yes, Robbie. You're one of us, too. A very special one." He fixed me with a stare.

149

I pushed the wine back toward Courtney. "Jesus." I was still in shock. "I want to stay sober to hear what you have to tell me. But hold on." I wondered how deep the deception went. "What about the newspaper clippings, Jonathan's warnings. Was that all a charade?"

"Well"—Courtney watched me, an anxious expression crossing her face—"We had to be sure of you. We threw things in your way—mysteries, clues, obstacles. If they'd frightened you or driven you away, we would have modified our plan." She stopped, shaking her head. "But I knew from the moment I saw you that we were..." Her words trailed off. "Let's just say I never had any doubt." Courtney reached over and ran her fingers into mine, squeezing my hand.

Clues, obstacles, frightened me away, modified the plan? I suppose that made sense. To them. To me, this was uncharted territory. I was confused, curious, and more than a little frightened. My brother and the girl I loved were staring at me, involved in something mysterious and unless I was off *my* nut, supernatural. My throat tightened.

"Robbie, please, trust me. There's absolutely nothing to be afraid of." Courtney looked at Michael.

I sat staring, frozen, shaking my head.

"Please believe me. What I told you today was the truth about my state of mind, my mother's ashes, all of it. The wine was mead—an ancient drink made from honey and spices. We've used it for centuries. It is very strong, but it wasn't drugged. I have *never* lied to you," she assured me. "There are things that I haven't told you—about who and what we really are." She gestured toward Michael.

I looked back and forth between them. "What if I told you I don't want to hear any more? That I want to get up, head down the mountain, and go back to my life—the dull, normal life I had when I arrived here four days ago."

Courtney looked toward Michael, then at the ground, bringing her hand to her cheek.

"Go ahead. If that's what you want." She frowned, her head sinking lower. "I won't stop you and neither will Michael. But if you stay, we'll tell you everything and remember, I promised that you wouldn't be disappointed," she continued.

Damn! I looked into her velvet-brown eyes, reflecting the moon rising behind me.

Michael nodded.

I grabbed the wine and took a swallow.

"All right." I shrugged. "Whatever you have to tell me can't be any stranger than what's going through my head."

Courtney moved closer, taking my hand again.

"Robbie, do you believe that good and evil exist in the universe?" she asked, eyes focused and intense.

"I don't know. Are you talking good and bad people, like the Allies and Nazis, or something more abstract?"

She looked at Michael. "Both. The World War II analogy is all right, but it's oversimplified." Courtney took a deep breath. "Our family worships the good in our world, the beauty and purity of nature. We love and respect one another, living in harmony the way the gods and goddesses intended."

"Gods and goddesses?" I asked.

"Yes," Michael answered. "We believe in nature, the Earth, and all living things. Not one omniscient being who controls the universe."

"All right." I nodded. "So this is a religion? Like Judaism or Christianity?"

"Yes." She nodded. "Only more so. We have a unique philosophy and strict code of behavior. It demands far more discipline and study than anything Sunday-morning Christians observe. Those of us descended from the ancient ones have special abilities." She smiled. "But we've had a long time to refine them. The essence of our being, what you'd call our soul, has been reborn many times. We spend years studying our craft—the practice that you know as witchcraft. You might find the things we do difficult to grasp, darling." She shrugged, looking at Michael. "Let's leave that for another time."

I sat looking at the two of them, wondering if I was going to wake up in my apartment. "That's fine. But what does any of this have to do with me?"

"There are thousands of us, but we are a tight-knit group, a very tight-knit group." She gave me a kind, patronizing smile like one would a slow student. "And the truth, the reason that we kept challenging you, testing you, is that we need you." She sighed deeply. "*I* need you. To be my consort. My lover, if that makes it more graphic."

Courtney's voice grew soft. She blushed. "You and I must celebrate my emergence into womanhood by joining on litha, the night of the summer solstice, when the full moon rises." Her fingers wrapped around mine as she squeezed my hand tightly.

Was I really hearing this? No, I'd gone insane. It was the only explanation. "All right, all right. Nice try. You had me going for a while. I think this charade has gone on long enough. Any second you're both going to laugh and tell me this is an elaborate joke." I searched their eyes but saw no humor. "Aren't you?"

Courtney looked at Michael. "No, Robbie. This is what you Yanks call the real deal. I know it's difficult to process and you need time to grasp it, but I swear this is no joke."

I looked at Michael. He nodded. "The lovely lady speaks the truth. That birthmark on your shoulder? It identifies you. You're special. We both are. But you're the chosen one. I understand how hard this is for you, but like Courtney, you were destined for this since birth."

"Since birth?" I was dumbfounded. This could not be happening. Could it? "All right. I'm the chosen one. Now that I've heard the punch line, suppose I decide to go back to the estate and head home?"

"You can leave, Robbie. You're not a prisoner. We'd erase your memory. We'd have to. You'd never remember any of this, meeting me, Simon, Michael's true identity. You'd simply remember a pleasant weekend in the country," Courtney whispered, her eyes studying the ground again. Her words stung. The thought of losing Courtney, of erasing any memory of her and everything that accompanied this surreal weekend was something I refused to think about. Whatever else it was, I found it fascinating beyond anything my imagination could have conjured up. I had to admit, I wanted to know more.

"You can really do that? Make me forget all this?"

She nodded.

"All right." I shrugged, still unconvinced. "If I'm free to leave, and I won't remember any of this, why all the scheming, subterfuge, and mystery? What's the punch line?"

Courtney frowned, perhaps afraid I was about to get up and leave. She had no worries. I was completely captivated. By Courtney and the strange fascination for the occult that had risen and stirred me in ways I could never have imagined. It was heady, like an adrenaline surge that kept growing as they spoke. Leaving was the farthest thing from my mind. Even if I was put off by the danger I suspected was involved, I was so much in love with her and so intrigued by their story, heading back to my former reality was not an option.

"Robbie, dear, I asked you before about good and evil. Our family and thousands of other witches

represent good. But evil does exist. It's insidious and
pervasive. Let me explain. There's a prophecy that
dates to antiquity. It foretells the coming of a very
powerful witch—my coming—and warns that if I
don't join with my chosen mate on the night of the
solstice, evil will have free rein to loose itself on the
world. Even we don't know what that may mean. We
do know that it may lead to chaos and anarchy to
make past evils pale by comparison."

"Courtney. I trust you and Michael, but please
understand this sounds like something out of a
cheap horror movie. And why me? How is it that I've
been thrust into the role of savior?"

"I know this is difficult to grasp, darling, and
there isn't time to give you a primer tonight. Why
you? Because you fulfill the prophecy. Simon will
explain it to you in more detail. And as to evil, it not
only exists, it's been growing on an unprecedented
scale. Think about the evidence. The Great
Depression, the World Wars, the Holocaust. Michael
had a front row seat. He bore witness to man's
cruelty. Would you like him to relate what he saw at
Auschwitz and Belsen?"

I looked at my brother's face. He blanched and
looked away, his eyes moist in the moonlight.

"No."

"Wise choice." He nodded, touching my shoulder.
"What I saw defies description."

"And now a more sinister threat." Courtney
continued, sadness in her expressive eyes. "Unlike
anything we could ever have dreamt of. Atomic
energy could be a powerful tool, a windfall,
something wonderful to produce new science and
energy sources for humanity if used by good men in
the proper hands. But the atomic bomb is the most
destructive device ever created. One that could
destroy the world. And it's found its way into the
hands of cruel, aggressive, and greedy men. Please,

Robert. You must believe us."

"My God. You really are serious."

"Deadly serious." Courtney nodded.

"So I become your consort, or the world goes to hell." I clenched my fists. Confusion and anger swept over me. "That's some choice."

"I know, darling. I wish there was an easier way but..."

"You can stop using the endearing terms, Courtney. I understand. I'm the lucky one. I've been chosen as your mate for this bizarre ceremony. We're going to save the world. You don't have to play the affectionate admirer."

Courtney stood and turned, looking at me as she put her hands to her cheeks again. She walked to the edge of the small outcropping overlooking the lake. Shoulders dropping, she stared into the still night sky.

"You fool." Michael grabbed me by the arm, pulled me up and pushed me toward her. When she turned, her face was covered with tears. Falling into me, Courtney threw her arms around me tightly.

"Don't you understand what's going on here?" Michael's voice rose while she held me. "This has been the most difficult thing Courtney's ever had to do. It may mean nothing to you yet, but she'll be the embodiment of a goddess, the fortieth in a long line of goddesses. That's an extraordinary position. She's what Christians refer to as *divine*. But in the same way that Jesus was both human and divine, Courtney has a human side. A deeply sensitive and passionate human side. One that's fallen desperately in love with you, brother. She's a beautiful, sensitive young woman. The most difficult part of this is that the depth of her love has created a terrible conflict. Treat her with the respect she deserves!" His words were deadly serious. "She's willing to sacrifice everything to love you."

155

Courtney nodded shyly. "Oh Robbie," she whispered, face streaked with tears. "Robbie, dearest, there *are* things I kept from you, but not my feelings. Never my feelings. When I told you that I loved you more than I ever thought it possible to love anyone, it was the truth."

"It's your choice, brother. If you think she's lied, get in your convertible and go back to hobnobbing with your rich friends. The world will go on. At least for a while. But no one will ever love you the way Courtney does nor, I suspect, the way you love her.

"This union has been foretold for centuries. And no one and nothing can keep you two apart." He put his massive arms around us.

She looked back at me. "I don't blame you, Robbie. For not trusting me. I've botched this. I love you so much, I let my emotions muck it up." She looked up at the twinkling Milky Way, now dimmed by the bright circle of the moon. "We need you. But you mean so much to me." She lowered her eyes, a desperate smile crossing her face. "I want you to stay, Robbie. Not for any cosmic purpose but simply for me," she whispered, shoulders sagging as she looked at Michael. "I swear, if you doubt that, ask me to go anywhere with you. I'll be packed and ready in fifteen minutes. We'll find a way. We'll make a life for ourselves."

"Courtney!" Michael protested. "You can't do that. We need both of you to fulfill the prophecy."

"I'm sorry, Michael." She held up her hand. "I love him that much."

I looked at them. If this was rehearsed, they deserved the Academy Award. My eyes searched Courtney's. "So if we don't perform this ceremony, it could wreak havoc?"

She nodded. "Yes. The ritual and my ascendance will curb the evil or so the prophecy says. It's complicated. But I don't care anymore. I just want to be with you."

"I assume there's more to tell. But don't worry. I won't leave. I'm committed to you and the ritual. I've never felt anything like this before and I never want the feeling to end."

"Then you'll stay with me?" Courtney asked. I let her soft lips melt into mine.

"I never had any doubts." Michael ruined the idyllic moment, slapping me on the back so hard I almost fell.

I held Courtney, taking in her magnificent face and nodding.

Michael squeezed my shoulder and beamed. "That's my man."

Courtney closed her eyes, grinning as she clung to me. "No, Michael. He's all mine."

Chapter Twenty-Six

What had I promised? Was this real? I was tempted to run to a church and find a crucifix, but they were used to ward off vampires, not witches. There would be excuses, a conversation with Rachel. And yet somehow, despite the complications, I was at peace. Happy. I had no right to be, but I was. We saddled the horses, and the three of us walked back down the steep, rocky trail. Courtney and I led our mounts, Michael followed. No one spoke until we reached the clearing at the bottom. Michael patted me on the back and kissed Courtney on the cheek.

"Quite a night, huh?" He grinned as he hopped into his jeep. He looked at Courtney. "Now don't get lost on the way home." Michael narrowed his eyes and grinned. "You do make a handsome couple." He started the jeep, put it into gear, and headed north toward Route 302, throwing up a trail of gravel.

I watched and laughed, shaking my head. "My brother's a witch! I'm a witch?"

Courtney put her arm around me, squeezing me. She laughed. "Things are never what they appear. I promised you wouldn't be sorry." Courtney raised her eyebrows.

"I knew you were a goddess the moment I saw you." I beamed at her. "I suppose I should be overcome with fear, guilt, and misgivings."

"And?" She looked at me.

"I don't feel any of those things." I shrugged. "Actually, I feel energized. From the first time I heard about witchcraft and the fact that you might be connected, it's excited me."

She turned toward me, her eyes searching mine. "What I said at the stables—about stealing your life from you. I still feel that way. This is hard for me. I've never lied to you, Robert. It may be difficult to understand. While I may be the embodiment of a goddess, part of me is still a twenty-year-old girl." She took my hand, squeezing it. "One who's hopelessly in love with a divine young man."

I took her chin in my hand and studied her. "Suppose there was no greater purpose in our meeting. Imagine that we met at this reunion. Would you still feel the same way?"

Her lips curled into a smile and nodded. "You know I would."

Courtney's eyes dropped and we turned back to the trail. We held the reins loosely. Our mounts followed. Thanks to the silver moonlight, I bent and found her full lips, kissing them gently, then brushed the perfect nose that wore a generous sprinkle of freckles after our day in the sun.

"I just know I love you," I whispered. "So much."

She followed suit, playing, teasing my lips with hers. I thought about our first tentative kiss that afternoon. Courtney was a quick learner. It brought a question to mind.

"Courtney, when you're reincarnated, reborn, do you remember things you did or learned from your past life?" I wanted to understand everything about her and this strange new thing that captivated me.

She smiled softly. "No, not entirely. You retain certain abilities or skills you mastered in past lifetimes. In my case, a kinship for animals, my love for horses and my ability to ride, my love of music." She stopped and shrugged. "My mental abilities and telepathic powers have grown much stronger. But do I remember what I ate for breakfast the day we called down the storm that destroyed the Spanish Armada? No."

"Wait a minute!" I swallowed. "You're teasing me. That was in 1588. Don't tell me you had something to do with that?" I asked, laughing.

"Yes." She looked up at the moon casually, now almost full. "That's right." She turned, her lips still curled up in amusement, but her eyes were deadly serious. "We used our collective abilities to call down the storm that destroyed those ships and kept Britain safe."

"So you and your friends saved England?" I was dumbfounded. "All right. I'm in no position to argue. Are there things you've done recently to help save the world?"

"Actually several, one or two during the last war, but your expression says you don't believe me." She wore the look of a teacher with a new student. "I know this may be too much to absorb in one sitting, Robbie. Let's talk about something else."

I nodded. "All right, back to reincarnation. If you don't remember things from your past lives, what does it accomplish?"

"Well, let me add something. We retain and amplify our powers with each incarnation. Simon can read minds and manipulate groups of people through telepathy. He's incredible. Your brother has the ability to read other people's thoughts, project his into their minds and call forth spells. If we live our lives correctly, as the gods and goddesses direct, we evolve with each life, grow closer to living the ideal existence. Sainthood, your Christian brothers might call it." She sighed and continued the lesson. "There are three planes or realms of existence. The underworld is the place of darkness where nature's spirits dwell."

"You mean like hell?"

"Oh, no, darling. It's simply a place that exists. We don't believe in hell. No one is sentenced to eternity in some fiery underworld. Next there's the physical or manifest world—the world we live in—what we're seeing right now. We can touch and smell and feel things." She stood on tiptoes and gave my lips a quick brush. "Like that." She giggled. "And finally, there's the ethereal or celestial plane where the gods and goddesses dwell. But it takes many lifetimes for one's essence or soul to evolve to that level."

"All right. So if you're a goddess, your soul must have been in existence for—"

"More than eleven centuries," she interrupted.

The girl walking next to me was describing her supernatural existence as if she were describing what she was going to eat for breakfast.

"My God, or should I say, 'my goddess.'" I exhaled. "You're not going to leave me, are you? I mean to go to this…"

She kissed her fingers and put them gently to my lips. "Not if you're a good boy." She smiled and shook her head. "No, I promise. I will never leave *you!*"

I sighed and took her hand. "But what about *your* abilities? You described the powers the others have. What about you? If you're as powerful as Michael says, you must have incredible abilities."

She sighed back at me and looked up at the moon again. "My goodness, McGregor, you are the curious one. Well, I can communicate with other creatures. You already know that. I'm a telepath. I can heal. I did it the other day for you, though you don't remember." She laughed and pushed me. "And if you're not a good boy, I can even bring down some serious lightning on that lovely head of yours. But for something that serious, I need a tool." Her laugh grew louder as she touched the amulet around her neck. "And it would drain my energy." Courtney was enjoying herself, teaching and teasing me with each revelation.

Light dawned. "So that's why you fell asleep after the episode with the animals." I stopped, remembering her fatigue in Naples. It must have been when she did her healing.

She nodded. "Bingo."

We arrived at the stables. So many questions were unanswered. I decided to let it go for the evening. I wanted to be with Courtney. Not the high priestess or the nascent goddess. But Courtney, the sweet girl I loved. We took our horses inside and unsaddled them and put the tack away.

"Should we rub them down?" I asked.

"I'll do it in the morning." She took my fingers in hers. "Wendy will let me in very early. I really don't sleep much anyway. And after tonight"—she grinned and put her head on my chest—"I'll never be able to close my eyes." She pushed me and giggled again.

"Me neither." I paused. "There are so many things I want to know about you, about all of this." A question came to mind. "Wendy, is she one of you?"

"You mean one of *us*, darling." She took my arm.

I stood corrected.

Courtney continued, "She's what we call a convert. She wasn't born a witch. Many of our followers are like her, but she's become a devoted student of the craft. And of course, I understand your curiosity. Your head must be swimming. We have all the time in the world to talk." Suddenly her face took on a melancholy look. "That is, unless you want to leave after we're wed at the celebration."

"Well, I was thinking about it. I really miss my sailboat." I burst into laughter. She squeezed me so tightly I coughed.

"Robert, you are such a tease. I don't know if I'll ever get used to your fooling."

"You've got a lifetime to try." And with that, I took her in my arms and kissed her again, feeling the sweet taste of her tongue and lips mingling with mine, knowing they belonged together. "Remember, you promised. No flying off to that mysterious celestial world," I teased. My lips found her delicate ears, playing with them, working up and down their flawless shape as I inhaled the intoxicating scent that clung to them like fresh blossoms. We parted, knowing we couldn't fulfill our desires until the appointed time.

Courtney took my hand. "Come on, there's something I want to show you." And with that she led me up the gravel path and through the courtyard. She stopped, dipping her hands in the water, splashing me as she laughed. She pulled me toward the garage, switched on the light, and pushed me to the Jaguar. When we reached it, she pulled up the cloth cover. I broke into a wide grin. There, tied to the luggage rack on the boot was a large suitcase with her initials on it. She pulled it to the floor and opened it, showing me the contents.

"I told you, Robert." She lowered her dark lashes. "If you'd asked me, I would have gone anywhere. I will right now. Damn the world. Since the night we met, you are my world."

"I know that feeling," I assured her. I was not prone to sentiment. But there was something so genuine, so full of emotion in what she said I felt my throat tighten. For a moment I thought I might choke.

"I believe you. But we'd spend the rest of our lives questioning, running away. Not from Simon or the evil you talked about, but from ourselves. How many of us can say we've had the opportunity to make the world a better place? I promise to do whatever you ask." I took her hand. "Then, you have to promise me something."

She leaned into my chest. "Anything."

"Promise that we'll go somewhere far away and find peace, someplace where you and I can ride and play and swim, then lie in each others arms from sunset till sunrise, telling each other all the special, private things we feel."

"Oh, Robbie, I promise with all my heart that when this is over, I'll never leave—" She stopped. Courtney pulled away and whirled around.

"What's the matter?"

She shook her head violently. "I told you. I'm a telepath. I can sense emotions. I felt something or someone sinister, an evil like nothing I'd ever imagined."

"And?"

"Whoever or whatever it was is very close. I'm frightened. I thought we were safe. Now, I'm not sure."

We slowed, entering the courtyard. There, leaning on her cane, staring up as the moonlight reflected off her lined face, was Courtney's nanny, Mrs. McPherson.

Chapter Twenty-Seven

Courtney's eyes grew wide. She shivered and scanned the courtyard.

"Well, hello, you two," the older woman greeted us. "We missed you at the celebration."

"We watched from a nearby hill," Courtney volunteered. She tried to sound casual, but her voice shook.

"That's nice." Mrs. Mac approached and took Courtney's hand. "You two are such a wonderful pair." She backed away, releasing her grip. "You belong together."

I approached, sensing the tension as I brushed by Courtney. "Thank you. I hope we get a chance to talk. There are so many things about Courtney I want to know," I said with a smile. "She likes to keep her little secrets."

"You'd be surprised at what's hiding beneath that pretty outside." The older woman chuckled. "I'd love to spend time with you, Mr. Robert." She took my hand, whispering in her thick brogue, "I think you're good for her." She winked and turned as she walked slowly back toward the main house. "Good night."

Courtney stood, holding herself as she trembled, watching her nanny trudge out of sight.

"What was that about?" I asked. "I don't understand. I thought she was like your grandmother—your oldest friend?"

Courtney nodded, following the woman with her eyes. "She was. I mean she is. I don't understand it either. My instincts have never betrayed me. Hold

165

me." It was a plea. I took her in my arms, caressing her back as I kissed her hair. I remembered the expression I had seen on Mrs. McPherson's face at dinner.

"Well, come on. No one's perfect. Even goddesses." I offered an attempt at humor.

She clung to me. "You don't understand," she whispered into my chest. "I know you think this is fantasy, but this isn't some silly woman's intuition. My senses have been honed and refined over centuries. It's like saying that the law of gravity no longer applies."

"I believe you," I assured her, tightening my embrace, confused. Telepathy was not on the class list at Harvard.

"Hello, you two," a voice called from the entrance to the main house. It was Gretchen. She approached on tiptoes. "It was quite a night." She put a hand on each of our shoulders, beaming as she looked at us. "Oh, to be young again."

"Yes, life is good." I nodded, tightening my hold on Courtney.

Gretchen looked at me, her lips curling up as she tried to hide a smile. "Welcome to the family." She touched my forearm, studying me before turning her gaze toward Courtney. "Are you all right, my dear?"

"She'll be fine. Just got a chill," I said as Courtney snuggled close to me.

"Well, enjoy the rest of the night," Gretchen whispered and headed back to the entrance, disappearing inside.

I hoped Courtney was wrong, but there was something comforting in the fact that despite all her powers she felt safe and warm in my arms. I had no inkling how to argue the point, having no frame of reference.

I decided to change the subject. "Courtney, I've

never seen those people at dinner so happy."

She backed away and raised her eyebrows. The moonlight was so bright her face shone.

"Come on, you have to tell me," I prodded. "Did it have something to do with Simon? Does he have the ability to transform a whole room full of stogy seniors into a fraternity party?"

"Yes and no."

"Share it with me."

"Yes, he has incredible powers of suggestion, but I think it was just the spirit of friendship and warmth he brought to the group. Those people are all members of our family." She smiled. I could sense the tension leave her shoulders. "I don't think there were any spells employed. But then Simon is so powerful there are times when even I'm not sure whether he's using his abilities."

"I'm glad. I had the feeling he was manipulating the group."

"Looks like we're completely alone." She searched the courtyard. "My place or yours?"

"Pardon?"

"I don't want to leave you. Something's not right. I have a strange feeling. There's no one to tattle, so please let me stay with you tonight."

What an offer!

"I don't know about this." Sleeping would be difficult enough after the evening's revelations. With Courtney in the same room, it would be impossible.

"You don't understand, Robbie. I'm not frightened for myself. But if someone knows how I feel about you..." She twisted her lips, touching the beautiful pendant with the moonstone at its center. "The amulet not only gives me special powers, it protects me. That's why I wear it. It's been doing yeoman service for my ancestors for a thousand years. It's you I'm worried about. Please. I'll lie on the couch and won't do anything to tempt you," she said, crossing her heart. "Promise."

"Who are these mysterious people who might want to harm me?"

"I'm not sure. But I have a bad feeling. Please," she pleaded again. "Simon's been acting odd too. I think something's going on he's not telling me."

Mystery, danger, a beautiful damsel in distress. This is like the movies! How could I refuse?

I took her hand and we tiptoed to my door. With a look around I opened it, and we went inside. She sat on the couch as I pulled out two cigarettes, lit one and handed it to her. She inhaled deeply. I took the other. I sat on the floor next to her as she sat back, resting her feet on the coffee table. I felt slender fingers running through my hair. I took her hand and pulled it to me, kissing the palm.

"Courtney, what do you know about Mrs. Mac?"

"Other than the fact that she's been like a grandmother? What do you mean?" she asked, sounding annoyed as she crushed out her cigarette. "Why? You can't believe she had anything to do with what I felt."

"No, of course not," I assured her, still wondering.

She slid onto the floor next to me, resting her head on my shoulder.

"You two can become fast friends tomorrow." She yawned, closing her eyes.

I watched her for a few minutes, luxuriating in her being close. I wanted to ask her about my provocative dream. The one where she and I were joined. Had she put that image into my mind? I never had the chance. "Hey, I thought you witches didn't need to..." I stopped as I heard her gentle snoring.

Pulling off her boots, I picked her up and put her on my bed, covering her with the quilt. I kissed her lips softly.

Tomorrow held a series of challenges: calling my mother and friends to tell them I'd be staying, and the one I dreaded the most: trying to explain this to Rachel.

Chapter Twenty-Eight

Sometime in the early morning hours I awoke stiff and tired on the couch. My aching leg and back muscles signaled I'd spent too many hours in the saddle. No matter how I shifted positions it was impossible to get comfortable. When I turned and saw Courtney lying snug and cozy under the comforter, my resolve evaporated. I crossed to the bed, threw off the warm covering and lay down next to her. As I did, she moaned softly, letting her arm fall across my chest. I turned, letting my gaze wash over every inch of her face. Playing my game again, I lay, trying to find a flaw, a tiny defect in the perfection. There were none. The musky scent of sleep mingled with the delicious jasmine that always surrounded her.

I leaned over and kissed her nose, letting my lips drift to hers. She smiled sweetly but turned away. As I lay watching the outline of that lightly freckled nose, I knew there was no woman I had ever wanted as much. None I ever would. But that would have to wait till Friday evening. The girl lying next to me seemed so young, so sweet, so innocent. *Eleven centuries!* It was difficult to grasp she'd lived so many lives. I let my arousal fade and turned from the angel lying a scant twelve inches away.

****

Courtney lay awake, luxuriating in being close to him, the scent of his body, the secure feeling of his arm encircling her. She had to slip from underneath and go tend to the horses. It was the last thing she wanted to do. Courtney smiled briefly as she thought about using her powers. *A spell to put Romeo and Pumpkin Patch back in fighting form?* Then she could lie here next to him...forever. It occurred to her that she'd often been annoyed with her human side because it always seem to hinder her. Now, as she felt his warmth and felt him pressed against her, she basked in it. *Love,* Courtney thought. What a wonderful word. She brushed aside a tear as she thought of her mother, wishing she could have lived to meet Robbie.

Quickly and silently she turned and slid away from Robbie. As she stood, Courtney turned and bent over him, studying his handsome, aristocratic face. She brushed strands of dark hair off his forehead and kissed his lips softly. He made a soft noise and turned onto his back. She tiptoed to the couch and pulled her boots on.

Courtney looked at her watch as she stepped into the dawn: 5:35. In the east the sun broke over the White Mountains. Making her way across the courtyard, she saw fingers of mist rising from the pool in the still, gray air.

Before she went to the stables she had a visit to make. Tiptoeing up the stairway, Courtney reached the long, paneled hallway and stopped in front of the third door on the left. She closed her eyes and concentrated. No need to knock. Simon opened the door wearing his silk dressing gown.

He nodded and ushered her into his room. "I expected you."

Courtney sat down on the love seat that hugged the far wall.

"I had a vision last night," she whispered.

Simon nodded again. "I know. I felt it, too. About half an hour after the fireworks ended?"

"Yes." She studied her mentor, terrified by the implications of his confirmation.

He stood and paced, then proceeded to the

double windows and opened them to the dawn.

Courtney sat in silence, biting her lip as she closed her eyes and pictured Robbie.

"This is such a beautiful place. I've been absent far too long." Simon's words seemed casual and out of place. She knew better. His eyes wore dark shadows and his face looked drawn and weary. He must have been awake all night.

"Simon. I'm frightened." She sighed and stood, clutching his long arm as he focused on the sun climbing above the distant mountains. "Not for myself," she said, fingering the amulet. "For him. For Robbie." She turned toward the sunrise. "I love him so much. If anything happened to him..." she whispered, unable to articulate her fear.

"Everything will be fine, my dear." He turned, kissed her hair and gave her a confident smile.

"Did anyone at the Pagan Council have an inkling? Think anything out of order?" Courtney asked, not sure she wanted to hear his answer. The council was the supreme governing body for all pagans.

"Someone had mentioned a small sect of Druids that met at the ancient ritual site on Anglesey." He shrugged. "No one thought they represented a threat. It makes no sense. Why would anyone want to interfere with the ceremony?" he asked, more to himself than to her.

"I have to warn him. Tell him he may be in danger."

Simon held up his hand. "No. Not yet."

"But you and I know that evil exists. Robbie's a child. He believes in fairy tales. I'm so frightened that someone might..."

Simon shook his head. "Calm yourself, child. Let me talk to him. After you return this afternoon we'll draw down the circle and seek wisdom from the ancient ones."

"But Simon!"

"There is nothing to worry about. You and I are the most powerful witches to ever live." He squeezed her shoulder gently to calm her. "Even if someone tried to prevent or sabotage our plans and the ceremony"—he touched a finger to the amulet that adorned Courtney's neck—"we would defeat them."

****

I awakened to the pleasant chirping of birds outside my window. I smiled and turned, stretching out my hand, expecting to find Courtney snuggling under my comforter. My heart sank. She was gone.

It was almost eight. I jumped out of bed, showered in record time, and dressed in light cotton slacks, a plaid shirt, and my walking shoes. I ran across the courtyard to the main house. When I entered the dining room, Courtney was nowhere to be seen.

I saw Simon. He was entertaining Jon, Gretchen, and several others at a large round table. After my conversation with Courtney and Michael, I surveyed the scene, still amazed that these fine ladies and gentlemen were witches.

Sitting alone at a small table, watching the show with a bemused expression was Mrs. McPherson. I waved at the large group. Simon rose and crossed to meet me with his hand extended.

"Good morning, Robert." He nodded at me. "I understand you know who and what we are. And of the role we hope you'll play in our ceremony."

"Yes, sir. Courtney and Michael explained the...situation."

"I'd like to spend some time this morning answering the questions that I'm sure are running through that agile mind."

"Of course," I agreed. I wanted to hear everything, and I did have a lot of questions. "I'll eat breakfast and have to make some calls. How about

10:30 in the courtyard?"

"Fine." He shook my hand again, nodding.

I looked up and saw Mrs. McPherson. She smiled warmly, motioning for me to join her.

"Would you sit with me, Mr. Robert? I saved a place for you and my girl." She stood, leaning on her cane, motioning to the empty seat across from her. "I'd like to get to know you," she said. "That would make Courtney happy."

"Thanks. I'd love to talk to someone who's known her as long as you have," I said, looking around. "As a matter of fact, I was hoping to see her."

"I saw her heading to the stables. Said she had to take care of some horses. She'll be back shortly." The older woman had a thick Scottish burr I found delightful. She caught my expression.

"I love your accent," I explained, realizing I had just read her mind.

"You certainly are a fine-lookin' young man. I can see what Courtney finds so agreeable in you." She paused, motioning for a second cup of coffee. "I'm not used to being the one who's waited on," she confessed with a guilty smile. "So. What can I tell you about my girl?"

"I've heard that she lost several people who were close to her under strange circumstances?"

She fixed her coffee in a deliberate way, then turned watery gray eyes toward me. "Well, I can no talk for certain to the strange part. There was Mr. Phillips. He was killed in a terrible accident. It's no secret he was Miss Courtney's real father." The older woman scanned the room and reddened. "And then there was Meghan, of course, her best friend. The wee child drowned at the pond where they were swimmin'. So sad. My Courtney tried to save her, but there was nothing she could do, poor dear."

That was interesting. It raised a question. With

her extraordinary powers, I found it hard to see Courtney letting her best friend drown, even if she was a child. Should I ask Courtney?

Mrs. McPherson continued, "They were both so full of energy. Always taking chances, jumpin' their mares over stone walls they had no business tryin'. It was impossible to keep track of 'em." She shook her head. "They lived on their horses and it was very warm that day." Her eyes were moist and faraway. "They snuck off by themselves. The first we knew of trouble was when Courtney rode home cryin' for help. By the time we arrived it was too late."

"I heard that there were some strange markings near where the girl died."

She raised her thick gray eyebrows. "I had heard that, too. Somethin' about a sign or a symbol. The constable did come by, of course, but who knows? There's lots of country folk livin' out there." She shook her head. "They have funny ideas."

I found it difficult to believe that this wise old woman knew nothing about the markings. I was about to pursue the issue when a dreamlike touch rested on my shoulder. Courtney kissed my cheek and came around to sit in the chair between Mrs. McPherson and me. She was still dressed in her riding clothes.

"Hello there, sleepy head," she teased, a playful look in her soft, dark eyes. Just seeing her brightened my spirits. The conversation with Mrs. Mac faded to the recesses of my mind.

"Well, if you didn't keep me up so late, I could get up and help you with the horses. But I need my beauty sleep."

She studied my face, her eyes taking in every feature. She put her lips together and sighed. "No." She tilted her head. "You're beautiful enough."

I flushed and shot a look at her nanny. The older woman smiled.

We went to the breakfast buffet and gorged ourselves on poached eggs, freshwater salmon, and French toast. The conversation shifted to other topics. We discussed the weather, Courtney's party, and the trip the two of them were going on that morning.

"Mrs. Mac has never been to America before. I'm going to borrow Jon's Packard Victoria convertible. It's spectacular." She sneaked her fingers across the table, brushing mine. "I'll take her over that delightful road we took to Naples. But then, we've done so many things, haven't we, Robbie?"

Mrs. McPherson looked on like a proud grandmother.

"I cannot wait, darlin'." She stood up and touched Courtney's shoulder. "What time should I be ready?"

Courtney looked at her watch. "No rush. We have all day. I'll meet you in the garage at 10:30."

I stepped on her boot under the table.

"Ow," she complained, looking cross.

"I don't want you to be gone all day. I was hoping to sneak away." I groaned and held my sore back. "For a long...walk." I raised my eyebrows.

Courtney laughed. It was warm and delightful. Her eyes shone. She feigned a deep sigh. "You are incorrigible, Mr. McGregor. And here I thought you were a proper gentleman."

I looked around and seeing no one watching, I took her hand, letting our fingers meld.

"Besides, while I take Mrs. Mac around the lake, you and Simon are going to talk. He'll answer your questions, explain about our family and the ceremony." She blushed.

"Right. But how did you know?"

She wore that playful smile. The irresistible one I loved. "I'm sorry. I thought you knew, darling? *I'm a witch!*"

176

Chapter Twenty-Nine

Despite knowing that Rachel should have been my first call, I was a coward. I called two friends I'd made plans with and explained that I had to cancel. I apologized and promised to see them the following week, having no idea what or where I might be after Friday night. I reconnected with the operator, giving her my mother's number.

After three rings she picked up.

"Hello, Mother." I wondered about her reaction. She had a dinner party planned for Friday evening, and she adored Rachel.

"Hello, Robbie. How's the reunion?"

"Better than I expected." I swallowed and took the plunge. Being valedictorian, award-winning scholar, and All New-England athlete was one thing; telling my autocratic mother I was going to spoil her dinner party was another. "That's why I'm calling."

"That's wonderful, dear. I knew you'd enjoy yourself." She paused. "I can't wait to hear all about it." She stopped. I heard her Kerry blue terrier barking in the background. "Oh, be quiet, you naughty boy." Since my father died and Michael and I'd moved out, Churchill was her only companion.

"Sorry, Robbie," she continued. "You know Churchill. He hears a noise and he's off to the races." She laughed softly.

I pictured her standing in the narrow, paneled living room of the austere Mount Vernon Street townhouse our family had occupied since before the Civil War, shaking her fist at her precious pet.

"That's fine, Mom. I'd love to tell you

everything," I assured her. *I've fallen in love with a beautiful witch, and I'm about to save the world but of course it all involves an ancient wedding ritual!* I smiled envisioning that conversation.

"Robbie," she said quietly. "If you want to spend more time up there, it's fine."

I was about to launch into my elaborate set of excuses. Michael was sick and needed my help, my car had to be repaired. I hated lying, but I had a litany of stories prepared. Her nonchalance caught me off guard.

"Really?" I said, still in shock. "That's funny. I was going to tell you I wanted to stay for a few more days, but I'd have to miss your dinner party."

I waited for the explosion, the next shoe to drop, something. Instead she offered, "Come back when you can. And tell Jon and Gretchen I said hello."

"Mother, did you hear what I said? I'll be away on Friday evening."

"Yes, I did, dear. Do what you have to, Robbie."

I sat amazed, letting her reaction sink in.

I decided to pursue a more sensitive subject. "Mother, do you remember Gretchen's sister Ellen?"

"Of course, dear. Poor thing died in a dreadful riding accident."

"Yes." I paused, not sure whether to continue. Why not? My brother was a witch and the world had been turned upside down. "Well, she had a daughter named Courtney."

"Yes, that's right, Robbie. Do you…like her?"

I hesitated. "We've become good friends."

"Really. How's she dealing with her mother's death?"

"Remarkably well."

"Let's see, Courtney would be about…"

"Almost twenty-one, Mother."

There was a pause. I could hear her breathing into the phone. "You've become good friends?" she asked. "I met Courtney once or twice. What a beautiful child."

I held the phone, knowing she was putting the pieces together. "Yes. She still is," I agreed.

"Does she have something to do with your staying, Robert?"

She was using my full name. This was serious.

"Robert?" she repeated.

"You'd make a fine detective," I whispered.

"Sounds like you have some thinking to do."

"Mother," I began.

"I trust you, son. Follow where your heart leads you." She hung up the phone.

I walked out to the courtyard, trying to understand my mother's reaction. If Michael and I were witches then it stood to reason that my mother knew of the family. Was she a witch? Was it possible I'd been living in a fog for twenty-three years?

I checked my watch. I was a few minutes early, so I wandered to the garage. I had no idea why, but I had a colossal knot in my stomach. It had nothing to do with the talk with my mother. No. This was vague, an undefined sense of tension.

As I walked inside, I noticed a large yellow convertible parked in the door leading to the driveway—the Packard Victoria that Courtney and Mrs. McPherson were going to take. It was handsome; long, low, and sleek, it stood, adorned with silky ribbons of chrome and brown leather upholstery. The top was lowered, covered by a gleaming boot that matched the dark interior.

"Quite the ride, eh, McGregor?" Courtney asked, coming up behind me. She'd changed from her riding clothes into another of her wonderful outfits. Everything looked expensive and fit her to perfection. She wore the multicolored silk scarf. Tied loosely around her neck, it camouflaged the familiar pendant. Sunglasses rested atop her head.

179

I nodded in agreement. "I love my Jag, but this is spectacular."

"Robbie, is everything all right? You seem troubled."

"Courtney, try to imagine learning everything I have in the last"—I checked my watch—"twelve hours. Everything I believed has been thrown in the trash! You're a witch. My brother is a witch. And even I'm..." I gestured, unable to finish the thought.

She took my arm and squeezed it gently. "A witch, too?" Hearing the words still sounded strange, otherworldly. She nodded, searching my eyes. Hers stared back, full of sympathy, velvet-brown and large as saucers.

"We explained that last evening. But why don't you ask Simon about it."

I intended to but there was something else I had to ask her. "Courtney," I began. "Is Mrs. Mac a witch?"

"No. I told you that." She shook her head. "Of course, she must suspect what we are. But no, she is not a witch."

I accepted that. But there was something about the woman. I had no way of guessing what caused my discomfort, but I felt uneasy, as if she knew far more than Courtney gave her credit for.

"When you sensed evil last night, she was the only one around."

She raised her dark eyebrows. "Robbie, what is it? You said that last night. I can't accept that someone who's been so kind and caring could have any evil intentions. Besides, if that was the case, how is it I never noticed it in all the years she cared for me?" She shook her head. "And point of fact, Gretchen was nearby. Do you think she's evil? No one's been kinder or more supportive."

"No, of course not," I agreed, but remained unconvinced.

Courtney squeezed my arm and nodded in the direction of the courtyard door. I turned. Mrs. McPherson approached. She smiled and raised her hand. Limping across the cement floor, her cane rattled with each step. Courtney met her and took the old woman's arm, helping her cross the final few feet.

I walked with the two of them to the Packard, making conversation. I helped Mrs. McPherson into the passenger seat. Courtney hopped into the driver's seat.

"Did you speak to *her*?" Courtney asked, studying the upholstery.

"She has a name. It's Rachel, and no, she wasn't home." I was flattered by the show of jealousy. I closed the door. Courtney turned, giving me an I'm-sorry look.

"Have a wonderful time," I called as Courtney adjusted the seat and threw in the clutch to start the powerful six-cylinder engine.

"We will." Courtney put her hand out, adding, "Robbie. Be careful." Mrs. Mac smiled broadly.

"I'm always careful," I told her, not sure what she meant. "I'll see you at dinner," I told them, trying to shake my anxiety.

I looked at my watch. Exactly 10:30. Heading across the garage and out into the courtyard, I kept looking back until the large convertible was out of sight. As I got to the courtyard, Gretchen passed me dressed in her riding clothes. "Headed out for a ride?" I asked.

"Yes. I haven't had much chance lately, but I think I can sneak away for a couple of hours. Nothing like a brisk gallop on a sparkling day. Enjoy the morning and your talk with Simon." She waved and gave me a bright smile as she headed toward the stables. Apparently in the world of witchcraft everyone knew everything!

181

Chapter Thirty

"Simon."

He smiled as we shook hands.

"Take a walk with me?" He pointed to a path leading away from the courtyard and around the cove.

I nodded and fell into step. We walked up the inclined gravel path.

"You must be confused."

I nodded again. "That's an understatement. This is so much to believe." I felt exhilarated, alive in a strange new way. "To discover that witches exist. That I've fallen in love with one. That I'm one. That there are forces in the world that could destroy it." Fear and fascination mixed in equal parts. My adrenaline surged as I thought about the infinite possibilities.

"Sit down, please." He stopped and patted a large fallen log, overlooking the green of the surrounding grove and the gray-blue of the cove below. "Robert, witches have existed for thousands of years. Tens of thousands. Perhaps longer. I can't say who the first witch was. No one can. Cave paintings show ancient people engaged in spells and rituals. Scientists tell us those paintings are more than 25,000 years old."

I nodded. Simon had a soft, lyrical voice in counterpoint to his massive stature. He could read the dictionary backwards, and I could listen to him all day.

"Who the first witch was, none of us can say. There are many theories on what and who we really are, on how we came to be. Some say that our development was accidental. Two individuals with physical and mental powers beyond those of ordinary humans mated. Their children found others and did the same. Over many generations through a process akin to evolution we grew in number and strength, refining our special skills and abilities. Others say that we're descended from a powerful race that came here thousands of years ago and blended into the Earth's population." He raised his eyebrows as he smiled. "All I know is that we're different and very powerful."

I sat, listening in awe.

"Many centuries ago shamans and priests formed the basis for the belief system—the religion—that we practice today. Ancient Greeks and Romans practiced something called 'the mysteries.'"

"I remember studying that."

He nodded and continued. "Many sites have been excavated showing where rituals or ceremonies were performed. And most ancient religions worshipped many gods and goddesses. The female was usually the most important deity."

"Michael told me that you don't believe in monotheism."

"No. I know it's difficult for someone who's been taught that concept, but we don't believe divinity is restricted to one omniscient being. We think it exists in everything around us: the trees, the clouds, the mountains. Everything in nature, all of us, are interconnected in a divine, infinite way. Harm one"—he stared deeply into my eyes—"and you harm us all."

"I understand the concept. Sounds kind of..." I searched for the right word.

"Pagan," he said, looking amused again.

I nodded.

"Are you a student of Latin?"

"Three years in high school. Why?"

"Then perhaps you know the word, '*pagani*'?"

"Not really." I shrugged.

"It means 'one who lives in the country—a peasant' in Latin. No indication of evil or Satan. It's the word from which pagan is derived."

I shook my head. "Etymology wasn't my specialty."

"How about '*heathen*'?"

"Of course I've heard the word."

"It meant someone who dwelled on the heath, country folk, farmers, peasants. Another word used to misrepresent its original meaning and portray those being labeled into something mysterious and sinister."

"By who?"

He sighed and looked away. "The early Christian church. And sadly, most of it had to do with power and money. Our ancestors were persecuted because we were the competition. The church's practices were strict and frightening. They used fear and intimidation. We offered a more attractive alternative."

I raised my eyebrows.

"The history of our persecution is long and dark. Witchcraft never has been the evil or satanic ideology that's been portrayed in books or movies. There's nothing mysterious about the tenets we follow. Like every other belief system, we have our rituals, but when you understand them, they're no different than those practiced by Catholics or Jews."

"All right." He made it sound simple, almost pleasant. I nodded again. "But if that's the case, why this mysterious ceremony? What's the threat?"

He turned toward me again. "What's different about many who practice the craft is their innate ability to control and manipulate fellow beings and the surroundings." He stood and faced me. "That's what makes some pagans so dangerous. Evil does exist. I promise you. And there are those who've chosen to use their abilities for a dark purpose—to corrupt, control, or destroy mankind. Courtney's ascendance—her embodiment as a goddess—will prevent that."

"You keep referring to these special powers and abilities, Simon."

"Yes," he continued. "As I said a moment ago, we learned to develop and use our minds in ways that most people would find extraordinary. Courtney is still young, but she's incredibly powerful. She can call forth spells, create hallucinations, transmit her thoughts, make you do and say things you could never imagine."

He must have seen the look of concern cross my face.

Simon held up his hand. "No, Robert. I promise. She never used her powers on you."

"You read my thoughts?"

"It was a combination of reading your face and what I assumed would come to the mind of a young man in love. I've been doing this a very long time. The old adage is 'practice makes perfect.' Courtney would never use any of her powers to enlist your help," Simon continued. "She insisted. She genuinely loves you, Robert."

I felt my face flush.

"There's something I want to show you." He approached me and opened his shirt. My stomach churned.

"Simon," I began to protest as he pulled the material down below his left shoulder.

"Don't be alarmed," he assured me. When I saw what he revealed, I understood. It was a duplicate of my half-moon birthmark. He raised his thick eyebrows. "Does this answer why you were chosen for the ceremony?"

185

"What about Michael? He and Courtney are close. Is he one of the chosen ones?" I asked.

"I thought you'd ask that." He straightened his shirt and resumed his seat. "Actually yes, but you've seen Michael without his shirt on?"

"Of course."

"Does he bear the special birthmark that you and I do?"

I shook my head. "No."

"And even if he did, there's something else." He exhaled deeply. "My son, Courtney, was very powerful. He was strong, self-willed, very handsome. But he was also cruel and vicious. Even the most powerful of us has weaknesses. Courtney's was women." Simon drew teeth over his lower lip. "He used his powers to manipulate them."

"But I still don't understand." Suddenly it struck me. "Do you mean that Michael is…?"

He nodded. "Yes, Michael is one of his children. Courtney's half brother." He looked at me and smiled, lowering his eyes. "He was the son of Courtney and a woman who lived in Cornwall. A sad, sweet beauty, she died while giving my son's offspring birth. But my son wanted nothing to do with caring for a child, so for a time our family looked after the child. Your father and mother, who were dear friends and family members, had never been blessed with children. They took Michael in. As the gods and goddesses often do, they amused themselves by bringing them a second beautiful child. One of their own conception, Robert—you." He looked up at the high blue sky, his face a troubled mask. "So you see that would eliminate Michael as a potential mate for my granddaughter."

I stared at Simon for a long moment. "So Michael's…adopted?"

"That's correct," Simon replied quietly. He searched my eyes. "Does that make a difference?"

"It's a good question." And it was. One I was not sure I could answer in such a short span of time. Michael was more than just an older brother, a drinking buddy to share a few beers with. He'd been my hero, my moral compass when my father died suddenly.

Had Simon's revelation called that into question? I didn't think so, but it was something I needed to consider.

Simon watched me, closely. His gaze was hard and penetrating.

"Whatever the source of his birth, I've never known a finer man than your brother."

"My...adopted brother."

Simon nodded slowly. "Your adopted brother. That's correct."

The smile he wore was genuine, but I could detect a faint semblance of doubt.

His hand went to my shoulder. "I understand, Robert. It's something you may need some time to digest."

I shook my head. "I see no problem with it or with him, Simon. Michael is the same man I knew an hour ago. But my whole world has been turned on its head in a matter of days. And here's one more piece that needs to be reworked and refit."

Simon chuckled softly. "Nicely put, Robert. I'll do my best to help you see they all go back together in the right order."

We resumed our slow circuit, rounding the pristine waters of Sebago on a path that paralleled its ragged shoreline.

"All right, tell me," I began. "If I'm so...special, how is it I've never noticed anything unusual? Why don't I have those powers you spoke of?"

"Robert." He gave me a patronizing look, like one would a slow student. "You *do* have them. Have you ever thought you knew something before it happened, imagined what someone was thinking and found out it was true?"

I thought for a minute. "Yes. Of course. I guess I'd never thought about it like that."

"Of course you didn't. Why would you? But I promise that you have innate powers—amazing powers—you've never used."

And now the big question. The one that I'd been turning over in my mind since last night. "All right. I believe that." I fixed his eyes with mine. "But why didn't anyone tell me what I was? Why leave me in the dark for twenty-three years?"

He held my eyes. "A very good question and one I'd be disappointed if you hadn't asked." Simon seemed to be searching. For the right words perhaps? "Think about this. Courtney's been groomed for her role since birth. She's been steeped in our belief system, trained in how to become the embodiment of a goddess. But you, Robert." He placed a massive hand on my shoulder. "How would your life have been different if you'd known your true identity and destiny? Would you have attended Harvard? Been such an outstanding scholar or athlete? Courtney's been insulated, removed from the social system that you operate so well within."

I focused on the cove below. Of course he was right. My part in this magnificent drama was to be exactly what I was: a Boston Brahmin who attended the finest schools and had the finest friends. I was the given, the control part of the experiment. He had me.

I nodded as a reluctant smile crossed my face. "I understand."

He studied me. "Bravo, Robert. I knew you would. In time Courtney will teach you the intricacies of the craft, but she's such a child in so many ways—naïve about the intricacies of our social systems. You'll teach her to operate in *your* world."

****

Courtney directed the convertible around a bend in the road. A large Cadillac, parked at a clumsy angle on the shoulder, blocked their path. She stopped. The front doors were open on both sides of the large vehicle. Two women stood next to it. One of the women was bent over. Her companion seemed to be helping her. The first woman straightened up and put her hand to her friend's forehead.

"We best stop, dear," Mrs. McPherson suggested, putting her hand on Courtney's arm. "Someone may be hurt."

Courtney nodded and pulled the Packard onto the shoulder. "You wait here. I'll see if they need any help," she volunteered. Opening the door, she got out and headed toward the Cadillac.

As she approached, Courtney slowed. Fear gripped her as she felt the same sense of dread she had the night before. She stopped and turned. Mrs. Mac was out of their car and headed toward her. Behind her was a woman Courtney had never seen. Her hand was on her nanny's shoulder. Mrs. Mac stopped suddenly. A strange look crossed her face. Terror?

Courtney turned back toward the Cadillac. Both women had made a miraculous recovery and approached her. Courtney's stomach churned. Her mouth went dry. She put her hand on the amulet and closed her eyes. Suddenly, a voice she recognized called to her.

"I wouldn't do that if I were you, my dear. You'd be very sorry," the voice warned. "If you use your powers to do us harm, it will cost the life of someone you love very much."

****

We walked for another hour, Simon explaining while I questioned. The tutor and the student. The pupil and the teacher. As the sun rose overhead, he revealed more details of the craft, the enormous powers many of them possessed, and how they came to possess them. As he progressed through the explanation, it began to make sense.

I thought about Michael, where he'd come from and who he was. As I pictured his broad smile, thought of his robust laugh and his never-ending attempts to steer me down the right path, I knew nothing in our relationship had changed. In some ways, I saw this new relationship as a stronger one. A bond formed not from blood and necessity but one forged through loyalty and love.

"Simon." I hesitated. There was one more question I had to ask him. "Ellen, Courtney's mother. Could you tell me what happened to her?"

He stopped and turned, studying the lake through the pines. "Well, no one is exactly sure." He shrugged. "She and Courtney were out on a remote riding trail. Briarwood is crisscrossed with them. Courtney told me Ellen had given her the amulet, the Andromeda pendant with the moonstone at its center. I'm sure you've seen it. Well—"

Suddenly, we heard a noise from below. Someone was approaching rapidly, running up the path. When I turned, I saw Michael's stocky frame. I smiled, deciding to reveal my newfound knowledge of who he really was when he stopped abruptly, looking at Simon in a way that sent chills through me.

"What is it, Michael?"

He stood doubled over, breathless from his run. He opened his mouth, struggling to speak. Michael held something in his hand, looking back and forth between us. When I saw what dangled from his fingers, my legs grew weak. My breathing stopped. There in my brother's hand was something we knew well, too well. *A family heirloom* she called it. Michael squeezed the engraved silver and clamped his lips together. Something that protected her fellow goddesses for a thousand years, she'd told me: the Andromeda pendant with the moonstone at its center. The one that never left Courtney's neck.

Chapter Thirty-One

Simon gripped Michael by the shoulders. "Stay calm. Tell us what happened," he commanded.

"I was headed here to meet you." Michael stood wide-eyed, taking deep breaths. "I saw Jon's Victoria convertible by the side of the road. I recognized it. I knew Courtney and Mrs. Mac were taking it for a ride. I stopped to see if I could help."

I stood, frozen by fear. Every negative emotion Courtney talked about last night in the courtyard came flooding back, no longer theories. Something very terrifying and very real had happened to her. My pleasant, dreamlike world crumbled as I stared at the amulet dangling from my brother's hand.

"No one was there," Michael said. "I searched inside and found this on the driver's seat."

Simon looked at me then back at Michael. "Someone wanted to make sure we'd find the amulet," he said. "To send the message that Courtney is no longer protected."

Michael nodded.

"But I don't understand. Who's taken her and why?" I whispered.

"A small band of Druids," he answered and turned. "I'm not sure why." He shook his head slowly. "I should have foreseen this. All I know is they have plans for Courtney. Michael, we need you to focus," Simon instructed. "Concentrate."

"I've tried, Simon. I see nothing. I've never had this happen before." He shook his head. "I know Courtney's very powerful. She might be able to block my thoughts, but if she's in trouble, why would she

192

do that?"

"I don't know. She shouldn't." His eyes grew narrow. "Could someone else be blocking you?"

"I can't tell. All I know is I'm getting nothing." Michael shook his head.

"Courtney would never leave the amulet on her own," Simon continued. "But who could make her do that? She's young but she's so strong and has so many gifts, I can't imagine…"

"Mrs. McPherson," I heard myself saying.

"Yes, of course, Robert. If Courtney's missing, her nanny's gone as well," Simon agreed.

I shook my head. "No, you don't understand."

"What are you talking about, Robbie?" Michael took my arm.

"Last night Courtney had a premonition, a vision. I don't know what to call it. She was terrified. When we looked around, the only person there was her nanny."

"Really." Simon shook his head. "That makes no sense. The poor woman is old and infirm. Courtney's the most powerful member of our family."

"This morning at breakfast, she told me things about what had gone on at Briarwood. I had a strange sense of foreboding. I told Courtney, but she wouldn't listen."

Michael ignored me and turned toward Simon. "Maybe Courtney was…"

Simon stared at me. "Mrs. Mac insisted on making this trip," he whispered, fixing me with his eyes. "Wouldn't take no for an answer."

"Simon," Michael protested. "She's a feeble old woman, for God's sake."

"What better camouflage?" I volunteered. "Michael?"

He stared at me, his mind working. "Of course. The way they taught us in OSS," he whispered.

"What was that?" I probed.

193

"Hide in plain sight. In the midst of the enemy." He looked up at Simon. "Is it possible? That she fooled all of us?"

"But Courtney had the amulet." Simon shook his head. "She was protected. No wearer would surrender it, and no one wearing it has come to harm in a dozen centuries."

"It makes no sense," Michael agreed.

I was in over my head. Having been a witch for a day didn't qualify me to debate these two.

"Let's get back to her room. It's possible her familiars have picked up on something."

"Her familiars?" I asked.

"Animal partners, companions. We communicate with them through telepathy."

"You mean the cats?"

"Yes." Michael nodded as he pulled me down the path toward the house. "Simon has two mastiffs, I have a magnificent buck, Courtney used Cephy and Cassy. If anyone could pick up her thoughts it would be them."

Chapter Thirty-Two

We arrived at the courtyard, breathless. Either Simon or Michael had communicated with Jon and Gretchen. They were there, flanked by two dozen members of my new family and, I hoped, my allies. Despite their age, the guests showed a different face. Everyone assembled was alert and sober. I noticed that Wendy had joined the group.

"Michael found the amulet," Simon called, holding it up. "We're going to find Courtney's familiars and search her room. Everyone use your powers. See what you can discover. Gretchen, you're the high priestess. Get your tools and draw down the circle." He gave the group a brave smile.

This sounded like a foreign language. *Amulets, familiars, high priestess, draw down the circle?*

"Robbie, come with Michael and me," Simon commanded. "You possess gifts you may not be aware of." We headed toward Courtney's room. "Your father was gifted at sensing negative emotion."

My father? This just keeps getting stranger.

We ran upstairs to her bedroom door. Simon pushed it open and rushed inside. Nothing.

"Perhaps whoever took Courtney destroyed Cepheus and Cassiopeia," he whispered.

Michael went through the drawers of her dresser. Things emerged I had only seen in movies— a beautifully engraved silver knife, small silver bowls, candles of all colors and sizes, incense. Inside her closet, a small stand made of polished mahogany appeared with a pentacle inscribed in its surface.

Michael saw me staring. "These are her sacred implements: her athame, chalices, altar...all used in ritual when drawing down the witch's circle." He patted me on the back.

"Are you getting any impressions?" Simon asked Michael as my brother held each item and closed his eyes. He turned to me. "Michael has the ability to see things or draw images from objects. Everything has an aura surrounding it, even a rock. Michael has the ability to see things in that aura."

Michael scowled. "Nothing, Simon." He tossed the items on Courtney's comforter. "We need to find—"

He stopped as we all heard the sound of meowing.

Simon closed his eyes.

Michael's face grew a broad smile as the two majestic felines appeared in the doorway.

Simon approached them and knelt, closing his eyes again. He touched one then the other. When he stood, he looked grim. The two cats seemed agitated and glided up onto the bed.

"They're not sure, either, but both felt a sense of dread from Courtney. It was very brief but very strong. Whoever took her knew she'd try to communicate with us. Either they managed to silence her or forced her to be quiet."

"I don't understand. If the amulet protected her, why would she give it up?" I was confused and afraid for her. "What do they want?"

"The amulet has been in our family for longer than we can remember. It was always worn by the most powerful priestess. Soon Courtney will take her place as the earthly embodiment of a goddess. She'll have incredible power. Ellen wore the amulet and died right after she removed it. Perhaps the same people who took Courtney were responsible. There's a pattern I should have seen. It's all connected. I

196

blame myself for being so arrogant and blind."

"I still don't understand. Why did she give it up?"

"Simon. Robbie's right. It makes no sense," Michael agreed.

He looked at me, then put his massive hand on my shoulder. "I grasp what's happened. It's the only rationale. She wanted to protect someone. That's why she surrendered the amulet."

It took a moment for his words to penetrate. "No, please. Tell me it's not..." A sick feeling crept over me. I searched Simon's wise gray eyes.

"Yes, Robert," he whispered. "The only way she could be taken would be if they told her they'd harm the person she loves the most."

Michael turned.

I understood. Courtney had given herself up to save me.

****

Courtney sat silently in the back seat of the enormous Cadillac. Mrs. Mac sat next to her, squeezing her hand tightly. The women who had taken them captive wore sober expressions. She remembered the cruel smile on the face of the woman she had thought of as a confidant and friend. Courtney felt betrayed.

"Please, Courtney," said the large woman who seemed in charge. "We want your journey home to be as comfortable as possible." The woman studied her captive. Courtney sensed that the woman was tense and frightened. "We're aware of your extraordinary powers, but I have to warn you that if you try to influence us or communicate with your family, it will force us to resort to measures we'd rather avoid."

"I don't understand. What do you want? What can I possibly do for you?"

"I can tell you that when we reach our destination everything will be made clear. In the

197

meantime, if you make trouble or rebel, your charming old friend here"—the woman looked at Mrs. Mac with a cold smile—"will find life very uncomfortable. Do you understand?"

Courtney nodded. She was frightened, confused, and mad as hell.

****

I sat in the courtyard, lost in thought. I heard voices talking about Courtney—what they could do to find her, help her, save her. I jumped up. Whatever was going to happen I had to be part of it.

As soon as I stood, it struck me like a bolt of lightning. I could see something—the inside of an automobile. An older woman sat next to her. I saw a road sign out the window: *Boston 35 miles*. Just as suddenly the vision vanished.

"Where do you think you're going?" Michael grabbed my arm.

"Where's Simon?"

"Inside with Gretchen." Michael stared. "What happened? You look so pale, like you'd seen a ghost."

"Don't say that!" I grabbed his shoulders, pushing him away. "Not now. Not ever."

"Why? What the hell's going on?"

"I've just seen something—a vision, an image from Courtney." I ran into the house and found Simon.

Everyone assembled in the great room.

"Simon, how is it that he saw this vision?" Gretchen asked. "Perhaps it's just emotion. Robbie feels guilty—a sense of responsibility for Courtney's disappearance."

I took Gretchen's arm. "I swear. This is not wishful thinking."

"How can you be so sure, Rob?" asked Michael.

I searched the two dozen faces surrounding me. "Because it was more than a vision, Mike. I could feel her presence."

He frowned, looking at Simon.

"What do you mean, Robert? Explain. How could you feel her presence?" Simon asked.

"I mean what I experienced was more than just visual, Simon. I could actually feel her fear and her anger."

"It's possible," Gretchen offered. "They're incredibly close."

"I don't know." Michael shook his head.

"Robert, I want you to close your eyes and recall what you saw and felt when you had this vision," Simon said, placing his hands on my temples.

I did as he asked, closing my eyes as I recalled the image. Suddenly, my mind was consumed by a pleasant buzzing. I felt faint. Several sets of strong arms kept me from falling.

"What he says is true," Simon assured the others. "I caught the image clearly. I couldn't detect any emotion, but then I wouldn't since I experienced it secondhand."

"But why him? And how can she manage it?" Michael asked. He sounded frustrated.

"First, Gretchen's right. They have an extraordinary bond and awareness of each other. Unlike anything I've ever seen." He patted my shoulder. "And I think that she may be able to relay her thoughts to Robert for an instant without being blocked or detected. That's why she waited until she saw a sign to give us a landmark—a direction." He shook his head. "The problem is we don't know how often she'll be able to send clues."

They looked at Simon and then at me. Michael sighed and played with his lips.

I had to ask. "Simon, why did they kidnap her? I mean instead of..." I asked, unable to finish my thought. He grasped my meaning.

He raised his thick gray eyebrows, looking reluctant.

"They must have a ceremony of their own, Robert." He looked away. "I've heard rumblings." Simon finished in a whisper, "But I thought it was folklore."

I turned toward Michael. He stared at the floor. No one would meet my eyes.

Simon put his hand on my shoulder. "I'd rather not speculate. What we know is that Courtney is somewhere around Boston. But I'm positive that they have to return her to Great Britain. Wales, I believe."

I let it go. Whatever these people were planning for Courtney, I was better off in ignorance. I wanted to keep my mind uncluttered for any thoughts or visions she might send.

"The only place to get a transatlantic flight is New York City. They know our resources. They'll drive to avoid detection. If they took a plane from Boston we might intercept them." Simon looked at me. "But they have almost five days until her birthday. They may fly to somewhere on the Continent first. That'll make finding them difficult. We have a major task ahead of us. But I promise, we'll get her back."

Chapter Thirty-Three

The next few hours dragged. Sand through an hourglass. I heard hushed discussion between family members.

"Why aren't we doing something?" I asked, pounding the table. Four hours had passed. All these powerful witches and wizards were doing was drinking coffee and sitting on their behinds.

Simon took my arm and gently directed me to the ballroom. "We have an extensive network, Robert. We have to rely on them to help us determine where they've taken Courtney." He squeezed my shoulder. "After that first image, I was hoping you might receive something else to help us pinpoint where she is."

"Nothing since that first vision." I shook my head. "Why are you so sure they'll take her to Wales?"

"There's a strange Druid coven behind this. I'm certain of it. But still don't understand why. Wales is their home." He motioned for me to sit.

I had too much nervous energy. I paced in front of him.

"This group is small but powerful," he continued. "They're directly descended from the ancient leaders, the philosopher-priests who ruled much of England. They have a new leader—a high priest. I've heard about him, but discounted it. He has some agenda. I'm afraid Courtney and our ritual are part of it."

I concentrated, trying to see her, to make contact. The door flew open, followed by Michael and

Jonathan.

"We just got a call from one of our people in New York. Four women, one fitting Courtney's description, another Mrs. Mac's, bought tickets on this evening's flight to Bournemouth."

Simon nodded. "Interesting." He closed his eyes.

"This is a big break," Michael enthused. "The flight takes fourteen hours. It stops in Gander and Shannon before it gets to Hurn Airport. We can intercept them."

"First," Simon began. "It strikes me as odd that they could get to New York in that time." He looked at his watch. "Five hours? Second, this seems a little too obvious. These people knew our plans, where we were, every detail. They know the extent of our network. Would they parade someone like Courtney who's bound to attract attention to an airport ticket counter?"

Of course he was right. My heart sank. "He's right," I whispered. "Of course they wouldn't."

"I appreciate your opinion, Rob, but you're new to all this."

Simon held up his hand. "Let's give Robbie some credit. So far his instincts have proven accurate."

"All right. So what do we do?" Michael asked with a scowl.

"Follow the bait they've given us, but keep searching and hope Courtney can send another image or that we can figure out where they really are."

As if on cue, I felt weak and dizzy. An image appeared in my mind. It was faint and faded quickly, but there was no mistaking it. I saw whitecaps, heard the unmistakable call of seabirds and just before I lost it, I saw the cluttered deck of a large fishing vessel.

I staggered backward and sat down, breathing heavily. "You don't have to search. I know where she is."

****

We stood in the dining room gathered around the table. When I explained the details of what I saw, both Jonathan and Michael were certain the image was Portland Harbor. Gretchen was skeptical, explaining there were too many places on the Maine Coast that fit my description. Simon called a friend at the Portland harbormaster's office, telling him about the images I had seen. He asked the man if there was a fishing vessel that fit the description.

"The name is what?" He nodded, his look a mixture of anger and amusement as he hung up. "You'll like the irony." He shook his head. "The vessel we're looking for is called the *Sea Witch*. She left two hours ago. He came on duty after she left, so he couldn't tell us who boarded. The captain told someone they'd be gone for ten days."

The room had filled when word of my vision spread through the compound. Some shook their heads, others showed frustration.

"She regularly fishes well out into the Atlantic. She's well-built, eighty-five feet long, and my friend thinks she could make the British Isles by Friday."

"Damn," I said, looking at Michael.

He nodded. "That complicates our situation. They could put in anywhere."

"No." Simon concentrated. "It has to be somewhere in Wales. I'm sure of it. These Druids have too many ties to that country. But it's riddled with places of ancestral significance, places that they might use to..." He looked at me and stopped before completing his thought. I searched the other faces in the room. They were staring at each other or the floor.

"What? What aren't you telling me?" I stood toe-to-toe with Michael and took his shoulders. "What do they want Courtney for?"

Michael looked at Simon who came between us and pulled me away.

"Why won't you people tell me what's going on?" I pleaded with him. "I love her, Simon. I have to know."

He sighed. "I wish I could tell you. I'm at a loss to explain it. Druids are a peaceful group that reveres and worships nature. I'd been told about their new leader. He seems driven by some strange passion, but this…"

"Then this makes no sense." I shook my head, clenching my fists so tightly they hurt. "Is there some rationale for kidnapping Courtney?"

"I can't be sure. A dozen centuries ago, Ethwyn, a powerful and beautiful goddess, had a remarkable vision. She foresaw that the fortieth in her line would be a princess, beautiful, wise, and powerful beyond any that had come before. The number forty is significant in witchcraft."

"Go on," I prodded.

"She foretold the coming of this young woman before the end of the millennium, when the world was plagued by war, cruelty, and a terrible force that could destroy mankind."

"That could easily be today. World Wars, the Depression, the Holocaust. That force could be the atom bomb."

He nodded. "When we were blessed with Courtney, we knew she was the chosen one. But to assure that her power and goodness does not end with her, the prophecy commands she mate with a man. A very special man. That man must have all the physical attributes and beauty worthy of his mate."

My jaw dropped. "And you all decided that man was *me?*"

Simon nodded. "You not only met all the criteria but as you've discovered, you're one of us."

was Courtney. She was terrified. I tried to focus but all I saw was darkness. *Remember whatever happens—* For an instant I felt sharp pain, then nothing.

"What is it, Rob?" Michael saw I was shaking.

"Another message from Courtney. But it was strange. No image, just her voice and fear. She was frightened."

"Those *bastards*," Simon cursed. "I've never believed in violence, but if it takes the rest of my life, I'll find them!"

"What did you see?" Michael asked.

"Nothing. It was dark. She called my name. Then started to tell me something. I felt a sudden sharp pain." I was trembling I was so angry and frightened for Courtney. "What are we waiting for? Let's get going," I demanded.

"Robert, as much as I want to find her, there's nothing we can do tonight. Let's get something to eat and try to get some rest. The next few days are going to be long and difficult."

I wanted to protest. But he was right. "All right. What do we need for the trip? You mentioned a boat and I assume when we get to Wales we're going to be doing some hard overland traveling. I won't pack my dinner jacket."

"No." Simon patted my shoulder. "Here's what you'll need..."

****

I sat in Jonathan's office staring at the phone. I dreaded making this call. But I had to. I owed Rachel an explanation. The problem was I had no idea what to say. I could lie—tell her my car had broken down or that Michael needed my help to solve some imaginary crisis. I could tell her the truth. Was that really something I should do over the telephone? No. I had to do it in person. I picked up the receiver and gave the operator Rachel's number. I heard the sound of the phone ringing in her apartment.

"Hello," Rachel answered. I could hear anxiety and fatigue in her voice.

"Hi," I whispered into the phone.

"Well if it isn't my long-lost beau." She sounded angry. I understood. I should have been back in Boston. "I thought you'd abandoned me."

"No, Rachel, I haven't abandoned you."

"I'm glad to hear that. Where are you and what the hell's going on, Robbie?"

I decided on the truth with some adjustments.

"Rachel, please don't be angry." I began. "Remember the girl from England?"

"How could I forget?" she said in clipped tones.

"Something's happened to her. Something bad."

"So what?" She paused. Her tone remained confrontational.

"She went out for a drive this morning with her nanny and they went missing. Michael found the car abandoned. No trace of either one of them."

I heard a sigh. "Oh my God, Robbie, I'm sorry. That is terrible." Her voice softened.

"Yes, it is. The girl's grandfather's here, too. He and Jon have asked if Michael and I could help. Courtney—that's her name—was due to inherit a large estate. It's possible they were kidnapped."

"What do the police say?" she asked.

"I'm not sure. The grandfather's handling things."

"Okay." Her tone was still chilly. "Do what you have to and please, keep in touch."

Twisting the truth had worked. But I felt worse. How could I tell her the whole truth? Regardless of what happened I knew there had to be a reckoning. But as selfish as it was, for now, I had to keep Rachel in the dark. It was best for both of us.

"I'll keep in touch. Don't work too hard. You

sound tired."

"I'll see you at your mother's Friday night. Love you." She kissed the receiver.

"Love you, too," I said as I hung up the phone, ashamed for lying so often and so well. It was what we witches were best at.

Chapter Thirty-Five

I lay in my bed, tossing on rumpled sheets as I relived Courtney's last message. I closed my eyes and concentrated, hoping to hear her again. I tried the opposite tack and let my mind go blank. Still nothing. I turned and looked at the clock on the night table. One-fifteen. I willed the hours to pass, wanting our journey to begin. At 2:00 a.m. I rose and went to the bathroom. I stared at the sleeping pills in my medicine cabinet. *Take one as needed,* the instructions read. I saw Rachel's father's name on the bottle again. I opened the top and popped one in my mouth.

The medication overcame my adrenaline and anxiety. I recalled images of Courtney and Rachel laughing in my dreams. One galloped across a golden meadow while the other ran out the hospital door, breathless, taking me in her arms.

"Robbie. Robbie!" Michael's husky baritone called as he banged on my door. The sleeping pill had done its job too well.

"Coming," I answered as I stumbled out of bed, sunlight filtering through the sheer curtains. I looked at the clock. Eight-fifteen. We were supposed to meet at eight. "Give me a minute." I crossed the distance and pulled the door open.

"You look like hell."

"Thanks. Nice to see you, too. I took a sleeping pill. Give me ten minutes."

He looked at me rubbing his hand over his chin. "Okay, but get your ass in gear. We've gotta catch a plane."

I nodded and turned. In three minutes, I was in and out of the shower. I pushed my toothbrush around as quickly as possible, put on deodorant, and dressed. No need for other affectations. I was on a mission. In less than eight minutes I stood in the courtyard, overnight bag in hand.

"Quick recovery," Michael yelled as he motioned to the garage.

Simon paced. He was dressed in dark, simple clothing. So was Michael. We could have been agents heading out on a mission. Knowing our target, I welcomed the parallel. I'd never been in a tight spot with Simon, but if he was anything like Michael, the chances of rescuing Courtney were good.

Jon, Gretchen, Wendy, and a dozen other family members stood in the garage. An immaculate four-door Lincoln stood in the gravel driveway.

Jonathan approached and squeezed my shoulder. He gestured at the car. "She's got a V-12, Rob. Get you there in no time." He let out a long breath. "I'm sorry about all this. The way it's turned out."

"Not your fault, Jon." I forced a smile. Regrets had no place. "No one could have foreseen this."

Simon took my arm. "Let's go. We're wasting time." He nodded. "We'll get her back, Robert."

I turned and placed two envelopes in Gretchen's hands. One addressed to my mother, the other to Rachel. She looked down and rubbed her eyes. "If this doesn't turn out well..." I took her face, looking into damp gray eyes. "Deliver these for me?" I asked. She hugged me so hard it took my breath away.

"They'll be no need," she said as I pulled free.

"I'll take the first shift," Michael volunteered.

Simon looked at me. "Fine with me." I nodded, got into the back seat, and waved to the group. They stood, trying their best to look hopeful.

Simon got into the passenger seat. Michael put

213

in the clutch and started the powerful engine. I never looked back.

****

It was dark, very dark, and damp. Courtney was chained and gagged. She lay on a cot, shivering. From the motion it felt as if they were somewhere at sea on a large vessel, but she couldn't be sure. One of them had seen her communicating with Robbie. They struck her across the face with something sharp and took Mrs. Mac away with a noose around her neck. If Courtney used her powers again her nanny would pay the price.

Courtney feared for both of them. Her hands had been cuffed to the sides of her makeshift bed. She could have made easy work of freeing herself, but she had no idea what they might do to Mrs. Mac. The woman in charge told Courtney that they still had someone close to Robbie. If she tried to escape or communicate in any way they could do him harm or worse. She had to remain passive.

"I really need to use the bathroom," she told the woman who came into her tiny cell when she removed the gag and turned on the small, bare overhead bulb. Courtney offered her captor a weak smile, trying to look compliant. This woman seemed brusque and rude, but it was a mask. She always gave in to whatever her captive asked. She was an easy target for Courtney. The woman undid the handcuffs. Courtney massaged her wrists. They had marks where the metal had pulled and chafed her skin.

"Go ahead," the woman said, leaving the door open. Courtney knew the location of the head—the small ship's bathroom. It was dirty and held a stale odor but it served its purpose. She wanted to communicate with Robbie again, but thought better of it. Her cheek still stung from the bruise where the other woman had struck her. She returned and compliantly sat back on her cot. The woman had brought some water and a ham sandwich, both of which Courtney devoured.

"Thank you." She nodded with a warm smile. "Can you tell me why I'm here?" Courtney risked asking.

Her captor's face grew dark. She played with her lip. "I can't tell you anything, missy. But while you're under my care, I'll see to it that you and your friend are treated right."

"Then Mrs. Mac is all right?" Courtney needed to know.

"Yes. We need to make sure you behave yourself," she confided. The woman patted her captive on the shoulder and left. The light remained on and the handcuffs remained unattached. Courtney's subtle manipulation of the woman's mind had worked. But she still had no idea what their motive was. All she knew was that she had no intention of remaining docile for long.

****

Michael was the navigator. He had done his homework. The most direct route was through New Hampshire and central Massachusetts, but that would have bogged us down in endless small towns, halted us at traffic lights and forced us to slog along at forty miles an hour. He chose to go southeast to Portsmouth, then south along Route 1 around Boston. We hit fewer lights and were able to take advantage of the awesome power under the Lincoln's hood. We were intercepted once by a Massachusetts State Trooper. The poor officer was no match for Simon. He stepped out from behind the wheel and went to talk to the officer. He was back in two minutes. The trooper looked dazed. We sped off at twenty miles an hour over the speed limit.

I kept waiting, praying for a sign, any indication Courtney was alive and knew we were coming to her

215

rescue.

"They can't do anything until Friday evening. They have to keep her alive until then. It's essential," Simon assured me as I got behind the wheel for my turn driving.

"I know." I nodded. "But the last image was so dark, so frightening. I could sense fear and pain." I stopped. There were no words. They might have hurt her. The prophecy said they needed her alive on Friday evening. It did not guarantee her comfort.

Chapter Thirty-Six

We parked the Lincoln in front of the sign that read *Departures* at New York's Idlewild Airport. Michael handed the keys to a man waiting for us. A family member, I assumed. Entering the utilitarian concrete terminal the man who took the keys directed us toward the Pan American ticket counter. We were waved around the queue by another who handed each of us boarding passes. The thought crossed my mind that family members outnumbered the normal population.

"You're booked on a special flight," the man explained. "The first commercial flight to circumnavigate the globe. They're using the new Lockheed Constellation. It's quite the event. Only twenty-one passengers. Mostly press."

"I appreciate your efforts, but this flight is big news. I wanted to keep a low profile," Simon said with a frown.

"I understand, sir. But there were no other options." The man seemed frustrated. "It was either this flight or wait another day. That wouldn't leave any margin for error."

Simon put his hand on the man's shoulder. "It's all right." He turned toward us. "Here are your passports. Cover your faces when the cameras go off. Our enemies are clever. I don't want them seeing us in the *Times*."

Simon and Michael left me in the waiting area and went to the restaurant for a bite to eat before we boarded the plane. I had no appetite. I was desperate for another vision from Courtney.

Something to tell me she was alive. The thought of her fate if we failed haunted me.

"You okay?" Michael asked when he returned. "You look like hell."

I glared at him, shaking my head. "Thanks. You really know how to boost a guy's spirits."

"Seriously, you look like you've seen a ghost." Realizing what he had said, Michael lowered himself into the seat next to me. "I'm sorry. You know I didn't mean that."

"I know, Mike." I shook my head, forcing a smile. "It's just that, I don't know. I keep getting this terrible feeling that she's in trouble."

"Of course she's in trouble. I mean..."

Simon joined us, holding a cup of coffee.

"No, Michael," I stopped him. "I don't mean trouble with the Druids. It's something else. I can't explain it. She's there sometimes, like a buzz inside my head. Just beyond my reach, then she's gone."

"Is it possible they drugged her?" Simon asked. "Does the feeling you're getting seem like a dream, Robert?"

"It's possible. It's been happening since after lunch. I didn't say anything because I thought it might be my imagination. But it's not. I can sense her."

Michael exhaled and looked at Simon. He stood and crossed to the newsstand, returning with the *New York Times*. As he sat next to me, I turned, staring casually at the paper. I froze as an article jumped out at me.

"Oh my God." My throat tightened. I stopped breathing for a moment.

"What is it, Robert?" Simon stood and crossed the space separating us. He stared at me. I pointed to the headline that caught my attention. The desperate look in Simon's eyes told me he understood. Michael closed the paper to see what the commotion was about. I folded it so the headline stood out.

"She couldn't. Could she?" he asked. His face grew ashen as he looked up at Simon, then back at me.

"I don't think so, but..." Simon twisted his mouth into a scowl. "No," he said. "Courtney would never do that."

His words hung in the humid air, unconvincingly. Fear consumed me.

"That might explain what I felt earlier." I whispered. "I thought they might have hurt her, but maybe she..." I refused to finish the thought.

I stared at the newspaper. "Judge Rules Woman's Death a Suicide," the headline read. Suicide. The word screamed out at me. I swallowed and stood, fighting the sickening feeling as I headed to the men's room. I lurched into the first stall as nausea overtook me.

****

I checked my watch. Eleven twenty. We had left New York thirty minutes late due to the commotion over the flight. That pushed our arrival time at Gander back to half past midnight. I tried to convince myself that Courtney would never resort to taking her own life, but I was terrified by the reality that if she did, it would be to save me.

The thought tortured me, but I tried to put it out of my mind. My exhausted body drifted up and down with the turbulence. I looked down at the sparsely lit Maine coast 20,000 feet below. I found myself hoping, praying that whatever force controlled the universe would help us find her in time.

I closed my eyes, trying to sleep. I saw Rachel's face as the four supercharged Wright engines droned outside my window. I loved Courtney. There was no doubt of that. But I'd treated Rachel so badly. After thirty minutes, I stood and found my overnight bag.

Michael looked up from his magazine and nodded.

"You okay, brother?" he asked.

I pulled out the sleeping pills and took one in my hand. "Fine, Mike," I answered, trying to sound confident. "I'm going to take something to help me sleep. I think I'm going to need it."

He scanned the passengers scattered across the Constellation's well-appointed cabin. "No need," he told me, putting down his magazine. "Sit down," he whispered, gesturing to my seat.

I looked around. Simon was snoring softly in the row in front of us. Toward the rear of the plane, one or two of our fellow passengers were talking in muffled tones, but most sat, their seats reclined as they slept. The sound of the large engines pulling us toward Newfoundland drowned out what they were saying.

"What's up?" I raised my eyebrows and sat down.

He swept the cabin with his eyes a second time. Apparently satisfied, he took the seat next to me. "I can help you." He paused. "You shouldn't take any drugs. We all need to be sharp. Close your eyes and lean back in your seat."

I looked at him curiously but did as he asked. I could sense him leaning over me. I felt his hands on my temples. Calm swept through my body. A pleasant buzz ran through my head as the tension vanished. The sensation from Michael's touch ran down my spinal cord, sending a soft tingling as it exited through my legs. Somewhere in the back of my mind I had a foggy recollection of Courtney doing the same. I had no idea where or when.

"I want you to count very slowly to ten," Michael said softly. His words were resonant, hypnotic.

"One, two, three," I began. Before I got to five I was asleep.

Chapter Thirty-Seven

Michael's magic did its work.

"Sir." The dimpled stewardess shook me gently. "We're thirty minutes from Shannon. I believe that's where you'll be leaving us."

I coughed and cleared my throat. Sunlight and conversation filled the cabin. The inside of my mouth had the taste of an old riding boot again. "Yes, that's right." I answered, stretching and searching the adjacent seats for Simon and Michael. I checked my watch. Eight-thirty.

"Well, look who's decided to rejoin us." I turned to see Michael's broad face wearing a grin. He came up behind me and tapped me on the shoulder. "Well, I see that sleeping compound worked." He winked.

"Yeah. I feel great." And I did. I stood, rotating my torso to loosen the stiffness in my muscles after the long sleep. My mind immediately turned to Courtney. I wondered if Michael's spell might have blocked out any images.

Simon approached, using a towel to dry his hands. He stared at me. "No," he said.

I looked at him curiously. "Are you..." Seeing a dozen other passengers in our vicinity, I stopped.

"I know what you were thinking," Simon offered. "And the answer is no. It wouldn't have blocked"—he scanned the cabin before continuing—"any communication from her." He sat down next to me and patted my forearm. "Are you still sensing her presence?"

A strange feeling came over me. There was no image, but I could feel her. "Yes, I feel something.

But I'm worried it may be my imagination."

He studied me. "Are you familiar with Carl Jung, the psychologist?"

"Yes." I nodded, wondering what a renowned psychologist-philosopher had to do with our situation. But the last few days had taught me never to doubt Simon's wisdom.

"He was called the Darwin of the mind." Simon shrugged. "We're great believers in his work. Jung said, 'The debt we owe to the play of imagination is incalculable.'"

I stared at him. "I'm not sure I get your meaning."

"It's simple, Robert. We've come to understand the value of imagination, dreams, and what most of the world views as fantasy." He leaned over and lowered his voice. "Jung spoke of an inner world, calling it the collective unconscious."

I knew he had a point, but it was foggy. "Perhaps I'm missing something."

Simon held up his hand. "It's difficult for you, someone educated and surrounded by the analytical trappings of the manifest world—the physical. But all of us are connected to this vast inner world, a group mind if you like."

Suddenly it dawned on me. I wanted to shake his hand. I could feel a grin spread across my face. When I looked at Michael, he smiled at me.

"I think he understands," Simon said.

I nodded. "You're telling me that what I'm feeling isn't my imagination. It means Courtney's alive."

Michael nodded and shook my hand. "Yes. And we're gonna get her back safely."

We fastened our seat belts as the large plane bumped over the thick layer of clouds separating us from Shannon Airport.

Chapter Thirty-Eight

Drizzle and a cool breeze greeted us as we deplaned and walked through Shannon's international terminal. Several men stood waiting to meet us. I assumed all were family members or allies. That seemed an appropriate way to describe them since Michael and Simon had described the Druids as the enemy. The situation wore every earmark of a battle.

"This is my younger brother, Lionel." Simon gestured toward the striking middle-aged man holding out an enormous hand.

"Robert McGregor." I shook it. "It's a pleasure." Lionel was shorter than his older brother. He had brownish hair, curly and graying at the temples. It was combed back and long, hanging over the collar. Lionel brought Basil Rathbone's Sherlock Holmes to mind. If he possessed half the intellect and detecting skills, he'd be a fine addition to our team.

"Hello, Michael."

"Lionel." He nodded. "Where's the boat?"

"On the coast. We'll head straight there." Lionel moved us along. "We cleared your bags through customs. They're already in the Jag." He moved quickly toward the exit. Outside a Jaguar sedan waited. A man slammed the boot closed and nodded as he headed to the dull English Ford behind us.

Lionel caught me staring. "She's got a V-8 that would put most V-12s to shame. She's our trail car. The Druids are very active here. We want to make sure there are no incidents." He patted my back.

We were hustled into the vehicles. Lionel got

223

behind the wheel. Simon rode in the passenger seat. Michael and I shared the rear. I saw Lionel give a nod to the driver of the Ford and put the Jag in gear. We sped away, leaving a thick trail of exhaust in our wake. Lionel used the accelerator generously and we left the entrance at a dizzying speed. I noticed two police cars nearby. Lionel and Simon gave a discreet wave and the first bolted out in front of us.

"A police escort?" I whispered.

Michael chuckled softly. "The Phillips family knows how to travel."

I elbowed my brother. "Did they say we're going to catch a boat?"

He raised his eyebrows and gave me a shrug. "When it comes to planning and operations, these folks are no amateurs. I'm not sure of the plan, but I'll bet we're not picking up an old fishing smack."

I had no argument. Simon and company had orchestrated this like a well-planned military operation—without the snafus. I nodded at my friend and put my head back.

Robbie. Oh, Robbie, I love you. I heard her as if she sat next to me. I sensed fear, intense anger, and pain, but not the searing pain of two days ago.

"Simon, Mike," I yelled, unable to contain my excitement. "I heard her. No image, but it was Courtney."

"And?" Simon asked, his chiseled features taught.

I smiled. "Frightened, mad as hell, and in pain. But she's alive."

"I want you to close your eyes and think about her, nothing but her. Concentrate on the way you feel when you see her, touch her." He hesitated. "When you kiss. Block everything else out."

I did. Everyone sat silently. No one breathed. *Courtney, Courtney, I hear you. We're coming. Don't be afraid.*

Seconds went by. They became a minute. I sighed, certain my thoughts weren't strong enough, my skills not honed enough when suddenly—

I hear you, darling. I'm waiting—

"It worked. I could hear her for just a minute. Then she stopped and cried out in pain again."

Simon grabbed my hand and shook it. Michael slapped my back. "Most likely, they're watching her closely. Trying to keep her from communicating. I don't know what their telepathic abilities are. None that I know of. But telepathy isn't an exact science. Many things affect it, especially over the long distances we're dealing with."

There were times when I felt like a child, learning a whole new set of rules and behaviors.

Simon looked intense, as if calculating some arcane probability. "If they could block her thoughts," he said, "they would. They may be watching her. When they're distracted, she sends a message. If they see her they resort to something more primitive."

"I can't bear to think of her being hurt."

"I understand," Simon said, his jaw set. "Cruelty is alien to what we pagans believe. But to use an expression from your western movies, they have a new sheriff in town."

Chapter Thirty-Nine

We headed northwest on the N19 highway. At the city limits, the police waved us on with a salute. We made a sharp turn to the southwest on the N92 toward the town of Dingle seventy-five miles away. The trail car followed at a discreet distance. We made a stop in Tralee where Simon stopped to make a phone call.

"Everything's ready. My old friend Nigel Thomas has seen to that. He's a captain in the British Navy and has developed a plausible cover story for his superiors." Simon nodded to Michael and Lionel. "The fact that two members of the admiralty are family members doesn't hurt."

He turned to me. "We're going to leave from Dingle Harbor. It's not the perfect location. I'd rather leave from the east coast, but Dingle's where our ship is. She's something special, chosen for this mission. Nigel Thomas and I served together in the first war. He pulled some strings to get us this craft. You'll understand when you see her."

He herded us back into the cars and checked his watch. I did the same. Almost noon on Wednesday; only sixty hours until the full moon and the ritual. I swallowed hard. No new messages from Courtney. Despite the damp, cool air, sweat trickled between my shoulder blades.

I closed my eyes but found it impossible to doze as we sped over the last few miles to Dingle. I tried to open my mind and make contact again, but all I heard was the rhythm of my heart.

Michael must have noticed. He put his hand on

my shoulder and nodded. "Don't you ever doubt we're going to get her back and deal with these Druids."

Dingle was a sleepy fishing village. We passed through it at breakneck speed and headed toward a small collection of buildings hidden behind an eight-foot chain-link fence. As we approached, I could see a large sign, black letters on white, telling us to halt. *No One Will be Admitted Without Class I Security Pass,* the sign warned.

When we drew within a few yards of the well-manned guard post, the gate slid open. A British Marine showed himself, saluting smartly as he waved us through. Traveling with Simon and his family was like being a member of royalty. I would have enjoyed it had the stakes not been so high. The Jaguar entered. As I looked behind us, our shadow on the five-hour trip from Shannon turned back. The driver gave us thumbs up.

We drove through a maze of small derricks, mountains of supplies stored in neat rows, and two small oil tanks with all the attendant safety and delivery apparatus. When we emerged into the open, I knew why we were here. Tied up at the quay, a spanking-new patrol boat sat poised like a sleek predator ready to pounce.

"She's 110 feet of speed and intimidation. Cruising speed is thirty knots, but we'll push her to the edge to get to Wales." Simon looked at his watch. "We should be there just after midnight. We'll take the northern route. She's equipped with state-of-the-art radar and detection gear, so if the *Sea Witch* is actually chugging along out there, we'll find her."

He waved to an imposing man dressed in a captain's uniform. I assumed it was Nigel. Next to him a tall woman approached as well. Slender, with a tanned face and large, gray eyes, she wore the look of a hunter. She was stunning.

227

Simon did the introductions. "This is Nigel Thomas, my old comrade. We've known each other for longer than I care to remember." Simon slapped his back. "And this young lady is Gwyneth Montrose. She's our Druid expert—knows everything there is to know about them. Studied at Oxford, Cambridge, and has done extensive field work. She's also an empath. Gwyn has the ability to sense things—people, situations, the presence of good and evil, and a very close friend of..." Before he finished she ran to Michael, throwing her arms around his broad shoulders and kissing him. "Need I say more?" Simon added with a smile.

Michael and Gwyneth held each other for a long time, releasing each other when Simon gestured toward the waiting craft. We took our bags and double-timed it to the gangway.

"Well, I had no idea you were a man of such strong emotion and refined taste," I teased Michael.

"I met Gwynny when I was stationed over here with the Rangers and OSS. I specialized in dealing with the occult."

I must have looked skeptical.

"Hitler, Himmler, the whole Nazi inner crowd was preoccupied by spirits, spells, and the afterlife. They tried to link Jesus with the Aryans. Claimed that Parsifal—the Wagnerian hero—was a metaphor for Christ."

Gwyneth nodded. "We learned the craft together, Robbie." She smiled, her large gray eyes sparkled.

He returned her look with affection. I had never seen my brother display so much emotion. "One day a couple of years ago we suddenly realized that we were, you know." Michael's face reddened. "But my work for the family keeps us apart. When the ritual and all this is over, I hope..."

Gwyneth had been walking close, wearing a

brilliant smile. She interrupted, "He's going to steal me away and make an honest woman of me."

I slapped him on the back as I glanced at Gwyneth. "My God. Are all witches this lovely?" I asked. Despite my growing anguish over Courtney, I was happy Michael had someone he cared for.

"We'll find her, Robert. My oath as a high priestess." She flashed another bright smile as she squeezed my hand. "I know it."

I nodded my thanks and headed up the narrow gangplank. The sleek ship was running, pushing a thin plume of smoke from her rakish funnel. No sooner had we thrown our gear aboard then Nigel nodded to the deck officer. The lines dropped away as the svelte craft maneuvered away from the dock. We followed the narrow channel, heading out of the harbor and turned north, a fresh breeze blowing in our faces.

I whistled. "This is amazing," I said, looking at Michael. "We've commandeered a British naval vessel."

"It's quite an operation. Even I'm impressed."

"Is Nigel one of *us*?" I asked.

He shook his head. "No, but Simon's done a lot for Nigel. Actually fished him and his crew out of the Irish Sea after his ship was torpedoed in 1916."

"You people have an amazing network."

"That's right. With a lot more sex appeal," he said grinning as he hugged Gwyneth. "And it's 'we.' You're one of us." Michael nodded.

We cleared the breakwater and made our turn. The small warship picked up speed like a racehorse spurred by a hungry jockey. We slid over the four-foot swells like a speedboat cruising across a lake. Despite the gravity of our mission, I found myself exhilarated as we cruised, paralleling the Irish coast.

"Let's head to the wardroom. We have plans to

discuss," Simon ordered. I nodded and followed everyone through the hatch, down a spotless companionway, and into the officers' mess. We sat down at the oak table in the room's center. Nigel followed, carrying an armful of charts.

"There's no way they could make it," he said with a scowl. Simon spread a massive map of the North Atlantic before us. Nigel had penned the distances between the assumed starting point and Ireland. He circled possible destinations. He had done the same with locations on the west coast of Wales and England. "That fishing vessel can't manage more than fifteen knots, a little more if she's picked up a tailwind. That hasn't happened. I've checked with the boys at Naval Meteorology. She's been sailing into a stiff headwind for two days—if she's even out there." He shook his head.

"Alternatives?" Simon asked.

"You think they're heading for Wales, the Island of Anglesey?" Gwyneth asked, narrowing her eyes. "Are you sure, Simon?"

Simon nodded. "It makes sense. They have ties to that area—very strong ties. Their history dates to antiquity. I grant you it's a guess, but an educated one that their sanctuary and sacred altar would be there." His eyes searched the charts as he bit his lip. "Remember, this isn't a lark they chose on a whim. We have to assume they've been planning this for some time. They'll have a gathering of elders and others and they can't do what"—he looked away, his face hard and tight—"they intend to without resources, preparation, and solitude."

Gwyneth reached over and patted my hand. We looked at each other. His assessment made sense.

"I think they've pulled a fast one." Simon continued. "They can't control or override Courtney's telepathic abilities so they've used them, let her to send us tidbits. Pieces of information to tease us—

give us brief images leading us to believe they're trying to get to Wales by boat. Desperate for any information, we let ourselves be taken in."

"What do you think they've done?" Michael asked, looking back and forth between Simon and Nigel.

"Left Portland and traveled by boat long enough so Courtney could send an image. I'm guessing they drugged her, put into a small harbor along the Canadian coast, and took a long-range aircraft to Wales. That's the only way to get there in time," Simon said, looking at Nigel.

His comrade nodded. "Makes sense."

"I don't feel them anywhere near, and I can smell these bastards," Gwyneth added.

Simon stood and paced. "I blame myself for this. I wanted to find Courtney so badly I believed their tricks." He looked at each of us in turn, offering a quiet, "I'm sorry."

"But if we can get there—this place you think she'll be—we still have thirty-six hours to find them, don't we?" I asked.

He shrugged. His chiseled features looked vulnerable and tired. "Yes, Robert. Assuming they don't fool us again. I can see why they're successful. I underestimated them. I never imagined they'd be a match for us. I was wrong." He turned and left the wardroom.

I followed him with my eyes. I respected Simon, but hoped that his overconfidence had not cost Courtney's life.

****

Dusk approached. I stood on the windward side of the patrol boat, trying to let the stiff breeze and sea spray occupy my mind. It was a losing battle. Images of Courtney and her pain consumed me. I promised myself to punish those who kidnapped and tortured her. I would end their miserable existence. I looked forward to it.

I took a drag on my cigarette as I heard the sound of the hatch shut. I turned to see Michael. "What are you thinking?" he yelled over the sound of the wind and the twin, high-powered diesels.

"So many things," I responded, adding "I can't wait to get my hands on these creatures."

"I understand how you feel. But this will be tough. Don't let your emotions get in the way."

"I won't," I said in a voice tinged with anger and arrogance. "I can deal with them. They better pray that Courtney's all right."

Michael patted me on the back. "These people are dangerous." He looked out at the gray and pink of the darkening sky. "They've out-thought Simon and kept Gwynny from detecting them. Those two are as shrewd and powerful as they come."

"Give me a shot," I yelled as a sudden wave pushed our sleek vessel to starboard.

Michael checked his watch. I did the same. Eight-twenty. I noticed his utilitarian timepiece was gone. He wore his Ranger chronometer. "Simon wants to meet at 2100 hours to go over the latest info and plan our landing." He started to turn and walk back inside. He put his hand on my shoulder. "We're gonna get Courtney back. I promise."

"Damn straight," I called to him. I had never been so determined. When the moon rose on Friday evening, she would be with me, or I would have died trying.

Chapter Forty

Courtney studied the tall stranger who met them when they deplaned in Gloucester. She needed to determine who he was and what he wanted. He had a familiar look. But reading his thoughts was impossible. Surprising. She had discovered that these people were Druids and to her knowledge, telepathy was not one of their skills.

"From this point on, Courtney, they'll be no more questions." He nodded to one of his associates and a tight leather gag was strapped in place. Her hands were pulled behind her and tied. Her ankles were also bound and she was placed into the large boot of a Jaguar limousine.

Courtney struggled despite her restraints, fighting her captors furiously. Too furiously.

"Enough of this foolishness," the large man with the strangely familiar voice whispered. "I want her in one piece for the ritual." It was the last thing she heard. A long needle pierced the cloth of her dirty hacking jacket and entered her arm. In a matter of seconds, blackness overtook her.

****

We sat around the oak table in the wardroom. Simon stood arrow-straight at the head, studying the papers arrayed in his hands. The look of quiet self-assurance had returned.

He cleared his throat. "Our friends on Anglesey tell us they've discovered a hidden sanctuary a few miles from Beaumaris Castle and the strait." He picked up a piece of paper, studying it. "I believe this is the site where they intend to perform the"—the words seemed to stick in his throat—"the ritual. They tell us there's been activity there recently."

I scanned the room. Everyone stared at Simon.

"We have several choices. We can anchor a few miles off the coast and take a launch into the harbor, or…"

Suddenly everyone turned toward me. I reached out, grasping blindly. I sensed Courtney. Felt myself mouthing my name, followed by a weak plea. *"No, Wendy…Help Mrs. Mac."* There was a weak cry, then silence. The words *Home* and *Romeo* ran through my mind. Just as quickly she was gone.

"Robbie," Michael cried out as they gathered round me.

I looked up at their faces, their eyes searching mine. The message was brief, dreamlike, and disoriented. More than anything the tone was one of sadness and betrayal. *Betrayal.* That was the only way to describe the sense Courtney communicated.

"Robert, how did she seem?" Simon grasped my shoulders.

I shook my head. "Not good. She's weak, very weak. Everything was blurred, fuzzy, like I was hearing it underwater. Just random thoughts, but there was something. It's difficult to explain. She was sad and frightened. And there was a feeling of hurt and terrible disappointment, as if someone had betrayed or deceived her." I related the disjointed words from her message.

"Was she coherent, awake?" It was Gwyneth.

"No, she was definitely drugged or unconscious. Maybe that's how she was able to get through. If they'd drugged her or knocked her out, they might have been asleep at the switch," I suggested.

"She said, 'Wendy,' then 'help Mrs. Mac'?" Simon asked.

I nodded. "Yes. Very clearly. The word 'no' and then the names." I was as mystified as they were.

"She and Wendy were close, but not as close as she was to Mrs. Mac. And I don't know about her nanny. She may have been calling out for help or trying to tell us who took her."

"It's possible. But all along she's been calling out to you. Betrayal, Robert?" Simon looked confused. "You spoke of Mrs. Mac. Do you suppose she's part of this? That might explain what you felt. And what about her reference to 'home' and 'Romeo'?"

"I have no idea. All I know is what I told you two days ago. Courtney felt a strange sensation, something that frightened her badly and the only one close by was Mrs. Mac." Suddenly I stopped, realizing that was not entirely true. Gretchen had been there that night, and the morning she was taken, but the thought teasing me was too bizarre, too strange to contemplate.

"Go on, Rob." Michael said with a look of frustration.

"It's nothing." I tried to ignore what I was thinking. "She's weak, frightened, but still alive. As far as 'home' and 'Romeo,' if she was drugged or knocked out, they may be random images in her mind. Maybe that's why she called out to Wendy." I shook my head. "Let's get back to our plans."

Everyone looked at Simon. "You could be right. But Courtney's so powerful, so intelligent. It's hard to believe there was no meaning in her communication. There had to be something in the images you received." He shrugged and looked at us. "But our job now is to get her back. Here are the alternatives."

Simon explained the choices. We could lay off the northeast coast of Anglesey and go into the harbor at Beaumaris, a quaint village known for its twelfth-century castle and its yachting population. Our arrival in the early hours of Thursday morning might give us some anonymity, but in boating season there was no guarantee. Anglesey had wide sandy beaches. We could land at one and hike inland. The cliffs were shallow and easily climbed. Several were secluded. Our final alternative was to take the motor launch south on the Menai, the strait that separated the island from the Welsh mainland. We could put in at one of the small quays upriver. Several were near the site of the sanctuary that Simon's people had scouted. The final alternative offered the quickest and most covert entry onto the island. We could make our way inland and wait at their camp for our chance to intercept them. We chose the third.

"We should be within sight of the Welsh coast around 12:30," Simon told us. "We could wait until morning, but let's make sure we're in the right place. No more miscues. We'll leave the patrol boat at two. That should get us up the Menai by three and to our rendezvous by four. Try to get some rest. We'll meet on deck at 1:45." We all checked our watches and nodded.

Simon's manner was quiet and serious, almost military. I looked at Michael and nodded. He smiled. With luck, by tomorrow at this time, Courtney would be safe again, and those who took her and caused her pain would be repaid for their treachery.

****

I lay in the lower bunk while Michael tossed in the upper one. Nigel had given his cabin to Gwyneth. Michael had spent the better part of the previous two hours showing me weapons, how to use, aim, and load them. We'd repeated the drill endlessly. I'd been hunting with Michael and my father and could shoot well, but despite my contempt and anger for the people who had taken Courtney, firing a bullet at one of them would be a new and frightening experience.

My mind overflowed with so many thoughts. I recalled with a sense of irony that six nights ago I lay in my apartment with Rachel. She slept beside me, her arm draped lazily across my chest. I remembered thinking how grand my life was and dreading the next day's drive to the reunion. In the next day my life would take a turn so unexpected and strange no one would believe it. I knew. I found it difficult to believe myself.

As sleep began to take hold, I vowed to sacrifice anything, give my life if it meant saving Courtney or my comrades. I would never look back and ask myself what I could have done to make this come out right. In the days since that Thursday evening, Courtney was not part of my life, she was my life, the beacon that lit my way. If that beacon were extinguished, my existence would be pointless.

Chapter Forty-One

The dawn crept over the range of low hills to our front, its gray reluctantly giving way to a hint of pink beyond the forest. We had been in position since 4:30, resting on a low ridge a hundred yards from the site. Two local family members had delivered a sturdy duffel bag full of weapons. Adrenaline surged at the prospect of finding Courtney. But my mouth was dry and my palms sweaty. Despite my earlier bravado, the thought of taking a life left a dark, hollow feeling in my gut. The alternative could be worse.

Michael lay next to Gwyneth. He held up his field glasses, surveying the site. It looked still and empty. A hundred yards to the right of the clearing and the semicircle of stone benches that apparently served as seats stood a sturdy shack I assumed housed the tools and implements used when they performed their magic. But like the ritual site, it looked abandoned. If they were expecting a grand gathering to witness a sacrifice on the following evening, it seemed suspiciously absent of people or activity.

"Mike, are you getting the feeling I am?" I whispered as he continued to scan the area. "They have no idea we're here. Wouldn't they be making preparations, be involved in some movement if this thing was only thirty-six hours away?"

"I don't know." He shook his head. "But yeah. I think there should be some activity." His words died as he shushed me. Two women appeared from the thicket in back of what looked like an altar. As he stared, his shoulders sagged. He handed me the binoculars. These women wore hiking shorts, knee socks, and boots. Each carried a backpack. Upon seeing the stone amphitheater, they stopped and pointed. They seemed to be examining it. One produced a camera and took her friend's picture in front of a gray monolith. Michael shook his head as they moved on. Why these women were in the woods at this hour I had no idea, but they weren't planning human sacrifice.

Simon and Michael watched Gwyneth. She shook her head. "I'm getting nothing." She shrugged and squinted. "No feelings of any kind. If they *were* here, they've gone. At least for now."

"Simon, let Michael and me go down and check out that shed. If it's full, we may be in the right place. If not, we may have been mislead." I wanted to add the word "again" but thought better of it. I was getting the sinking feeling that we may have been duped a second time. All Simon's logic about this place and its significance made perfect sense. That troubled me. It was too sensible, too logical. To date, their cunning had been masterful. How better to draw us away from the real site than to create a feint, show a host of activity where none existed, and steal away.

Simon looked at me. His face registered frustration. He nodded. "Be casual. Put on these backpacks and try to look like hikers out for a jaunt in the country." He reached into the large bag, handing each of us a .45 automatic. "Just in case," he whispered. I checked to make sure it was loaded, the safety was on, and had a round chambered—the way Michael had taught me. He handed me a small pry bar. "This may come in handy on the shed." I put it in my belt. We tucked the weapons into our waistbands and headed down the low rise toward the shed.

We avoided walking on anything that might leave a trail, threading our way over the pine needles. When we reached the small outbuilding we scanned the area. A heavy padlock and hasp secured the door. Michael tried pulling it. No luck. I used the pry bar, pulling on it until it began to give way, then gave the plank door a yank.

"Shhh," Michael warned, scanning the forest surrounding us.

I nodded. We waited for thirty seconds with our backs against the shed before moving again. The hasp pulled free and the door flew open. My heart sank as I surveyed the contents in the early morning light. Nothing but a few old relics, some burned candles, and used torches. I stepped into the gloom, hoping to find a trapdoor or some evidence of activity. Nothing. If this was to be the site of a highly anticipated ritual, the implements were lacking.

"Damn," I said through clenched teeth. I slammed the shaky door. It vibrated and flew back toward us.

Michael's eyes registered his disappointment. We'd been fooled again. Turning, we looked toward the ridge, thumbs down. I caught sight of Simon's massive frame rising, head hung low as he spoke to Lionel and Gwyneth. As we plodded up to meet them, I felt empty and desperate. Had I been prone to tears, they would have flowed. But my anger and determination refused to let a sense of hopelessness cloud my vision.

"Damn them, where can she be?" Something dawned on me belatedly.

Gwyneth noticed. "What is it, Robbie? Are you thinking what I am?" She smiled.

Simon picked up on it, too.

"I hope so." I nodded.

"Would you like to let us in on the secret?"

Michael asked, looking irritable. "All I see is that we've lost any hope of finding Courtney."

"How long to Briarwood? If we left now?" I asked.

"I don't know. Hours. Twelve or fourteen and that's if everything went like clockwork, and we had some way to get there. Why?" Michael asked.

"Because." Simon looked at me. "That's where we'll find her."

"What?" Michael asked. Lionel stood mute but I saw him nodding.

"The message about home, Romeo, and Mrs. Mac. She was unconscious but she was telling us where to find her. Don't you see?" Simon had been right. "Those weren't random thoughts. It was a message."

"Damn." Michael snapped his fingers. "Of course. Hide in plain sight. They've taken her home." He smiled and squeezed Gwyneth tightly.

Simon already had the two-way radio out. He nodded. "Let's go. The launch will pick us up in an hour at the quay and by nightfall we'll land in Cornwall. When we get to the ship, I'll tell our people to search Briarwood and get a lorry to take us there. By morning we'll be in position."

I hoped desperately that the final leg of our journey was at hand. I knew if we were wrong again it meant a terrible fate for Courtney. One I refused to think about. All I could remember was the way she looked the first night I saw her and how much I loved her.

We sat in the launch. I closed my eyes, blocking out the world. I focused on her image. *We're coming for you, darling. Be strong and don't be afraid. No harm will come to you as long as I draw breath.*

Chapter Forty-Two

The estate sat like a jewel, acres of beautiful thickets and forest, hidden deep within the western English countryside. I could have called forth imaginings of Robin Hood and Arthurian knights had I not been so worried about Courtney. The family members from this part of Gloucestershire had scoured every acre of Briarwood. Furious activity was apparent on one of the distant sections of the estate. Another ruse? I hoped it sprang from overconfidence, thinking they'd planted so many false leads we'd never find them.

It had taken eight unbearable hours, two hundred and forty miles on the patrol boat. We landed in the late afternoon under the cover of threatening clouds. They gave the landscape the look of night. Our landing site was a deserted beach on the coast south of Newport. We spent the next three hours avoiding the highways, driving over uneven country roads to make sure we hid our approach.

As sunset descended our trek came to an end. We parked the vehicles near the River Severn and followed it northeast toward Briarwood. Dusk was followed by a gray, heavy darkness. Thick underbrush and uneven ground covered with deep ruts made the final two miles a difficult test, especially after days of frustration, little sleep, and gnawing fear. I walked over and around the obstacles. Branches slapped at my face. My mind was on Courtney, not plant life or the geography. My empty stomach did somersaults. More than once I had the urge to step into the underbrush and throw up the remains of my last meal. Instead, I summoned my newfound powers of mental acuity.

Images of Courtney's face helped me ignore the frightening possibilities if we were late or tricked again. I glanced at my watch, knowing that we had no margin for error. *She* had no margin for error. I found myself thinking about the possibilities if our small window of opportunity proved too miniscule, wondering as we traversed over the clumsy ground— had the Druids outsmarted us one last time? No. Courtney had to be somewhere ahead.

The local family members directed us toward one final rise and wished us luck. They offered to stay and summon their allies. Simon refused. He had been acting distant for the last few hours. Lionel had stayed behind with no explanation and there had been a long, private conversation with Simon and Nigel before we left the patrol boat. I wondered if our leader was feeling anxiety or doubt after the past miscues. Whatever happened tonight, he seemed to want as few witnesses as possible. Our work would be brutal but necessary, like using a strong insecticide to eradicate crops from a blight of pests. I was terrified—of our enemies, using weapons to harm them, and most importantly, of not finding Courtney in time.

For the first mile, I had a sinking feeling. Nothing but darkness showed ahead in the deepening twilight. The small path was lit by our infiltration lamps, powerful flashlights fitted with special covers that directed their light downward in a focused beam.

Suddenly, I felt a strong grip on my arm. "She's here." It was Gwyneth. She patted my back and returned to Michael's side. As she spoke, in the distance I caught sight of a dim glow above the low rise ahead. I shined my light on my chronometer— 9:30. We had two hours and thirty minutes to get in position, scout the layout, and arrive at a plan to save Courtney.

****

I lay prone, peering over the small crest of the ridge where we waited. This was the place. There was no doubt. I breathed more easily, found myself able to swallow without choking. Below us a massive circle of small granite monoliths stood in a semicircle facing a tall stake. A series of steps lead to a small platform, where I assumed the victim would stand. Below the stake was a growing pile of brush and sticks. Was this to be the source of the fire they would use to sacrifice her? A chill ran through me as I thought of the possibilities if she hadn't sent that dreamlike message two nights ago.

Protruding from each of the monoliths was a large torch giving the setting an eerie, surreal quality. In the center of the circle stood a large altar. My stomach tightened into a knot. To the right lay a path that disappeared into the thick forest. For a distance of a hundred yards the entryway was lit by torches in the ground, fading into darkness amongst the oaks. Three hooded figures attended the ritual area. One lit the torches on the approach, while the second and third added more kindling to the pile beneath the stake. I clenched my fists.

As if sensing my anger and frustration, Simon put a firm hand on my shoulder. "It will be over soon," he said, displaying a confidence absent during the walk from the lorry. Michael opened the large duffel bag we had taken turns carrying. The local family members had given it to us when we began our trek to the ritual site. Laid out before us was a stock of weaponry that would have made Al Capone blush. Simon and I each took a Thompson submachine gun. He gave me a quick refresher. Basically, pull the cocking lever back and squeeze the trigger in short bursts. Aim low since it tended to rise as it fired. I'd never seen one before, but after surveying the scene where they intended to sacrifice the girl I loved, I no longer had any anxiety at destroying these fiends. Besides, our mission was to frighten and delay. To rescue Courtney. Mass murder was not part of the plan. Michael picked up an Enfield rifle with a sniper scope. Gwyneth shouldered a Weatherby hunting rifle, this one equipped with a night vision scope. I still had the .45 tucked into my belt. I felt as if I was playing a role. I was a bona fide human arsenal—a stereotype from a John Garfield crime drama or a John Wayne horse opera. Simon and Gwyneth stayed true to their British heritage by each drawing a Webley Mark VI revolver. They had explained that these massive handguns were a favorite of English officers and could bring down an elephant at seventy-five yards. We all picked up extra ammunition and positioned ourselves.

Michael covered the left flank with his rifle, handgun, and a half dozen smoke grenades. Gwyneth headed across to a thick stand of trees on the right. As I watched, she positioned her weapon using the sling for support and leverage. She sighted the infrared scope, expertly fine-tuning its delicate mechanism. Michael's beautiful witch was a warrior, no stranger to battle.

I checked my watch. Twenty-two minutes after eleven. Just as I put down my arm, I heard someone coming. I raised my eyes and checked through the field glasses. In ten minutes, the Druids would get the biggest surprise of their lives. As quietly as possible, I checked my Thompson for the third time. Michael and Gwyneth made slight adjustments to their weapons.

I looked down at the procession of Druids. Their approaching resembled a pageant in a cathedral. Had I not known the epic circumstances I might have found the whole thing graceful, even inspiring. I counted two, four, six, finally stopping at twelve. They filled the semicircle, each standing in front of one of the stone monoliths. They let the hoods fall from their heads. But as I looked at each face, a wave of anger and fear spread through me. I spotted Michael. He was twenty-five yards away to my left. He shrugged. Courtney was no where to be seen. When I glanced behind me, neither was Simon.

Chapter Forty-Three

I looked at Gwyneth, then back at Michael. He seemed to be watching the path leading to the ritual site. Still no sign of Courtney, Mrs. Mac, or Simon. This had to be the right location. There was no way these creatures would be meeting tonight with a stake and a massive fire unless it was to sacrifice Courtney.

I kept a low profile, craning my neck to follow Michael's eyes. Something was happening. Gwyneth had hidden her weapon and was hunkered down, facing away from me. Where had Simon disappeared to? He was no coward. And no one was more intent on rescuing Courtney. Why had he vanished without a word?

I turned toward Michael again. He gave me a series of hand signals he'd learned as a Ranger. Translation: he could see five individuals approaching but couldn't tell if they were our targets or more Druids. They were slowing. I swallowed hard and exhaled, holding the Thompson on a fallen log with sweaty hands.

Suddenly, I felt a gentle tap on my shoulder. Relief washed over me as I saw Simon, his aristocratic face fixed in a hard stare. He put his fingers to his lips and gave me thumbs-up. When I turned toward the front, my heart stopped. Courtney was being pushed toward the ritual circle. Her hands were bound. She staggered. I picked up the field glasses, hungry to see her face. Her eyes were open, wearing a look of resignation. She glanced at the stake and the wood beneath but turned back to face her captors without flinching. Dirty, bruised, and bound, she wore a sheer white gown and bare feet. Courtney held her head high. In spite of my fear, my heart soared with pride and love. She carried herself with dignity and grace. At that moment I had no doubt. Courtney was a goddess.

As I watched through the binoculars, she closed her eyes. She smiled. Suddenly, I could hear her as if she stood next to me. *Robbie, I know you're here. I knew you'd come. You'll never know how much I love you.* She opened her eyes and looked up the low ridge toward me. The crone behind her gave Courtney a push so rough she tripped and fell to the ground. As she struggled to stand, the one who pushed her and a second woman yanked her to her feet and directed her to the set of stairs leading to the stake.

As she mounted them, I noticed two women behind Courtney for the first time. I'd been so anxious and preoccupied watching her, I hadn't noticed the poor woman being dragged by a tall member of their group. Mrs. Mac. When they reached the large stone altar she fell to the ground. I heard her pained cry from fifty yards away.

I owe you an apology, I thought, staring at her lying crumpled in front of this macabre scene. *She was one of the good guys after all.* They dragged the old woman to her feet and forced her to kneel facing the stake. She would witness the death of the young woman she loved. When Courtney reached the top of the steps her arms and legs were fastened to the stake with chains and padlocks.

Watching this cruel scene, I moved instinctively, but Simon held me in place. "Everything will be all right," he whispered and gave my shoulder a squeeze.

I had confidence in him. But as we watched a sick feeling grew in my stomach. The woman who brought Courtney to the site, a young Druid who seemed in charge, picked up a torch and headed toward the nearest monolith to light it.

I turned toward Simon again. He leaned closer. "I know this is difficult. But this all has to play out a certain way." I trusted him, but as the torch took flame, I held up the Thompson and put my finger inside the trigger guard. "Robbie, please, just a minute and we'll be ..." He stopped in mid-sentence, eyes darting toward the rear.

As he spoke I heard movement behind us. I scanned the scene in front. Michael stood, his Enfield poised in the firing position, Gwyneth crouched to my right, her weapon in position on a low branch. If Simon and I were next to each other then...

The leaves rustled behind us. The sound of a twig breaking was unmistakable. Damn them! Had we come all this way only to fail? These people were devils. I had no doubt of that.

"Well, well. I've been expecting you. *We've* been expecting you." The sick feeling grew. My stomach fell into emptiness. That voice sent chills through me. Not because of its frightening quality, but because I had heard it often in the last week. I had no need to turn. Suddenly, so many things made sense.

I tightened my grip on my weapon, poised to turn. If we were all going to die, I would take some of them with me, including the woman who mocked us. "Don't, Robbie. I know how much you love her. I want you to know it's been very difficult for me—playing two roles."

Simon grabbed my forearm, forcing me to release the Thompson. It fell to the ground. "He really doesn't understand the import of what's going on here," Simon explained as he released my arm. We turned in unison. The hooded figure of Wendy

Wilkins showed a crooked smile. She held a large revolver, a .45. The two creatures flanking her held twelve-gauge sawed-off shotguns.

Simon nodded as he surveyed the others. "It's all right, Duncan, you can lower your hood." We'd found where Duncan Wellington had vanished to. He stood on Wendy's right—a middle-aged man of impressive stature and bearing. His face showed strain. It was pudgy, drawn, and lined, but evident that Duncan Wellington had once been a man to make hearts swoon. The third figure had a low hood over his or her head, giving no hint of their identity.

"But I'm waiting to meet the mastermind. The man whose extraordinary powers and cruelty managed all this," Simon said in a low voice.

"Let's go down and meet my *real* family. I know you won't enjoy our little ceremony, but it is something that we need to do in"—Wendy checked her watch—"fifteen minutes. And our high priest, the one who's made this all possible, is approaching as we speak."

With that they pushed us over the low ridge heading toward the ritual circle. Anger and frustration swept over me. Surely we were not going to give up and simply watch Courtney being sacrificed. I glanced to my right. I wanted to rush at them, but strangely, Simon still wore that look of confidence. He'd expected all this. His compliance was part of the plan. I understood. We hadn't chased Courtney and her would-be executioners three-thousand miles to watch as they sacrificed her.

Simon held up his hands. "Certainly, Wendy. We're your prisoners." He walked slowly down the incline leading toward the circle. "We'll do as you say. Just don't do anything foolish."

"Have no fear, old man." She shrugged. "I'm not impetuous. And our leader is thrilled you've found us so you can watch his beautiful child die in agony."

Simon led me up and over the low ridge, then down the trail to what—I had no idea. "Perhaps we can come to an agreement." Simon suggested. "Some mutual pledge or... "

Wendy stopped, staring with raised eyebrows. "I've told you, this is difficult for me. I have affection for your family and its members." She exhaled deeply and shook her head. "Robbie may be ignorant of the true meaning of what's about to happen." She gave him a patronizing look. "But you're not. So please, don't try a feeble attempt at negotiation." She gave him a push toward the ritual circle. "Move!"

Chapter Forty-Four

Wendy looked left and right, finding our comrades. "Michael, I need you and Gwyneth to stand up and put down your weapons or Simon and your lovesick brother will be scattered across this lovely grove," she commanded, offering no hint of compromise. Duncan surveyed us and nodded, cocking the pump-action twelve-gauge shotgun expertly. There was something surreal about being surrounded by the world's most powerful pagans and having them resort to weapons to enforce their will. The thought passed quickly. No time for dialectic while the fate of my beloved and the world lay at hand!

I studied Wendy's face as we took the last few strides to the circle. She looked drawn and anxious, apparently conflicted by our predicament and the fact that she found herself in this situation.

When we reached the center of the circle, a tall, robed figure stopped in front of Simon. "Hello, son," Simon said with no emotion.

The man pushed his hood down, wearing a sneer. "I should have guessed you'd figure it out, old man." There was venom in his voice. "What did you expect? Calling down that spell to cause my death. My mechanic drove the car that afternoon. He was old and lived alone. No one missed him."

"You were my son. Despite all your cruelty and misdeeds, I loved you. The spell you imagined was in your mind. I wanted to help you—not destroy you."

A strange look crossed the tall man's face. His eyes narrowed and burned, his lips drew tight.

"Nonsense. You called down that spell to..."

Simon held up his hand and stared at him. "You're a fool, Courtney. You always were." Simon laughed. "I suspected the deaths on Briarwood were your doing." He shook his head slowly. "So you made it your mission to isolate this beautiful child. Your child." He pointed to my Courtney. "And destroy anyone who got close to her."

The tall man shook his head violently. He opened his mouth to speak. But Simon continued. "That poor child, Meghan, the stable hand, the teacher, and *even her mother*, your beautiful consort, your partner! What a pathetic excuse for existence. I always knew you were alive. Still doing evil. But burning your own daughter at the stake? That's a bit brutal even for you."

"I did it all for you, *dear father!* And the fact that you and the foolish boy you've chosen as her mate will hear her screams makes it all the sweeter."

"Of course, Duncan enlisted out of greed. When Courtney dies, he inherits her millions and has the added benefit of watching his illegitimate offspring die."

Simon's son sneered and nodded. "Of course."

"But what about Wendy? She did this out of some perverse form of love. She doesn't know you plan to disappear with that lovely girl." Simon pointed to the tall Druidess. "Brighid?"

Wendy looked pale as she turned toward the striking young woman with the torch in her hand. "No, he wouldn't do that to me," she whispered.

"Ask Brighid," Simon said in a level voice.

I shifted my gaze to my Courtney. Streaks of dried tears were apparent below her enormous eyes. I could sense the terror and pain that had been her constant companion. But despite her bruised countenance she was still the most exquisite creature on Earth.

I saw her lips twist and curl momentarily. The ties between us created a bond so strong, so impenetrable that it overcame the powers of our enemies. We communicated once again. Her thoughts and the images they carried were transmitted clearly—too clearly. Violent, vivid pictures of pain and humiliation filled my mind. I could see Courtney beaten, imprisoned, and bound with manacles that cut into her flesh. Suddenly, my only thought was revenge. A swift and painful punishment for these creatures. But how? In my peripheral vision I saw Michael and Gwyneth stand and let their rifles drop to the blanket of leaves.

"The circle you've surrounded us with seems impenetrable," Simon offered. "There's no way we can break through it. My compliments." He showed no indication of anger or fear, but flashed me an imperceptible nod. Our leader was a cool customer. "So tell me. To satisfy an old man's curiosity. Are you really one of them?" He directed the question to his son. "Because the Druids believe in peace and nature. But through those extraordinary powers you inherited and used so cruelly, you've convinced these poor creatures of something that has no basis in fact."

His son's smirked. "You lie, old man. You're the one misleading everyone."

Simon put his hand to his jacket. "May I?" he asked.

His son nodded. "What could you have in there that would make any difference?"

He removed an envelope. A murmur ran through the assembled Druids.

Simon removed a document from the envelope. "This is a sworn statement from the head of the Royal Observatory, Damien Woodbury. He certifies that the event you've threatened these people with, the Cardinal Cross, will occur when originally foretold. Years in the future. They'll be no cosmic crisis tonight." Simon scanned the crowd.

The murmur grew. The young girl replaced the torch in its holder. She turned toward Courtney Phillips. "But how can this be, master?"

"It isn't, my dear. This witch is playing mind games with you."

Simon took two steps and placed the document on the altar. His son snatched it and put it to the torch. "That's what we think of your falsehoods, old man. Let's begin the ceremony. We only have five minutes."

"I have another copy if you'd like." Simon produced a second paper.

The small band of Druids remained mute, frozen in place.

Courtney Phillips could wait no longer. He lunged for the torch and ran toward his daughter. "I've waited too long for this. I will not be denied!" he screamed. Just as he reached the foot of the platform, I lunged and pushed him and the torch into the dry kindling. In a matter of seconds, his robe and the tinder were an inferno. His anguished screams rose into the still of the damp English night. Wendy approached and made a vain attempt to extinguish the flames. It was too late for the sadistic witch who had cast a spell of evil across two continents.

I stole a look at Courtney. She struggled furiously, trying to free herself from the chains that held her. Everyone remained frozen, transfixed as they watched the terrible spectacle of Courtney Phillip's smoldering body.

Simon lifted his head scanning the low ridges surrounding the ritual circle. Looking, I hoped, for someone or something, but as I scanned the tree-filled landscape there was no sign of anyone.

But as I ran through the flames licking at Courtney's feet, I glanced back to see a group of men descending from every direction. Like vengeful angels, men wearing the battle dress of the Royal Marines showed on the ridge, weapons poised. The figure standing next to a horrified Duncan threw off his hood and raised his weapon. None other than our companion, Lionel.

"I wouldn't move if I were you." He gave me a cheerful nod as he sneered at Duncan. "Robbie." Lionel nodded and shook his head. "Damn hot under that robe."

"Save yourselves! Get away from here as quickly as possible," Wendy screamed. As the Druids ran, they found their escape blocked in every direction. One or two managed to evade the Marines. I quickly turned my attention to the beautiful girl chained to the cross.

Chapter Forty-Five

The sickening smell of burning flesh filled my nostrils. Courtney Phillips's young acolyte scrambled frantically, trying to find escape. I lost track of her, my attention fixed on the massive pile of dry twigs and logs flaming out of control. They crackled and sent sparks into the moonlit sky.

I shot a look at Courtney. She hung chained and unconscious. Someone had struck her. A large bruise showed on her right cheek and blood ran from a gash over her eye.

"Michael, Gwyn! Help me," I yelled. Gunfire erupted on the ridge and the entry path. I ran down the hill and up the steps, furiously kicking away the flaming kindling and small logs from the pyre beneath Courtney. Phillips's remains lay immobile, smoldering below us. Too late for the man who orchestrated this cruel adventure.

Michael retrieved his handgun and ran to join me next to Courtney. He aimed at the tempered steel padlocks but shook his head. "Too dangerous. I'm shaking. I may blow her hand off. Find something to loosen the stake."

I stood, searched and found two long poles. We dug feverishly around the base of the stake while Marines sprayed the flames with water, bringing the fire under control. Simon and Nigel had thought of everything. How could I have doubted them?

The fire had been extinguished by the time we freed the stake and placed it and Courtney gently on the ground. "Courtney. Courtney, darling, can you hear me?"

She moaned and opened her eyes for a moment. "Robbie," she whispered. "You did come. You are my Perseus. I knew you would be. Hold me." And I did, bending over, struggling to put my arms around her. A Marine captain appeared with bolt cutters. In a few seconds, Courtney was free.

Her wrists were bruised, discolored, and cut, as were her lips and arms. She had been no willing captive. I kissed her gently and pulled the Smith and Wesson from my belt, then rose. "Gwyn, watch her. I have something to do."

"No, Robbie. Please. That's not our way." She shook her head violently, grabbing for my handgun. I turned in search of Duncan. "Please, Robbie. You'll be—" Before I got ten feet several shots rang out. As I looked up, Simon and Michael stood over the twitching remains of Duncan Wellington. Each held their handguns loosely by their sides. As he fell to the ground, a shot rang out from a weapon Duncan had concealed beneath his robe. Simon flinched and grabbed his arm.

Michael approached him but Simon shook his head. "It's nothing," I heard him say as he covered the flesh wound with his hand.

Simon looked toward the sky, made almost daytime bright by the light of the full moon. The light Courtney and I were to celebrate our union beneath. Wellington lay lifeless on the blanket of pine needles and leaves. I walked deliberately across the distance that separated us. When I arrived at the scene, I raised the handgun in my belt—a .45 automatic. I cocked it and with hands shaking, threw it away.

It was over.

"Robbie, she's calling you and Simon." It was Gwyneth.

I ran back to Courtney. I wanted no more of this. My only concern was Courtney. Her face wore a gray pallor.

"No, no," I screamed. "I didn't travel halfway around the world to lose you."

As I watched, a young lieutenant wearing the insignia of the medical corps ran up to us. The medic working with him had a bag with plasma and attached it to Courtney's arm. I clenched my fists as I saw her dark bruises. The doctor began examining her, taking off the cotton sacrificial robe that she wore, covering her with thick woolen blankets.

I grabbed his arm. "She seemed so strong, so defiant only a few minutes ago," I pleaded. "She's going to be all right, isn't she?"

"'They'"—he gestured toward the remnants of the Druids now being herded like sheep by the company of Royal Marines—"mistreated her badly. How long was she their prisoner?"

"Four days, maybe more," Michael answered.

"Doesn't look like they gave her much to eat or drink. They wanted to keep her docile and weak. She's suffering from severe dehydration and—"

"They kept my angel in a dark cell with no food, water, or clothing." It was Mrs. Mac. She lay on a stretcher with an IV in her arm. "When they thought she was trying to communicate with one of you, they beat her—*those animals.*" She raised her head and spat the words as she scanned the area for the Druids that remained alive. I crossed the few feet and squeezed her hand. "Will she be all right, Mr. Robert?"

I looked back at Courtney, lying on the stretcher, her breathing shallow and labored. "I know she will," I answered, swallowing deeply. "She has to be."

"Let's get her to the hospital. She'll need all the help we can give her." With that they carried her up the low ridge to an ambulance waiting on the access road we had followed in. I got in and rode the few miles to the estate where a helicopter waited. She remained unconscious for most of the trip, opening her soft, dark eyes twice. I dabbed her swollen lips with a moist towel.

"I knew you'd come, Robbie," she whispered, voice barely audible. "Always knew. Never doubted." Then she lost consciousness.

****

Courtney lay in her room. The Royal Marine medical officer had relinquished her care to a team of specialists. Simon explained they were family members—experts at dealing with the special characteristics of witches.

"Remember, Courtney had not become a goddess. That would have happened on the night..." Simon turned away, unable to complete his thought. "Courtney was so powerful and so good." He shook his head. "But in so many ways, Robert, she was still a young woman, innocent, a child really. Using her powers to heal and communicate took a great deal of energy. It sapped her life force."

I remembered the day—had it only been a week ago—when she communicated with the animals at the petting zoo. In no time, she fell asleep as we rode toward Naples.

"I understand. It all makes sense now," I said as a frightening thought crossed my mind. "She tried so hard to communicate with us."

Simon held up his hand. "Not with us, Robbie." He took my hand, squeezing it. I realized he had never called me "Robbie" before. "With you."

"And yes, she was trying so desperately to reach you it took so much of her strength."

I looked at her, ghostly pale, lying quietly, breathing still shallow and labored. Michael entered the room, his arm around Gwyneth. Behind them, Jonathan, Gretchen, and several other family members from the States crowded in.

Jon raised his eyes, then backed away hesitantly. I walked to him and held out my arms. "I'm so sorry, Robbie. I had no idea how this would turn out, about Duncan, any of it." He broke down, sobs wracking his body. I found myself patting his thick gray hair, consoling him, trying to ease his guilt.

"I know, Jon. I know," I assured him as Gretchen joined in, hugging us both. I realized what the import of this powerful gathering implied. Courtney, my beautiful angel, the soul mate with whom I hoped to spend eternity was very, very weak, hovering near death. It would take a miracle for her to survive the night.

I asked the others to leave. They balked, but Simon smiled kindly and herded the others from Courtney's room, adding, "Do your best, son." It was a gamble worth taking. I covered her with blankets, gave her sips of water and ice chips, then lay down beside her, cradling her slender frame, sharing the warmth and energy from my body. I did my best to transmit my thoughts, constantly telling her how much I loved her, that she was safe, and that I would never leave her again. I willed her strength and life force to return.

Sometime in the middle of the night, the effort overcame me. I lost consciousness. The next thing I remember was Michael and Gwynny gently shaking me as the sun streamed in through the curtains. A gentle breeze brought the familiar scent of jasmine to the hospital room.

"She looks wonderful," Gwynny said beaming as she watched Courtney. "You're good medicine."

"Very good medicine." Michael nodded and smiled.

I sat up and looked over at Courtney. She was breathing deeply and regularly. Her color had returned. As I stood up, she let out a groan and opened her eyes. She looked briefly at Mike and Gwynneth, giving them a warm smile. But she reserved her special smile for me.

"Thank you, darling. I heard every thought you sent. They helped more than you'll ever know. Now." She looked up at me. "If our friends will give us a private moment, I want to kiss you."

****

Courtney lay sleeping peacefully. I kissed her softly and left the room. Gwynny, Michael, and other family members would join me in taking turns sitting by her bedside while she regained her strength.

Simon stood at a long window, his regal features posed in a pensive expression. His look caught me by surprise. "Simon?"

"Yes, son. You've done wonders with Courtney. She seems much stronger," he said as he turned and gave me a curious smile. "But you must have questions."

I nodded. "We defeated the Druids, but Courtney and I were never joined in the ceremony. What will happen to the world, to mankind? Does this mean chaos and anarchy will have free rein?"

"Walk with me." He put his arm around my shoulder.

We went down the steps and out into the sunny dampness of the English dawn as light filtered through the tall maples and oaks. He led me to a small garden and a marble bench. He motioned and we sat down.

"I've been meditating on that all night." He wore a serene look. "Are you familiar with Edmund Burke, Robbie?"

"An Irish statesman and philosopher from the late eighteenth century, if I remember my history correctly."

"Very good. Yes, Burke was a sage intellect." He

nodded and paused. "As I was meditating his most famous quote came to mind."

I searched my memory but came up empty.

He saw I didn't understand. "Burke said 'All that is necessary for evil to triumph is that good men do nothing.'"

"I still don't understand, sir."

"For generations—hundreds, perhaps thousands of years—we who practice the craft have been using our special powers to help mankind. But as I meditated, it suddenly struck me that whatever force created this planet and those who inhabit it, also gave them free will." Simon searched the morning sky and sighed deeply. "Mankind has a great capacity for evil, but it's my hope that it has a greater capacity for good. We've done enough, Robert. It's time for the Burke's 'good men' to stand on their own."

Epilogue
Late August, 1947

Wendy Wilkins would spend the rest of her life in a facility for the criminally insane. Duncan Wellington and Courtney Phillips had paid the ultimate price for their greed, hatred, and treachery. Once Phillips's spell was broken, the Druids of his group were stunned and ashamed. They returned to their peaceful ways, angered and chagrined that they had almost destroyed a beautiful young witch. Despite their regrets, they would still face the wrath of the pagan council. That secretive, somber body of venerable shamans would decide their fate.

Another chapter was added to the growing book that formed my education about my pagan peers and the world we inhabited. Simon explained, "When you have people with the kind of awesome power and abilities that we do, you can't allow them to go through the world wreaking havoc. So during the Renaissance, after the terror of the Inquisition, and the Burning Times, our ancestors established a ruling body to assure that none of us used our powers for evil. Witches, Druids, shamans from all pagan beliefs comprise the council. I'm a member but will recuse myself from this tribunal because of my personal involvement."

"How many will go before the council?" I asked.

"Fewer than a dozen were actually complicit in my son's wild scheme. Most of them were under his spell, so their punishment may be light. Three escaped—including the girl Brighid. She was very close to him." Simon shrugged. "Our brothers and sisters will search for them but no one knows where they've gone." He patted my shoulder. "Have no fear. You and Courtney are safe. I guarantee it."

****

Courtney and I galloped across the luxuriant high meadow we had ridden in June. Courtney rode her splendid gelding, as I followed gamely on Pumpkin Patch. Courtney now lived with Jon and Gretchen, managing Wendy's stable and giving riding lessons. Thanks to some help from Michael, she was enrolling in Dartmouth's new equestrienne program in the fall. By another strange coincidence I chose to transfer from the Crimson to the Big Green myself.

The grass in the meadow was taller and wore a dark, golden hue. It smelled sweet and warm. Courtney and I dismounted. She took the small urn from her saddlebags and walked past the beautiful lake vista and waterfall toward the natural altar where Ellen's ashes were buried.

"I do *not* understand why you're doing this. He was a cruel, vicious man who wanted to see you burned at the stake. To make you suffer to pay Simon back for what he imagined was an injustice."

"That's right and he was wrong, but he was still my father. We witches revere our family, no matter how corrupt or distasteful. And part of our philosophy is unconditional love and forgiveness. Turn the other cheek." She gave me a stern look. "Not so different, if I recall, from the practices of Jesus and your conventional religions." She frowned and shook her head.

"You're right. I still have a lot to learn." I shrugged and plodded along behind her. When we arrived at the burial spot, she turned to me wearing an I'm-sorry look. Despite the depth of our love, the burial ceremony was still a private one.

"I understand. I'll wait back at our picnic spot."

"Oh, don't think you're getting off that easily. I've packed another lunch for today."

Twenty minutes later she returned, eyes glistening. She went by me and returned with the saddlebags. The sparkling afternoon felt cooler than the day of our first adventure.

"I tested your abilities the other day," I said, looking up at the spanking white clouds as they played across the deep blue of the August sky.

"Tested them? Really. How?" She put down the saddlebags and watched me. I suspected she was reading my thoughts, but I went along with the game.

"I called Rachel."

"And?" Courtney pushed her lips into a pout.

"She seemed mystified. Had no idea who I was. Politely told me she'd never heard of a Robert McGregor."

The look that crossed Courtney's face was difficult to read. Part victory, part regret.

"I'm so sorry, Robbie," she whispered, finding my eyes. Hers looked damp.

"I'm not. You know I could never love anyone more than you. It's better she not remember than be heartbroken. And my mother tells me there's a splendid young intern she's been seeing."

"I'm glad." She squeezed my hand, laid out her picnic spread, and came across the blanket to sit next to me. "Do you remember what we did after lunch the first time we came here?"

"How could I forget?" I smiled, recalling our incredible kiss.

"Well, you have asked me to marry you?"

"Yes, of course. I want your inheritance," I teased.

"So that's it then. I'm nothing more than what you Yanks call a meal ticket?"

"That's all. You're just a scrawny little English

girl with a big...fat...inheritance."

"Simon and Michael warned me you were nothing but a gold digger." She gave me a mock frown and swatted my arm.

"I mean you can ride pretty well, can tell what I'm thinking, and you're not bad to look at. And God knows, you have the most expensive wardrobe I've ever seen."

She slowly put her hand on my shoulder. "Are you *really* feeling hungry?" She gave me a delicious smile. "*Really?*"

I shrugged, hoping I caught her meaning.

"I'm not." She put her lips together and found my eyes. "Do we have to wait until we're married before, you know, we finish that pleasant business we began in June?"

"Well"—I put my hand to my chin—"I could use a spell so you wouldn't remember my taking advantage of you."

"Really?" A broad grin spread across her face. "And how do you propose to do that?" she asked as she ran her hands slowly down my arms and brought her lips very close.

"Oh, haven't I told you, darling? I'm a witch!"

267

A word about the author...

Writer, college faculty member, and president of one of the Northeast's most respected writing organizations, Kevin Symmons has crafted a paranormal tale to keep you turning pages late into the night.

His other efforts include *Voices*, a sweeping women's fiction work that brings to light the tragic problem of domestic violence in contemporary America.

He has also collaborated with award-winning screenwriter, playwright, and professor Barry Brodsky, who has adapted one of Kevin's story ideas to the screen.

Kevin is currently at work on his next novel, a romantic thriller set near his Cape Cod home.